APR 0 5

DATE DUE

The Secret Under My Skin

Also by Janet McNaughton

AN EARTHLY KNIGHT

THE
SECRET
UNDER
MY SKIN

Janet McNaughton

An Imprint of HarperCollins*Publishers*

Library of Congress Cataloging-in-Publication Data
McNaughton, Janet Elizabeth, 1953–
    The secret under my skin / Janet McNaughton.—1st
U.S. ed.
        p.   cm.
    Summary: In the year 2368, humans exist under dire
environmental conditions and one young woman, res-
cued from a work camp and chosen for a special duty,
uses her love of learning to discover the truth about the
planet's future and her own dark past.
    ISBN 0-06-008989-X — 0-06-008990-3 (lib. bdg.)
    [1. Science fiction.   2. Environmental degradation—
Fiction.   3. Books and reading—Fiction.   4. Orphans—
Fiction.   5. Child labor—Fiction.]   I. Title.
PZ7.M23257Se 2005   2004012373
[Fic]—dc22

First U.S. edition, HarperCollins Publishers Inc., 2005
Originally published in Canada by HarperCollins Publishers Ltd., 2000
Typography by Rob Hult
1   2   3   4   5   6   7   8   9   10
❖

For Michael,
who is my window
on the future
and my future itself

THE SECRET UNDER MY SKIN

The Grand Hotel

At night I listen while some of the kids whisper their stories, from before. When they had families and homes. One after another. "I had a mother and she loved me. . . ." "My father had a job. He used to bring us candy. . . ." "My grandmother sang this song. . . ." And I believe them because kids who hit the streets too young never make it here.

We sleep in the basement of the grand hotel. It had a name once, but no one remembers now. The warders call it the Model Social Welfare Project. We call it the work camp. But the walls keep out the rain and snow. We sleep on beds. I don't have to beg or lift scrip cards or satisfy the stranger whims of strangers to earn my food like I did when the Tribe had me, when I lived in the Core.

The others talk about the past, but I don't. Not ever. If asked, I say I don't remember. But that's not true. I keep my memories to myself because they aren't like anyone else's. Not comforting. Not beautiful. Others cling to the past like shreds of an old blanket. My memories are more like shards of glass. I drift off to sleep tonight hoping I can take the others' memories with me to make my dreams. Hoping I will not fall into the same loop of haunting shadows that cannot be understood. But tonight is no different from any other. Once again, I'm in the strange city. The air is hot and breathless. We are at the edge of a green field enclosed by fine buildings—some made of stone. One has a rounded, green roof. I look around without straining because my head is resting on Someone's arm.

Suddenly I'm in another place. Darkness crowds the circle of bright light that holds me. There is music and noise. I am captivated by a yellow bowl on the table in front of me, bright in the unfamiliar lights of nighttime. Without warning, arms rip me from my chair. I hear a woman howl after me, a wordless wail. Then only darkness and the sound of running. I wake with a jolt.

Those are my memories. If I told them, who would believe me? What do they mean? I only know that I was once held by Someone. Who? If I could just shift my gaze a few centimeters, what would I see? When my heart is quiet again, I lie awake wishing I knew. If I had a memory of Someone—a mother or a father—maybe I would be someone too. But I am nothing. Just a voice inside my head. I only know that Someone once held me safe, even if I got lost after. Even if I was left behind. And Someone gave me my Object, the only thing I've managed to keep with me all this time. Whatever it is.

As I lie thinking, a sound creeps into the darkness. It grows until I recognize the hum of a fuel cell. The lights of a vehicle sweep past the frosted basement windows. Who would come here so late? But the sound doesn't stop. It continues up the hill. The only house up there belongs to a Master of the Way. I've never seen a vehicle go there before. A little kid whimpers. Before anyone else hears, I slip out of bed and find her. She's sitting up, her eyes wide. "The lights," she whispers. "Are they coming for us?"

I smooth the sweat-flattened hair off her face. "No. Don't worry. Lie down."

She shakes her head. "I'm scared."

"Lie down," I say again. "I'll stay, all right?" She nods. After a few minutes, her eyes start to close. She puts her thumb in her mouth and goes to sleep, but I stay with her. Just in case.

The Rumor

When the warders turn the arc-lights on in the morning, some girls groan and cover their heads. I'm tired from the sleep I lost last night, but I reach for my gloves almost before I'm awake. Gloves are the most important thing. I tie mine to the bed frame while I sleep, but as soon as I get up they go around my neck. These gloves are made out of kevlar. I got them when another kid was chosen for food service. She threw her gloves into the air and said, "I'm out of here." They landed at my feet. Other kids reached for them, but I was faster. I never let go.

When my gloves are safe, I shuffle into my UV suit and follow the others to the latrines.

Most mornings are flat. This one isn't. Excited whispers buzz back and forth. ". . . late last night, after lights out." I remember the vehicle and listen hard. "She'll have a U-R of nine," a girl says. "They all do."

"Right. Nine," someone snorts, "and what's she do? Nothing."

U-R. Use-Rating. We all have them. Kids say, "You are what U-R." Ten is tops. Working in the landfill, you never get past two. Kids with more specialized jobs, the gardeners, the food servers, get to three or even four. Street kids have no U-R. No one worries if they disappear, if they're taken for organs or if the death squads "retire" them. Death squad. The memory opens like a tear in my mind, and out of that blackness comes Hilary, pushing me to the darkest corner of our hiding hole while black-gloved hands reached for her. Hilary, putting a finger to her lips to keep me quiet. And me understanding, understanding everything. Hilary, looking back just once, then disappearing forever into the harsh light of day. The shell of something that looked like Hilary lying in the street when we came out at sunset.

Don't think. Don't think. Don't think.

I open my eyes. I have not crumpled into a ball on the floor. Hours have not passed. I let myself breathe again. I haven't been swallowed by that blackness for a long time now. Not like before. When I start to listen again, the kids are still talking. "What do we need a bio-indicator for anyway?" one says.

"I don't know. Maybe they do some good."

Now I know what they're talking about.

The Landfill

We leave after breakfast, grabbing UV visors at the door. Because the ozone layer is degraded, it isn't safe to let the sun touch your skin. We live daytime in the work camp because they give us protective clothing. In the Core of St. Pearl, people like us live nighttime, sleeping through the harmful light of day. My first few years here, I used to think I'd go blind. Daytime still seems strange to me.

About sixty of us kids and three warders walk down the road that leads to Kildevil. We never actually go to town, though. The way the people there feel about us, that would be a big mistake. Instead, after a few hundred meters, we turn into the landfill. The UV visors don't filter the air, only the light. The air is sweet with the smell of grass and trees. When I first came here, I was afraid of all this living stuff, but now I like it. Even the landfill looks nice today, like somewhere you wouldn't mind being. It's springy under my feet, layer upon layer of stuff people once threw away. How could their lives be filled with so much that they could throw all this away? No one knows.

We fan out. I always find a place alone at the edge of an excavation and work hard so no one bothers me. I take my gloves off the string around my neck, fit my hands into the stiff fingers that still hold the shape of yesterday's work, and begin.

Our job is to find anything useful. Plastic bottles, bottle caps, glass. Bundles of papers. Styrofoam. We work with our hands so things don't get more damaged than they already are. That's our job in summer. In winter we help with the hydroponic trays. It's nice in the middle of the winter to be in rooms filled with trays of lettuce and tomatoes. That's why they heat the hotel in winter. Hydroponic work doesn't take as much time, so we have classes in the mornings. They like to say we are educated here. We learn to read and write and add and subtract, things I already knew before I came here. They also teach us how the environment was degraded by the techies.

I've hit a good patch in the landfill today. Lots of bags of high-grade paper, clean and dry. After about an hour, one of the little kids notices, a new kid named Alice. She works her way over and moves in on me. I don't mind. The landfill is hard work for little kids. But then Melissa sees us. "That's too easy for you," she says to us. "Clear out." This happens all the time. There's no point in trying to argue. The tattoos on Mel's face show how important she was in her Tribe. They must have turned her out for her to end up here, and they would only do that if she did something really bad, like kill another Tribe member. I start to move away, but Alice doesn't.

"That's not fair," she said. "We found this first." Alice doesn't know anything about the Tribes. She has a real name, Alice Icecutter. That means she came directly here when her family failed. She never lived on the streets. She has no idea how dangerous it is to stand up to Mel.

Mel faces Alice down, standing head and shoulders above her. "Forget it, kid," she says. "This patch is mine now." Everyone waits to see what will happen. The warders watch, but they don't move. My spine coils into my body. It's stupid to stand up to Mel, but if Alice doesn't back down, I'll have to help her. I can't just watch.

After a long moment, Alice turns to me. "All right," she says, her back to Mel. "It's yours."

Mel grins, showing several broken teeth. "Good thinking, kid," she says. "I'm personal friends with Lem Howl. Make me mad and one night he'll get you." Her laughter follows us all the way to the patch she left, which turns out to be mostly broken glass.

I don't believe Mel for a minute. Nobody knows Lem Howl. He lives up the valley, past the Master's house, on a place called Ski Slope. We never see him, but kids say he's crazy. Worse. They say he eats anyone who gets close to his house. But he wasn't always like that. Every year on Memory Day, they tell us the story of the technocost and how Lem Howl went crazy. Memory Day is almost here.

Memory Day

Memory Day is the last day in October. It's a turning point in the year. The week before, we close the landfill for winter and spend days in the sorting sheds, packing the things we collected all summer to be sent away. After supper they keep us in our sleeping rooms in the basement so the warders can seal off the top floors and disinfect the growing areas. Most kids don't mind. They spend evenings making little dolls called "guys" out of scraps of cloth and paper. Some guys are just twists of paper with faces drawn on, but some are real dolls. Kids who've never been to a Memory Day before will spend hours sewing their guys. There's a girl named Poppy who has only been in my sleeping room a few months. She's given her guy arms and legs, sewn on a face, used dead grass to make hair. She hugs it at night when she sleeps. No one tells her not to. The guys are important to Memory Day. I hate them.

For me, the week before Memory Day means I lose my time with a lastbook. There are only ten lastbooks, but most kids never touch them. One has a page that stays blank no matter what you download into it. I've marked it now so I don't take it by mistake. No one takes care of the biblio-tech. Lately the lastbooks get stuck when I download new scripts. There aren't many titles, mostly reference scripts for schoolwork and stories about street kids who find happiness in Model Social Welfare Projects. I don't think the writers were ever street kids. I don't think they've even visited a place like this. But I love to read. The lastbook is my best friend.

After the second year, I'd read every script on the proscribed reading list. I didn't even know until I popped a lastbook into the biblio-tech and hit the "proscribed reading" pad on the wall. It flashed a message I'd never seen before: "Congratulations! Your proscribed reading program is complete. Take this message to your edu-warder and receive a certificate!" That hit me like a blast of cold water. I didn't want a certificate. I wanted more scripts. Those stories were barely interesting enough to read once. I couldn't read them over and over. I panicked, hit the topic pad, and held it down. A list of names I'd never seen before popped up. Shakespeare, Shelley, Yeats. That's how I found poetry.

There aren't a lot of poetry scripts. They all come from long ago. It only took a few months to finish every one in the biblio-tech, but that doesn't matter. Poetry isn't like stories that you only want to read once. Poetry reminds me of a jetty in St. Pearl. Every day something new would float up on it. Sometimes things you'd want to find and sometimes not, but always something new. I read the poems again and again. Not where anyone can see me, though. It isn't good to show you're different, so I usually take a lastbook into a hydroponic room where I can hide. At first I was afraid the warders would stop me from reading when I finished the proscribed program. They may not service the biblio-tech, but they do monitor it. After a while I realized they weren't going to bother. Readers don't make trouble. But the week before Memory Day, I can't hide and read, so I don't read at all.

It's important to keep what happens on Memory Day a secret from the new kids. If you told, and the other kids found out, they would beat you senseless. We have quite a few new kids this year, maybe fifty, and about half of those are little. Most have been here long enough to shift over to daytime and start working. The really new ones live nighttime in separate rooms while they switch over, but they will come for Memory Day too, even if they've never been with us before. The little ones don't stay for the bonfire, though, only the story.

It isn't an easy week. New kids get hints that something scary is going to happen, and there are fights and tears. Just being cooped up night after night is hard. It seems like the week will last forever but, finally, Memory Day is here. We work in the sorting sheds as usual, but the air feels thicker, like it does before a thunderstorm. Kids run around all day, waving their guys in everyone's faces. When it's dark, the warders herd us into the Rotunda.

The Rotunda still looks like it must have when the grand hotel was new. The room is large and there's a fireplace, so it's perfect for Memory Day. The high, domed ceiling is covered with three huge pictures made from pieces of colored stone. But tonight the light stays at the bottom of the room, and those pictures are as dark as the sky outside. There is never electricity at Memory Day. Torches flicker in brackets on the walls. As we file into the room, everyone looks to the huge fireplace at the far end of the hall where a bonfire has been made from scraps we saved all year. A single chair sits in front of the fireplace. The storyteller's chair.

The littlest kids are led into the Rotunda now, their faces decorated with orange and black paint. They carry orange lights instead of guys. They are very quiet, looking around with wide, staring eyes. They don't understand. Being scared isn't usually fun. I remember what that felt like. I would like to take one of those little kids into my arms to keep her from being afraid but, of course, I can't. We make a big circle on the floor in front of the fire. Normally the warders would have trouble getting everyone to sit down and be quiet. Tonight we do everything without being told.

Then the chief warder takes the chair. Her name is November. That means she came off the streets like most of us. When you come to a place like this without a name, they name you for the month you arrive. She is much younger than the last chief warder. The old one sounded like she was just saying the things she had to say, but Chief Warder November seems to believe everything she says. Her white-blonde hair is closely cropped. Tonight her eyes shine in a way I have seen before and learned to fear. "The story of the technocost is something we must all understand," she begins, "so you know why technology is dangerous and belongs in the hands of the Commission. Once upon a time, the sun did not burn our eyes, blind us with cataracts, blight us with cancers. . . ." After four years I know the story by heart. It seems hard to believe there was ever such a world, before the degradation of the environment filled the water and the soil and the air with toxins. My thoughts drift away.

". . . and then the techies decided they could get rich by selling their secrets to the evil Monopoly, and the worst of all was Lem Howl." When she says this, all the older kids hold up their guys and shake them. The warders show the younger kids how to flash their orange lights. "Lem Howl and his wife lived up on Ski Slope in a house filled with advanced technology, just right for destroying the environment. They thought they could get rich, but the Monopoly agents tricked them. They took the secrets, but instead of scrip, they gave them poison. Lem Howl's wife died when she took the poison, but it didn't work with Lem Howl. No, he didn't die at all. When he drank the poison, he began to glow with an orange light." Suddenly an eerie orange light glows up into Warder November's face, making it horrible. Little kids scream. Now I know there are diodes implanted in her clothes, but I still feel a shiver of terror. "Lem Howl went mad, but he didn't go away. He's out there, waiting for you. If you go out at night alone . . . HE'LL GET YOU!" She shouts these last words, and kids scream again. The older ones raise their guys and roar. Before the noise dies down, the littlest kids, the ones with the orange lights, are herded from the room. For them, Memory Day is over.

When Warder November speaks again, she sounds normal. "Now you understand what caused the technocost," she says, "and why the techies had to die. Because of them, the earth was sadly degraded. Terra Nova Prefecture is lucky. We are far from the desert zones. We did not disappear beneath the sea when the polar ice caps melted. The industrial zones are far away, so we can breathe the air." She smiles, a thin, hard smile as she moves away from the fire. "Always remember technology is dangerous and must be controlled by the Commission. Now," she says, her voice rising, "show us how the techies died."

Kids rush forward to throw their guys into the fire. The warders make sure they don't get too close, but every year I'm amazed no one gets pushed in. To me, this is the really scary part of Memory Day. I hang back, waiting for the rush to end. My guy is just a scrap of paper, made at the last minute. Some of the newer kids are startled and confused. I see Poppy with her beautiful guy, the one she spent days sewing. She clutches it to her heart now, her eyes filling with tears. An older kid grabs her and drags her to the fire. "Come on," she says. "It's either the guy or you." It's a joke, but Poppy doesn't know that. She screams as other kids wrench the guy from her. It lands on the fire with a shower of sparks. Kids cheer. The look on Poppy's face makes me turn away. It happens every year. The first year I was here, it happened to me.

When the guys are all thrown into the fire, the warders bring us to the other end of the room, where they've set out a hot drink called cider. It has the flavor of a fruit called apple. We never see real apples, but I'd like to taste one someday. Poppy is still upset, her face swollen from crying, her breathing shaky. A warder comes over to her with a cup. "Drink this, dear," she says. "It will make you feel better." Poppy shakes her head. The warder puts the cup into Poppy's hands. "I must insist," she says. There is a threat under her friendly tone. Poppy must hear it too, because she gulps the drink without another word. "Good girl," the warder says.

After we stack our dirty cups, we go to our sleeping rooms,

all except the kids who do food service. The new kids think Memory Day is over, but they are wrong. When the lights go out, we all lie awake. This isn't the ordinary, end-of-day wakefulness, though. It's different. I feel like something is wound up tight inside of me. We all do. Of course, we're keyed up from the bonfire and the story, but now I wonder if the cider has something to do with it. No one ever refused to drink it before. I think that warder would have forced Poppy if she had to.

I lie watching the windows, knowing what comes next. Still, the hairs on the back of my neck prickle when I see the orange light lazily swooping closer and closer until everyone notices, even the new kids who weren't expecting it. A cry goes up from the room, as if we were a single creature. The light passes. "That's why you have to keep away from Ski Slope," one of the older kids whispers. "Lem Howl is out there, and he'll eat you!" We hear the kids in the next room and know they have seen the light as well. Some of the newer kids, the younger ones and the ones who are easily frightened, are crying. I am fairly sure now that the orange light is carried by warders or maybe the kids who do food service. It's just another part of Memory Day, but maybe the useful part. Because it isn't always possible to make sure everyone stays in at night. And it isn't always safe out there. Maybe Lem Howl is a real person who catches kids. Maybe not. But there are people who trade in kids, healthy kids with organs sick people need, kids to do work I don't like to think about. We were as careful as we could be when I lived on the streets, but kids still disappeared. So maybe scaring us into staying in our beds at night is not so bad.

Chosen

After Memory Day we settle into the winter routine. The kids who are gardeners start the propagation trays. As long as the seedlings are germinating, the rest of us just clean trays and cut mats—easy work. It's the best time of year. We have classes every morning. I already know everything they teach, but I make sure no one finds out.

Hilary taught me how to read. She sat me in her lap, working with papers she had scrounged or stolen. I can still see her grubby, gentle fingers, patiently tracing the letters. "Every kid should know how to read," she said. She never told me who taught her. Almost since the first day, I slipped into a page of print like a fish in a stream. As if words were the water that carried me, that I drew my breath from.

Afternoons, this time of year, it isn't hard to hurry through my work and slip away with a lastbook. The hydroponic rooms are filled with empty tables waiting for the seedlings that are still crowded together in warm propagation trays, so it's easy to find a place to read. I sit with the lastbook in my lap, my back against the wall beneath the window, hidden by a forest of table legs. I am trying to read a poem by a man named Shakespeare.

Somehow, he makes words do things I've never seen them do before, as if they were alive. This makes the poems difficult, but it draws me back again and again. Today I read:

Shall I compare thee to a summer's day?
Thou art more lovely and more temperate:
Rough winds do shake the darling buds of May,
And summer's lease hath all too short a date;
Sometimes too hot the eye of heaven shines,
And often is his gold complexion dimmed. . . .

I'm about to call up the hypertext to unravel the metaphors when suddenly I'm looking at a pair of warder's boots. I think I must be in trouble for skipping off early, but she consults a list and says, "Are you Lobelia September?" I hate the name they gave me when I came here, but I nod. "You're wanted in the Rotunda tonight after supper. Seven. Don't be late." I expect that will be all, but she doesn't leave. "Don't you want to know why?" she asks. I look at her for the first time. She's new, hardly older than the oldest girls. She doesn't look unkind, so I nod.

Her eyes light with excitement. "Well, this is really something. The Master up the hill and the bio-indicator are coming tonight to choose someone to help her with her work." She waves the list. "It took us all morning to go through the biblio-tech records and pick the most likely girls."

I can't believe this. "How many are there on the list?" I ask.

"Fifteen, and that was stretching it. So you have a one in

fifteen chance of being chosen. Good luck," she says, and she's gone. I wonder how someone like that became a warder, but then the importance of what's happening hits me. Helping the bio-indicator might be a way out of here. But why would a bio-indicator pick one of us?

The Master and the bio-indicator are here for the towns-people, not street kids like us, so even though the Master's cabin is just up the hill, we never see him. I don't know much about the Way, but bio-indicators are people with special sensitivities. When they react to toxins in the environment, there's an eco-warning. Living on the streets in St. Pearl, I thought eco-warnings were just a nuisance that made it hard to get around without being noticed. I wonder now why more of us didn't die. It's a long time before I go back to my Shakespeare.

I'm almost too excited to eat dinner. When we are called into the Rotunda, I fall in line, curious to see the Master and the bio-indicator, to see who will be chosen. I barely know the other kids who use the lastbooks. It's bad enough to be different. Grouping together would make us too easy to target. But I'm sure the bio-indicator will want someone who is strong and pretty. I am small and ugly. No one would ever pick me.

The Rotunda is fully lit tonight. You would not guess it was the same room we came to on Memory Day. No one even glances at the empty fireplace now. I look at the pictures made from inlaid stone that cover the domed ceiling high above us, so high I have to steady myself when I look up. One picture is of Western Bay Pond, one of Gros Morne Mountain, and one of the Tablelands. Places people visited when they came to stay in the grand hotel.

I've never seen any of them.

Warder November seems unusually nervous as other warders line us up. "Listen now," she says, "there isn't much time. All of you are wards of the Commission. Do you understand? The Commission rescued you, feeds and clothes you, educates you. Never forget that you owe everything to—" She stops abruptly and colors, looking past us to the other side of the room. Without meaning to, we turn and follow her gaze. A man stands in the doorway. Beside him is a young woman dressed in white robes. "But you are early," Warder November cries. "Seven-thirty was the time we agreed upon."

The man is tall and powerful and not young. He crosses the room before he speaks. He seems perfectly calm. "Then I must have been mistaken. I apologize. But the children are assembled. Is there any reason why we cannot begin?"

"No," Warder November says, but she turns to us again looking very unhappy. "As you know," she says, "bio-indicators protect us from the toxins that surround us. They are very important. This is why, when the Master asked for our help, we could not refuse."

The man smiles at us. Not just with his mouth the way most visitors do. "My name," he says, "is William Morgan. I am a Master of the Way, but I grew up just down the road, in Kildevil." He surprises me. The few people who visit here rarely really look at us. They keep their distance as if we are unclean. This man talks to us like we're real people. "I would like to introduce our new bio-indicator. Her name is Marrella."

The girl in long white robes steps forward. Wisps of pale hair escape from a cloud of some fine material that wraps her head. She flows when she walks. When I look at her face, my breath catches in my throat. Her eyes are sea blue, like Hilary's. She's beautiful.

The Master speaks again. "Soon Marrella will undergo her initiation ceremony, her investiture as a bio-indicator. We find she needs someone to tutor her." She scowls slightly when the Master says this, but he doesn't appear to notice. "You have all been asked here because you use the biblio-tech and read. Tonight she will choose one of you. The person she selects will come to live with us."

An excited murmur goes through the group. This is more than any of us expected. And I know I would give my life to help this girl who looks like Hilary, to escape this terrible place, but I shove those thoughts aside. In my life, to hope is to be disappointed. I must protect myself from hope.

Warder November steps forward. "Maybe the girl you choose should sleep here, after all . . ." she begins.

The Master looks mildly surprised. "But Warder November, you agreed. The training will be intensive." He is polite, but even I can see he's determined to have his way. Warder November backs down reluctantly, and he nods to the bio-indicator, who steps forward to have a better look at us. A little space opens around her wherever she walks, as if we know we are not good enough to touch her. I cannot bear to think she will look at me. I only stare at my feet, waiting for this moment to be over so I can go downstairs, wait for everyone else to go to sleep, and cry because she didn't choose me.

Then I hear her say, "This one." And it is over. But no one moves. She says, "Is there something wrong with her? Doesn't she hear me?" When I look up, everyone is staring at me.

"There is nothing wrong with her," the chief warder says. "She must be shy."

The bio-indicator speaks to me. "What is your name, girl?" Her voice is impatient.

The first time I try, nothing comes out. I try again. "Blay Raytee," I croak. Such a funny sound that some kids laugh.

"Is that some kind of made-up name?" she asks. She isn't talking to me now.

There is some shuffling while the warders confer. "Yes," one says after a moment. "We named her Lobelia September. She claims that's her real name, but it's just something she picked up on the street." I say nothing. We've had this conversation many times. I never win.

"Well, she's the one," the bio-indicator Marrella says.

"Is she a good reader?" the Master asks.

"Oh, yes," one of the warders says.

"Then she will do." The Master adds his approval.

"We'll deliver her to your house."

"No, she will come with me now," the Master says in that calm, insistent tone.

I remember my Object. "But my things," I say. The warders laugh. I look directly at the Master. "Please. I don't have much, but I want to take it with me." I'm begging.

I expect him to ignore me but, to my surprise, he softens. "Yes, of course," he says.

21

Warder November steps forward, too quickly I think. "We'll bring her to you soon."

"No," he replies, "I will come with you." I feel like a bone caught between two dogs. There's some kind of struggle going on here and I am at the center, but I don't know why.

I move like a sleepwalker as we go downstairs. Why would anyone choose me? Why would *she*? In the sleeping room, I gather my few clothes, sliding my Object out of its hiding place in my sleeping bag and into the bundle. A warder points to the gloves around my neck. "You won't need those now," she says.

Poppy, the girl who lost her handmade guy on Memory Day, is nearby. Her gloves are already full of holes. I lift the gloves from my neck and offer them to her, a gift. She looks afraid. "Take them," I say. She says nothing, but her eyes thank me as she takes the gloves.

I hold my head up as we leave. I was chosen. Nothing will ever be the same.

The Master's House

When the door to the Master's house opens, the housekeeper frowns. "This one?" she asks. Her nose wrinkles. I hardly know where to look. The house is all wood and warmth, filled with bright colors and pretty things. I don't belong here. The bio-indicator has not spoken to me since we left the Rotunda. The feeling of being chosen is gone. I want to bolt out the door and back to safety. The woman is old, perhaps fifty. She is spotlessly clean and stout, a thick, graying braid down her back. She looks puzzled rather than angry.

"Just show her to my rooms," Marrella says. She doesn't even glance at me.

The older woman hesitates, then speaks firmly. "She must bathe before she can be part of this household. And she must have new clothes." She gestures toward the bundle in my arms. "These I will burn."

The bio-indicator looks annoyed, but before she can speak, the Master's voice flows between the two women like soothing oil. "Of course, Erica. Do whatever's necessary. She can begin her duties tomorrow."

I follow this woman through the bright kitchen and into the

basement, which smells earthy but is just as warm as the rest of the house. "The bathrooms are upstairs," the woman called Erica says, "but I wouldn't trust you to them yet. Here's the hot tub. I'll put you in it now. Get you all scrubbed." The big wooden tub is already full of steaming water. "I suppose you have lice," she adds.

I am not sure I like this woman, who my bio-indicator seems to dislike. I shake my head. "We were treated just last week. I don't have lice." I have had, but I'm almost certain I don't now.

She purses her lips. "Well, we can't be too careful. Do you know how old you are?"

I shake my head. "Not for certain. The warders say about thirteen."

She makes a *tsking* sound as she gingerly peels my clothes away. "Undernourished. How long have you been at that work camp?" It surprises me to hear her call it a work camp. Most adults say Model Social Welfare Project.

"Four years in September. That's why they called me Lobelia September."

"Is it what you'd like to be called?"

A tight knot loosens in my throat. No one ever asked me this before. "No. It's not my name. I have a name. Not much of one, but it's mine." The words pour out in a grateful rush.

"And what is this name?" I hear the smile in her voice.

"Blay Raytee."

"A strange name. How old were you when you landed on the streets?"

"It's hard to say. Very little. I was just beginning to talk."

"Maybe Blay Raytee was as close as you could come to your real name," she says.

I nod. That fits with what I remember. I wait for her to ask the questions I do not want to answer. I cannot speak of Hilary.

"And how long were you on the streets?"

I am naked now. "I don't know," I say. I shiver a little even in the warm air.

"You're cold, poor thing. Get into the tub." I am relieved to obey. She hands me a cloth and a piece of something hard, white, and fragrant.

"What's this?"

She gives me a funny look. "Soap. What did you wash with in that place?"

"They have showers by the spirulina tank. We get one every week. The soap comes through with the water first, and then we rinse in plain water." I do not tell her how badly this system worked. Most of us ended up with a scalp full of soap for the rest of the week. Instead, I sit on the bench in the tub up to my neck in hot water. "I like this," I tell her.

"Good," she says. "You can bathe as often as you want in this house. More than once a week. Here." She shows me how to use the cloth and soap. "Now you wash. I'll get rid of these clothes. I have others that should fit you." As she gathers my clothes, my Object falls to the tiles with a clatter. "This is strange," she says, picking it up. I wish I could grab it back. I never show my Object to anyone. She turns the flat black case, which is held together by small metal screws. Shiny brown ribbon runs between two spools inside. "What is it?"

Too late to hide it now. "I don't know," I tell her truthfully. "I've had it as long as I can remember. It's the only thing I've always had." I wonder if I should trust her, then plunge on. "Maybe . . . maybe it came from my parents. But I don't know what it is."

"Looks like some kind of obsolete technology," she says. She lays it on a shelf by some clean cloths. "It will be safe here. I'll be back in a minute to help you wash your hair."

"I can use the soap."

"No. Don't. We have something else for hair."

When she leaves, I sink in right up to the tips of my ears and sigh. I can never remember being so comfortable. Could Blay Raytee be a childish version of my real name? It makes sense. Hilary told me over and over how she found me. It was one of my favorite bedtime stories. "I had a name all picked out for you, sweetie," she would say, smoothing my hair back as I settled down to sleep. "I was going to call you Honey-Pie. But you just insisted you already had a name. 'Blay Raytee, Blay Raytee, my name Blay Raytee!' You yelled until I was afraid someone would hear you and find us. So that's your name. Blay Raytee." And I would fall asleep in her arms, happy that she was the one who'd found me.

I scrub myself. Erica notices when she returns. "You look ten shades cleaner," she says. "Duck your head under." She takes a bottle from a shelf and pours something cool and sweet smelling into my hair. As she rubs my head, it foams. It feels wonderful.

"What is that?" I ask.

"Shampoo. We can have things ordinary people never see," she says, "because of the bio-indicator. Any soap, any cream or

26

medicine she needs. Tip your head back now." She rinses my hair, then washes it again until it's so clean it squeaks. I am in heaven. She lifts a strand of my hair, as if weighing it. "Your hair would look quite nice with a proper cut." She's kinder than she seemed at first. I'm starting to like her.

As she finishes washing my hair, she says, "Marrella is not what we expected. Bio-indicators are usually eager to learn, but she resists. William finds her difficult to teach. Still, we have great hopes for her." Her sigh does not sound hopeful. I find it odd that she should criticize my bio-indicator and call the Master by his first name.

"Out you come now," she says. "It's getting late." She hands me a large, soft cloth and a white robe and cloak, then turns to give me privacy. I grab my Object as we leave the basement.

In the kitchen she opens a doorway. "These are the servants' stairs," she says. "They lead to your room." We climb to a room with bare white walls. It is more comfortable than I could have imagined. There is a bed, a chest of drawers, and a window with white curtains. She shows me a little bathroom, then points to a door opposite the one we entered. "Those are the bio-indicator's quarters."

"But where do you sleep?" I didn't mean to ask. The question just slipped out.

She smiles. "With William, of course. Across the hall."

Shock must show in my face. She laughs. "Did you think I was a servant? Child, I am Erica Townsend, the Master's wife." But she's not laughing at me, and I find I can return her smile.

When Erica leaves, I wonder if this can be real. For as long as

I can remember, I slept in makeshift hiding places with Hilary,
and after, in big spaces crowded with strangers. This room is plain
and small, but it's mine alone. The bed is clean, soft, and comfortable. There are sheets instead of a sleeping bag, even a pillow.
My body is relaxed from the easy day, from the bath. But I run
over the events of this evening again and again. I am almost afraid
if I sleep, I will wake up back in the basement of the grand hotel.
After a while I hear the Master, Erica, and my bio-indicator come
upstairs. Then I hear Marrella's voice, but her voice alone. It goes
on and on without stopping, like a song without music. The
house powers down, and everything is still. I pull the clean blankets over my clean ears. I will do everything I can to help
Marrella. We might even become friends. Finally I sleep.

Green Tea

When I wake, someone is trying to rip my ear off. It must be one of the older girls. I open my mouth to scream loud enough to be heard by the warders, but another hand covers my mouth. "Don't you dare," a voice says. I fall back onto the bed, rubbing my ear, trying to remember how to breathe. I am in the room where Erica left me. Soft light filters through the white curtains. Marrella stands beside my bed. She is already dressed in her bio-indicator robes, her head wrapped in cloth.

"I have been awake for fifteen minutes," she says. "This must never happen again. Do you understand?" I'd like to tell her I didn't know what she expected of me, but I'm afraid to contradict her, so I nod instead. "Good," she says. "Now get out of bed."

When she closes the door, I realize I haven't any daytime clothes. But, in the top drawer of the dresser, I find clean underclothes. The next drawer holds tunics and leggings that almost fit. Erica must have brought them here last night while I was washing. I pull the clothes on and hurry through the door.

Two filtered skylights pour pale gold light into the bio-indicator's room. A bright coverlet is flung across her bed, tangled with blankets and pillows. The furniture is made of beautifully

29

carved wood. Strange, pretty objects decorate the room, brightly colored glass and lumps of glittering stone. I cannot see Marrella, but then I hear a noise. Looking around the corner, I find an alcove beside the wall where my bedroom juts into this space. It is bright with windows. Marrella sits at a small table looking out toward Ski Slope. As I approach, I see a kitchen counter built into the nearest wall. "You may make tea," she says. I have no idea what this means. In the work camp, food service was job training for some of the older ones. My confusion seems to please her.

"My, you are ignorant. I will show you this one time." She stresses the last three words. "Then, you will wake me up every morning with a pot of green tea. Is that clear?" I nod, following the swift movements of her hands. When she is finished, she says, "Tell me how I made it." When I do, she smiles a thin smile. "Now you are good for something." She sits at the table. I don't know what to do. "Bring me the tray," she says, "then tidy my room." The table is not two meters from where she stood, but I carry the tray to her. When I have picked up her clothes and made the bed, she comes back from the kitchen area. "I am going to have breakfast now," she says. "Wash my dishes, then you can see Erica." She leaves through the door that leads into the central hall.

I wash the dishes, then tidy my room, trying, all the while, to push my disappointment aside. Marrella is not kind, but why should she be? Just because she chose me, I let myself hope we might be friends. When I first came to the work camp, I'd hoped to find someone like Hilary, but I never did. The warders keep as far away from the kids as they can, and the other kids look out for themselves. I should have learned by now. I give my little room one last glance, then take the servants' stairs, my stairs, to the kitchen.

Erica is already at work pushing a large lump of something soft around on a board. "Those two may relax before lessons begin, but I have work to do." She pounds the lump with such violence that I jump. "Bread will not make itself." She pounds again. I begin to realize she means no harm.

"What is that?" I ask.

"Bread dough, child." She pauses, then gives me another of her looks. "You do know what bread is, don't you?"

As I nod, a lump rises in my throat, forcing me to turn away. Hilary was a master thief. That was what kept us under the protection of a Tribe. She could steal almost anything, but she loved bread most. Hot and fresh from alleys behind the bakeries. She would run back to our hiding place, tear the loaf open, and give great, steaming chunks of it to me. We could eat a loaf, the two of us, in just a few minutes. She was also good at trading for things we needed. Once she even got a funny-looking doll in a bright pink dress for me. "Every kid should have a doll, sweetie," she said.

Erica did not notice when I turned away. "What did you eat in that work camp?"

"Texturized vegetable protein, processed kelp, spirulina, and vegetables from the gardens." With or without permission, I do not add.

She purses her lips. "Spirulina. People shouldn't have to eat algae. It's impossible for people with low U-Rs to get real food. No wonder you're so small." She punches the lump again. It doesn't look like the bread I remember. "Our food is much better." She runs a critical eye over me. "So it should be possible to fatten you up. Sit down."

I do. I wonder what she means by "real food." When I lived on the streets, I ate anything, but in the work camp, they taught us that civilized people only eat plant products, never the flesh of animals. Spirulina tastes awful, but I thought eating it made us more like ordinary people. Erica brings me slabs of bread on a plate. Not the spongy stuff she is working with now, but bread as I remember it. Then she hands me a glass filled with something white. A real glass, not the chipped and scratched celluloid containers they gave us at the work camp.

"What is this?" I ask.

"Milk."

"What is milk?"

This time, she just sighs. "Milk is a protein. It will help you grow. It has calcium to make your bones strong."

I slosh the liquid around in my glass. I pretend to sip but only smell it. It has no smell. It doesn't look like something anyone would eat. "How do you make it?"

"We don't make it. Cows and goats do. They make milk inside their bodies to feed their young." She's beginning to sound annoyed.

My stomach heaves. "You want me to drink something made inside the body of a cow?" I push the glass away. "I can't." The idea is disgusting.

Erica looks angry. For a moment I am afraid she will force me, then she relaxes. "I cannot make you do things that are good for you." She takes the milk away. "Tea?" she asks.

"Yes, please." At least I know tea is not made inside the body of a cow. The bread is delicious. I have to stop myself from cramming it into my mouth, the way Hilary and I did. Erica puts a mug full of tea in front of me. It is not pale green like Marrella's tea, but dark brown like bog water. I take a big mouthful. It burns my throat all the way down. "Hot," I gasp.

"Most people," Erica says, "put milk in their tea." She turns to some food containers on the counter. She runs each past a built-in scanner, which beeps. When she's finished, she packs the containers into a basket. "William won't need you until this afternoon. When you've eaten, you can do something for me. You know where the ski slope is?" I nod. "Good. You can take this food up to Lem Howell."

A crust of bread just about to go into my mouth falls to the plate, but Erica has her back to me. How foolish I was to fuss over food. She is already annoyed with me. If I refuse to do this, will they let me stay here? Would I rather be eaten by Lem Howl or go back to the work camp? My answer surprises me. "All right," I say. But I push the plate away.

Erica sniffs. "For someone who looks to be starving, you're an awfully fussy eater." I would like to tell her the bread tasted wonderful until I was asked to risk my life, but I say nothing. "You look pale," Erica says. "Are you feeling ill?" I shake my head. She holds the full basket out to me. It's heavy. As I take it, I wonder if this is some kind of test. But Erica looks so unconcerned. Could it be that she has no idea what she's asking me to do?

I pause at the back door. "Where are the UV visors?"

"Oh, you don't need one," Erica says. The alarm must show on my face, because she continues. "Really, Blay. They aren't necessary." She hands me a bottle. "Put some of this on your face, and I'll find you some glasses."

The bottle contains a thin lotion. "What is it?" I ask.

"Sunscreen. It will protect your skin from the UV rays."

"Really?"

"Yes. And take these." She hands me a pair of dark glasses. The idea of going out without a UV visor seems so dangerous, I can't bring myself to do it. Erica notices. "I'm not lying, Blay. You'll be safe, I promise."

"Then why do they make us wear visors in the camp?"

Erica frowns and quickly glances over her shoulder as if someone might be listening. "I'll explain later," she says, and I am out the door. It's so strange to be outside without a UV visor that I have to stop to orient myself. The grand hotel is down the hill. Just yesterday, it was my home. Just a few minutes ago, I thought I was lucky to be free of it. Now I'm not sure. I know where the path to Ski Slope is. They made sure we knew so we'd never wander up there by mistake. Yesterday, if anyone had told me I would willingly go to Lem Howl's house, I would have laughed. I am not laughing now. The path is steep, sheltered by birches, maples, and spruce. It's beautiful, but it fills me with dread. Somewhere from deep inside my memory, I find pieces of a story about a girl walking through the woods, just like this, carrying a basket of food. And she is going to a house where someone dangerous waits, someone with big teeth who wants to eat her. Maybe does eat her. But the memory is so faint, I can barely hold on to it.

I wonder if I should throw the basket into the woods and lie to Erica. But again I think, Maybe this is a test. I'd do anything to keep myself out of that work camp.

At the fork that leads to Ski Slope, an old metal sign reads "Ski Lift." I force myself to put one foot before the other. This path leads toward two rusting metal towers, the first of many pairs that travel up Ski Slope. The tops are visible above the trees from the upper windows of the grand hotel. Why are they here? Maybe it had something to do with an advanced technology. If the stories are right, Lem Howl's house is at the base of the first towers. When I see them ahead, I duck into the brush so I can at least approach from an unexpected angle. It isn't easy, dragging this heavy basket through the undergrowth. Branches snag my new tunic and scratch my face, making me wish for the protection of a UV visor. Then I see the clearing ahead. I move up cautiously behind a big spruce, removing the dark glasses so the light can't reflect off them. Lem Howl's house is just where the stories say it should be.

Two huge, rusting metal posts support the front wall. It's the strangest house I've ever seen. It reminds me of shacks in the barrio on the South Side of St. Pearl. Kids who went there would disappear without a trace. This house has that homemade look, but it's different, made mostly of wood, not chunks of cement and sheet metal. The strangeness comes from what's been added. Some things, like the solar collectors, I recognize, but there are more than this small house could possibly need, at least three different kinds of windmills and other things. Cones with wires coming out of them, metal grids that must have some purpose. Or maybe not. Maybe crazy Lem Howl just put them up because he likes the way they look.

Suddenly the door swings open and there is Lem Howl. I freeze. I am well hidden behind the spruce, but my heart pounds so loudly I'm afraid he'll hear. He looks just as I imagined. His clothes are patchy. His long, frizzy hair is reddish but graying. He sniffs the air like an animal. I'm afraid he'll sniff me out. Then he stretches and gives out a yawn that sounds like an animal's roar. He has big, yellow teeth. They look sharp. I wonder if I should drop the basket and run, but he turns and walks from the house to a small, wooden building. A latrine. The door shuts firmly, and I hear it latch. Why would a crazy man latch a latrine in the bush? I don't even stop to wonder.

I run from my hiding place as fast as the heavy basket allows. I fling it onto the step, turn, and run down the path without looking back, so quickly I am afraid I will lose control and tumble down the steep hill, but somehow I keep my footing. I am positive Lem Howl must be at my heels, but at the fork in the path, when I finally pause to look back, I am alone. Clinging to the signpost, I clutch my side, which feels sliced open with a stitch. I gasp for breath, but I am smiling. Lem Howl has his food, and I am not it. If this was a test, I passed. Suddenly a branch snaps on the hill above me. I run to the Master's house without looking back again.

Erica is still in the kitchen. She looks surprised. "Goodness, Blay, you didn't have to hurry back like that. Such a lovely day. You might have enjoyed your walk." She doesn't seem to understand I've just done something dangerous and brave. "Where's the basket? Did you leave it there?" she asks.

"You wanted it back?" I manage to say. How could I have brought it back?

"Yes. I'll fill it again in a few days. It isn't much of a walk. You can get it later."

My knees almost collapse when she says this, but Erica is looking out the window and doesn't notice. "Never mind. It's such a lovely day. I'll fetch it myself." I sit down, overcome with relief. Erica gives me a sharp look. "You're exhausted, aren't you? You didn't eat enough for breakfast. What would you eat, I wonder." She takes a round, red fruit from a basket on the counter and hands it to me. "Here," she says.

I take it in my hand. It's smooth and lovely. "What is it?"

Erica sighs. "You've never seen an apple?"

"Oh, an apple. I've heard of these." My teeth break the skin and sink into the sweet flesh. "It's good," I say with my mouth full, and Erica laughs.

She turns her soft and rubbery bread onto the board again. The thought of eating it makes me want to gag, but I love the apple. I bite again and again until only the stem and seeds are left. The kitchen is bright with morning sun. It's quiet, except for the thunk of Erica's bread on the wooden board.

"I went up to Marrella's room and yours while you were gone," she says. "You did a good job on them, Blay. I'm sure you're going to fit in here." Her praise makes me feel like I did in that hot bath last night. Warm and peaceful. The feeling is so good, it scares me. I must not believe that I could belong here. It is dangerous to even pretend. What am I doing here, really? My curiosity overcomes me. "Erica, why am I here? Last night, the Master said Marrella needed help with learning."

Before she answers, Erica presses a few keys on a panel in the wall. The kitchen powers down. "We've been having trouble with the power," she says, then she continues. "William and Marrella are isolated from the townspeople now until her investiture. It's part of a ritual that goes back centuries. So we can't ask anyone from Kildevil to help her, but things have not been going well."

"So I'll help her prepare for the ceremony?"

Erica hesitates. "Not exactly. The Commission encourages us to train bio-indicators because they remind people how degraded the environment has been. In the Dark Times, when clouds of poison blew over from the industrial zones, bio-indicators exposed themselves to the toxins to show when it was unsafe for ordinary people to go out, and eco-warnings were then issued. It was simply a biological reaction to the environment." I wonder what Erica means by "the Dark Times," but I don't want to interrupt. "Things are different now," she continues, "and we hope bio-indicators can play another role. To show she can adapt, Marrella must learn to use important equipment and collect knowledge that may help the earth. But she's always making mistakes. Over the next few weeks, she will also undergo some tests to see if she is capable of assuming new responsibilities, but she's reluctant to learn anything and she seems to clash with William. We're hoping you can help her learn. Is that clear?"

"I think so," I say. There's so much I want to know. I struggle for the right questions. "I remember the eco-warnings in St.

Pearl. We ignored them, but I never knew anyone who got sick because of them. Since I came here, there haven't been any eco-warnings at all."

Erica gives me a look I cannot read. "You're a clever girl," she says. "I might as well be honest with you. In the Dark Times, the eco-warnings were real. The air from the industrial zones killed people. Bio-indicators died so often, they could hardly be replaced. That doesn't happen now."

"Because of the technocost?"

A curtain comes down behind Erica's eyes. I have said something very wrong. When she speaks again, her voice is quiet. "That's what they teach you down there, isn't it?"

My throat is so tight, I can only nod. Silence fills the room until I think this conversation, perhaps all conversation, has ended between us. I am just about to creep away when she finally speaks again. "I cannot talk to you about the technocaust, Blay, but you should know that the things you've been taught at the work camp are not all true. Please believe me when I say that you don't have the whole story. You will learn many new things in this house. We might as well start now. Blay, the eco-warnings in the city aren't real anymore. The Commission uses them."

"What do you mean?"

"The Commission finds it useful to empty the streets of St. Pearl at times, to make people think it's too dangerous to move around. As long as people fear the eco-warnings, they depend upon the Commission to protect them. They don't mind giving the Commission extra powers."

"But why do bio-indicators cooperate?"

"They don't. There are no bio-indicators in the city now. No Masters. They have withdrawn. To places like this."

I remember the tension between the Master and Warder November last night. It begins to make sense. "You mean you're at war with the Commission?"

Erica laughs. "I wouldn't go that far. We live just up the hill from a Commission-run complex. Bio-indicators have always reinforced the Commission's power. For a long time, the Way cooperated with the Commission. But the technocaust caused a split. It's a kind of war, but no one dies. Call it a power struggle."

"But if we don't need bio-indicators, why do we still have them?"

"People would feel lost without them. Every month after her investiture, Marrella will be exposed to the water, the air, and the produce of the land in the bio-indicator's Sacrifice, a ritual dating back to the Dark Times. People still need the Sacrifice to make them feel secure.

"Besides, all creatures adapt when the environment changes. The Way is helping bio-indicators to accept a new role." She pushes her bread into pans, then wipes her hands on her apron. "All this must seem strange to you. It will be stranger yet."

"What do you mean?"

"Remember what I said about tests? William is trying to discover if Marrella has special talents. You will help her prepare for these tests and accompany her to see she comes to no harm. I suspect she chose you partly because you look as if you could survive anything."

I feel a chill on the back of my neck. How strange will these tests be? I wonder. "What kind of tests?"

Erica begins to speak, then clamps her mouth shut. "It's better for William to tell you," she says. "I have probably already said more than I should." She adjusts the panel on the wall again, and the power comes on. She turns on the oven and places the pans of bread on top. "There," she says. "Soon we'll have bread."

I stare at her. "You mean you bake it? I thought we were going to eat it like that."

She laughs. "Eat bread dough? What an idea! You must think we're barbarians." She is not angry. "I'll try to find something you can eat. Ever try fish?" I shake my head. Isn't it wrong to eat animals? I want to ask, but I don't want to upset her again.

"Well, I'm not surprised. Fish is so rare." She takes something from a package in the food storage unit and puts it in a pan on the methane burner. The smell is strong but wonderful, like smoke, like the sea. When it's ready, she puts a fragment on a piece of bread and gives it to me.

I do not like the way it looks, like the body of a living creature, but the smell makes my mouth water so I take a bite. It tastes smoky and salty, warm and soft, like nothing I have eaten before. "I love it," I tell her through the food.

She grins. "You have expensive taste, but it's a good protein. That's called kipper. Smoked herring. A very rare food. Before I was born, herring were thought to be extinct. The fishery is tightly controlled, but we get some from time to time. Now, help me get the rest of this food ready."

Later, when Erica takes the meal to the dining room, I stay at the kitchen table.

"Wouldn't you like to eat with us?" she asks. "You don't have to sit alone."

"I'm fine," I say. I'm not sure Marrella would welcome me. "I really don't mind," I add when Erica hesitates.

"As you wish," she says finally, and leaves. We made a huge salad for lunch. Erica left more than I could possibly eat, the rest of the fish and half a loaf of fresh bread. Lunch passes quickly. I do not mind being alone with food. When Erica returns with the plates, I have already taken care of my dishes. "Good girl," she says. "Now you're wanted in William's study."

The study is at the front of the house. Passing through the door, I think, Now my real work begins. They sit at his desk, the Master with his back to the window, Marrella opposite, with a book turned between them. "Ah, Blay," he says. "Please wait while I finish explaining this." It is his habit to make orders sound like requests, but he expects to be obeyed without question. I sit in a semisolid chair. It forms itself around my body like a cloud and begins to pulse a pattern in vivid blues and greens. Ordinarily I'd be interested, but now I ignore it. Instead, I study the Master. His eyes are the gray of a sea that is distant, but calm. His eyebrows are heavy. His gray hair has thinned to a fringe around his ears. He is older than Erica, but powerful and tall. He looks like someone who might have been a soldier. No. A warrior. That's the word. Marrella does not look at me. It seems I am not worthy of her notice.

"You see," the Master says, "this one, *Marrella splendens*, is the creature you were named for."

Marrella draws back. "It's very ugly." She sounds horrified.

"Oh, no, it's quite beautiful in its way," the Master says. His voice is filled with humor and patience. "We learned many things from the Burgess Shale. But you won't need this book until the final test." As he closes the book I note the title, *Geology Lessons for Bio-indicators*. He takes another book from the shelf. "This is the one you must read before the first test. Take it with you now."

Marrella does not touch the book. "I still don't understand why I have to do these tests," she says. "I want my investiture."

"I know you are anxious for the ceremony, but I've explained all this before. The tests will determine your aptitude for the role." He turns to me. "There are two small tests, Blay, and a more extended one. They seem simple, but from them I will know if Marrella has the talent we are looking for. The final test is the greatest and is particular to the landscape of each area. On this part of the island, we've chosen the Tablelands. If we proceed to this test, Marrella will go into the Tablelands and you will go with her. She will listen to the earth, and we will see what happens."

Marrella interrupts. "I have always wanted to see the Tablelands." She is as delighted as a child. She asks nothing about the tests themselves.

The Master nods. "And you will if you pass the first tests."

Even I know about the Tablelands. In the picture on the ceiling of the Rotunda, they rise from the green hills around them like a chunk of the moon. Barren orange rock with not a plant to cover the naked ground. It's place of desolation, and no one I've ever talked to can say why. I feel a cold wind at my back. Perhaps Marrella will fail the first tests. Then we would be safe. But she is the one who chose me. How can I wish her to fail?

The Master continues. "Normally I could leave these tests until after your investiture, but winter is coming and there is a sense of urgency about this now. So we begin tomorrow, at dawn. I will not bother to describe what you must do until then. Just make sure you read the book."

Marrella begins to rise, but the Master stops her. "Before you leave, Marrella, we must discuss your UV readings. You're still making careless mistakes. I have told you, repeatedly, to make two sets of readings for each observation, and yet I'm only seeing data for one. I also thought you understood the importance of taking a zenith observation as well as direct sun observations. I find them missing from most of your observation sets. The UV readings are very important. Such carelessness cannot be tolerated. Tomorrow we will run through the entire process again with Blay. Then perhaps she can help you."

Marrella has stopped smiling. "I thought," she says, "that being a bio-indicator was a natural talent. I did not know I'd have to learn all this stuff." She spits the last word out.

The Master's face darkens. "Marrella, being a bio-indicator can be a blessing or a curse. You must decide. To this point, I would say you have seen few of the blessings."

He pauses to give Marrella a chance to reply, but she scowls and says nothing, so he goes on. "In the Dark Times, bio-indicators were like sacrificial victims, like those put to death in ancient days to stop the gods from being angry. The role was altogether automatic, as you wish it now to be." His voice tightens. "At that time, the life expectancy of a bio-indicator was a few years at most." He pauses to rein in his anger. Although he is not young, there is power in his body. If he loses his temper, he could do great harm. Marrella has not flinched, but I hold my breath. He continues. "Things are different now. Bio-indicators collect information. Some do UV readings all over the planet every day, looking for changes in the ozone layer. Others collect information on greenhouse gases. They all learn and try to contribute to our store of knowledge. It's your job. Is this clear?" His eyes blaze.

Marrella meets his gaze steadily, then shrugs one shoulder slightly. Her defiance takes my breath away. I am sure they will come to blows. I move to the edge of my chair. The Master is twice my size, but I will throw myself between them to protect her if I must. When he speaks again, his voice is filled with controlled anger. "I have never seen such disrespect in a bio-indicator. Your performance in this house has been disgraceful. If you fail these tests, Marrella, there will be no investiture. You will leave here in shame." He turns away. "Go now," he says. "Learn what you need to know. Take this." Without looking at her, he pushes the lastbook across his desk. "It will make you a better bio-indicator." His voice is bitter.

Marrella takes the book and storms from the room. I am swept along in her wake. At the foot of the central staircase, I hesitate, uncertain if I should follow. "Come," she calls back over her shoulder, so I do. In her bedroom, she throws the lastbook against the wall. It lands on the floor with a loud thud that must certainly be heard throughout the house. I wonder if she's broken it.

"Learn this, Marrella. Do that." She mimics William's voice. I am horrified. In the work camp, anyone who spoke like that would be punished. Severely. I wait for the Master, but nothing

45

happens. Marrella turns to me, still fueled by anger. "Can you shampoo my hair?" I nod. Until last night, I didn't even know what shampoo was. "Good. I'm finished listening to that stupid old man for today." She leaves, and I can only follow.

This bathroom is much finer than the basement where I bathed last night. Everything is green and white, the smooth surfaces spotless. I understand why Erica didn't want me in here until I was clean. Marrella sweeps around like a whirlwind, gathering towels, setting a chair in front of the sink. She sits. "Unwrap my turban," she commands. I find the tucked-up end with no help from her and begin to unwind. The cloth falls away. I gasp before I can stop myself. "Pretty, isn't it?" Marrella says bitterly. "Did you think I was chosen as bio-indicator for my beauty?"

I don't reply. I had thought only wisps of hair escaped from her turban. I see now that those wisps are all the hair she has. Her bare scalp is red, cracked, and scabbed. I force myself not to look away.

"It isn't catching," she says. "My skin reacts to everything. Before this started, my hair was beautiful. This is what made me a bio-indicator. At the time, I thought I was so lucky to get away from those dreary weavers." She points to a bottle of shampoo. "That's the only one that helps." I test the water as she leans back on the basin. I wet her poor, sparse strands of hair, then pour the shampoo. It has a sharp, medicinal smell. Gathering my courage, I smooth it as gently as I can over her red, cracked scalp. Flakes of dead skin wash away, and I remember what the Master said a few moments before. Being a bio-indicator could be a blessing or a curse. His words come back to me: "To this point, I would say you have seen few of the blessings." Now I understand.

When I am finished, her scalp seems less inflamed, although it still looks nothing like skin. "That's better," she says. "I feel better. Thank you." It's the first kind thing she's said to me. "Now clean up in here and come back to my room."

I scoop the dead skin and few hairs from the basin into a disposal unit. Then I scrub the basin and hang up the towels Marrella dropped on the floor. When I return to her room, she is sitting on her bed. She hands me scissors. "It's silly for me to pretend I still have hair. Cut it off." I hesitate, but she says, "Go on. I won't change my mind." It only takes a moment to snip what's left away. Then she gives me a tube of cream. "Put this on my head, and I'll show you how to fix my turban." As I work, I catch sight of the lastbook lying open on the floor, the one she threw against the wall. Its pages are still covered in print. When we have finished, she turns to the kitchen area. "That's all for now." I scoop the book off the floor in one fluid movement on the way to my room. The maneuver reminds me of lifting scrip cards on the street, something I was very bad at in spite of Hilary's coaching. But I'm not really stealing now. I know she won't read the book tonight, and I'll return it to the Master's study. After I've read it.

The house falls into a kind of brooding quiet after the confrontation. I sit in my room, enjoying the luxury of idle time alone. The lastbook is unharmed. Its title is *Plant Life: A Natural History for Bio-indicators*. When it grows dark, Erica calls me to the kitchen, which is lit with candles.

"Power trouble again," Erica explains. "Here's a meal for you, Blay. Eat while I fix a tray for Marrella. William is too angry to share a table with her tonight, and I imagine she feels the same way." She sighs. "I've never heard of a bio-indicator acting like this. She's only interested in the investiture ceremony and the status the role will give her. She won't learn anything. William and I have no children. We have no idea how to deal with her."

There is a glass of something white by my plate. I look at it dubiously. "Soy milk," Erica says. "Untouched by the body of a cow."

I take a big gulp to show my gratitude. It tastes terrible. "It's wonderful," I say. She rewards me with a smile. The basket is on the counter, the one I took up the hill just this morning, although it seems like weeks ago. "You got the basket," I say before I can stop myself. She smiles. "Yes. I told Lem about you. You'll have to meet him." Have to meet him. What does she mean?

"Poor Lem," Erica continues. "He's never recovered from what happened."

I'm too curious to be quiet now. "Why don't they retire him?"

"Retire him? He has a U-R of nine! They don't tell you anything in that work camp, do they?" I shake my head. I'm not sure Erica would like to know what they do tell us.

"Lem Howell calculated all the settings for the hydroponics. Light levels, temperatures, ventilation, growing schedules, concentrations of nutrient mediums, everything. Without him, the hydroponic project would fail, and the Commission would close the work camp. They call it a welfare project, but they'd shut it down if it cost them money. Lem Howell is the reason you've stayed off the street." She looks furious.

Once again I have made her angry. Once again she makes my head spin. "I'm sorry. I didn't know."

The edge comes off her anger. "How could you? They want

you to think the Commission is taking care of you. No one can blame you for not knowing the truth."

"But isn't Lem Howl a techie?"

"Of course he is. One of the best on the island. That's what I've been telling you."

"I thought that was bad."

"That's what they tell you down there, isn't it? Technology is so dangerous, it must be controlled by the state." Erica begins to pace as if pursued by the thoughts in her head. "That's the mentality that caused the technocaust. Blay, I have to make you understand that things are not as you've been told. You can start by meeting Lem Howell."

My heart lurches. "But isn't he . . . crazy?" I whisper this last word.

Erica laughs. "In his own way, yes. From what William tells me, Lem never was like other people." Then she grows more serious. "He's only forty, but his wife's death aged him terribly."

So some of the story is true. "But he won't hurt me?"

"Don't be silly. He doesn't eat children."

I stop myself from contradicting her just in time. I like Erica, and I want her to like me, so I try to believe her. "Would you come with me, when I meet him?" I ask. "I'm afraid to go alone."

"Is that why the basket was thrown down like that this morning?" I nod, looking down. My face is hot and red. "I thought there must be a reason. You don't seem like a careless child. Of course I'll go with you. I think you'll be surprised, though."

I am bound to be, but I don't say so.

When I finish eating, Erica hands me some containers off the table. "These go in that cupboard." As I open the cupboard, the scanner on the wall beside me beeps. "I didn't ask you to run them through the scanner, Blay," Erica says.

"I didn't. It beeped on its own." I lift my arm and it beeps again.

Erica laughs. "How odd. It seems to like you. Now take the tray up to Marrella."

I wonder if I should say anything about Marrella. Today's fight must have upset Erica, too. As I turn to the stairs, I think of something. "I have seen injured animals bite those who try to help them."

Erica looks at me strangely. "What do you mean?"

My heart is pounding now, but I continue. "The Core of St. Pearl was full of stray dogs. They got hit on the auto-routes all the time. But if you tried to help one, it might bite you."

"And?"

"And, Marrella is . . . injured. Have you seen her scalp? It must be painful."

Erica relaxes. For once I have not spoken wrongly. "Yes, I think it is. The medicines should have helped by now, but they aren't working. I think she is mourning the life she lost. A girl like you can't begin to imagine the world Marrella came from. She grew up in a gated community in St. Pearl. I doubt she ever even saw the Core where you lived. She never worked; she only went to school when she felt like it. The first seventeen years of her life were filled with idle comfort.

"Then, last year, her grandmother died. She was Marrella's only relation. I'm sure that loss has a lot to do with what Marrella feels. I've tried to talk to her about it, but she just pushes me away.

I had hoped things would be so different." She sighs. "Take the tray to her now, and you can have the rest of the night to yourself. It's been a difficult day." She hesitates, then continues. "Blay, when you came to this house last night, I couldn't imagine why Marrella chose you. I thought she must have acted out of spite, picking such a sorry-looking child."

My hurt must show in my face because she quickly catches herself. "That was only my first impression." She reaches over and pats my hand. "That bath did wonders for you, dear. And now that I know you better, I think you may be the one wise choice that girl has made since she came to us."

I glow with the warmth of her words as I carry the tray upstairs.

At the door that leads from my room to Marrella's, I am stopped by the same tuneless song I heard last night. I'm afraid to interrupt, but I must give her the food, so I open the door and enter as quietly as possible. She is sitting cross-legged on a mat on the floor, palms upward on her knees. She chants softly, but clearly, ". . . come to me, guide me, oh, wise ones, oh, sisters of the earth. . . ." She stops abruptly and opens her eyes. "How long have you been spying on me?"

"I just entered your room this moment. The Master's wife sent me."

This seems to satisfy her. "Place the food on the table in the kitchenette," she says. "I am not finished." She closes her eyes again and continues her tuneless chanting, but this time quietly so I cannot hear her words. I fill the kettle and place it on the burner. When she sits down at the table, she seems calmer and more cheerful. "I wonder what I'll have to do tomorrow?" she says, almost to herself. "I suppose we'll find out soon enough."

"Would you like me to help you with the book?" I ask. I'm immediately sorry. She gives me a look full of scorn and doesn't even reply. As I turn to leave, she says, "Set your panel to wake you before sunrise."

"Set my panel?"

She looks exasperated, but only mildly so. "The control panel in your bedroom. I'll show you." I follow her. She points to a flat wall panel near her bed like the one in the kitchen. "It controls your environment. You can set the temperature, light levels. You can program music for your room, but don't. The noise would bother me. And you can set it to wake you, like this." She makes a few deft passes over the time display. "Set it for 6:00 A.M. Then I will not be forced to pull you from your bed by the ear." I recognize something like humor in her tone. She seems more at peace tonight. But as I leave the room, I remember what Erica said. "What if there are problems with the power overnight?"

"What do you mean?"

"There are problems with the power. Erica told me it goes out in the kitchen."

"There's a backup fuel cell in each panel. There are no problems with the power."

"Oh, fine." I leave the room confused, but afraid to contradict her. Erica said there were problems, and the kitchen powered down twice today. Maybe Marrella doesn't notice things like that. I set my panel, then open *Plant Life: A Natural History for Bioindicators*. I fall into the book effortlessly, learning things I never suspected. Plants too small to be seen by the naked eye, trees that grow hundreds of meters high and live for more than a thousand years. I learn how plants use sunlight, water, and carbon dioxide to make their own food, and how, in doing so, they free oxygen from water. This freeing of oxygen is the most important thing that ever happened on our planet. Life on land was not possible until plants freed oxygen for the atmosphere and the ozone layer was created. In the hologram pictures, I go into the cell of a plant to learn how this process, *photosynthesis*, takes place.

When I finally hear my name, it reaches me from very far away. I realize this is not the first time I was called. "Blay, where are you!" Marrella sounds impatient.

I glance at the page before I close the book. Two hundred and eleven. I must have been reading for hours. "Here," I say, quickly opening the door. "I am here."

Marrella is sitting on her bed, the empty tray nearby. "Where have you been?"

"Here," I say again, sounding like an idiot. I find it difficult to pull myself back to reality. "I must have fallen asleep," I add, excusing myself with a lie.

"You may take my tray now," she says, and she turns her face to the wall. I take the tray to the empty kitchen and go back to my book. After I finally finish, I drift into a happy, relaxed dream. I swim inside the cell of a plant, watching cytoplasts use light and water and carbon dioxide to make food. In doing so, just as a by-product, an accident almost, they liberate oxygen. I watch the tiny plants of the oceans breathe life into the atmosphere, 3.8 billion years ago. Millions of years pass. The sun's rays grow less deadly, and the barren, flat rocks of the earth are ready for life.

The First Test

I do not sleep long, but deeply, and wake feeling as if something good is about to happen. I can never remember feeling this way before. I don't know why I should, but the feeling doesn't leave me. Maybe it's because I spent all that time reading. "Photosynthesis," I whisper to myself, remembering the accidental miracle that made life on land possible.

The green tea is made before Marrella stirs. She is pale against the unbleached sheets, her turban slightly crooked, her inflamed scalp just visible above one ear. I remember what Erica said last night, and I wonder if her hair will ever grow back. She frowns while she sleeps. Afraid to wake her with words, I let the cup and pot rattle as I put the tray down. She opens her eyes as I hoped she would.

"Oh," she says, "morning." Her voice is flat. "That test is today, whatever it is." She sits and pours herself tea. "I don't understand. Why can't he just let me be?"

The question isn't aimed at me, but I could answer it. I could tell her how it feels to long for books, how lucky she is to be one of the few chosen to learn, but I know better than to try. Instead, I leave her to finish her tea. When I return, she has dressed and departed. I quickly tidy her room and my own and rush down to the kitchen.

Marrella is eating breakfast. With a look, Erica warns me to be cautious. I need no warning, but I appreciate her concern. I take my place at the table quietly and as far away from Marrella as I can. Erica gives me bread, which I eat quickly. Too quickly, I guess from the looks Marrella casts my way. The way I eat must shock her. But she doesn't know what it's like to be so hungry you could never believe your belly will feel full again. And the bottomless hunger that makes inside, a hunger that cannot be filled by food. While I lick the last crumbs from my fingers, William enters from the back porch. His coat is wet. He looks like he hasn't slept at all, but he smiles. "I was hoping for a day like this. The UV levels will be low. You can do this test without protective glasses. That will make it easier." How? I wonder. "Marrella, you read that book I gave you, didn't you? Part of it, at least?"

"Of course I did." She lies so easily.

William smiles. "Very good. Now, the test is simple. Go outside, find a plant, and bring it back to me."

"A plant? What plant?"

"Any plant. That's the test."

Marrella stands, annoyed. "Is this some kind of joke?"

William's eyes are as calm and serious as his voice. "No joke, I assure you. The plant you bring will tell me what you've learned. I think you understand. Now go." He leaves before Marrella can speak again. Erica turns her back to the sink, pretending to be busy. "You may need rain gear," she says mildly. "You'll find it on the way out."

I follow Marrella to the porch. We take waterproof coats and shoes but nothing else. Stepping into the damp air with nothing to protect my face makes me shiver, not with cold, but with excitement. In spite of the waterproof coat, I feel naked. A cool wind touches my skin. The grass is wet, but the rain has stopped. Thick, gray clouds bring the sky down close, wisps of fog trailing through the trees. It is light, although the sun has not yet risen. And it seems to me the world has changed. Everything, at least every living thing, glows faintly with pale yellow light. Marrella clumps through the wet grass grumbling. The feeling of joy I woke with has not left me, but I keep it to myself.

Marrella kicks a loose rock. "Bring back a plant. What kind of a test is that? They are making fun of me." She turns to me. "Which way do you think we should go?"

My arm rises almost of its own accord and points up the hill. I have to think of a reason to justify this. "I saw some meadows yesterday when Erica sent me up Ski Slope. Perhaps you will find what you need there." Somehow, I know she will. We walk the damp, dim path in silence, and I think the world has never looked so lovely. Every raindrop on every leaf glistens. I hear music in the wind, in the leaves. The air holds so many delicate scents, each one a separate strand. I feel part of everything.

We stop at the first meadow. Marrella looks around. "There aren't any flowers. Most of these plants are already dead for the winter. How can I pick a plant?" Her mood grows worse as mine grows better. At the far edge of the meadow, there's a group of boulders. "Over here," she says. "At least I can sit down to think." The rocks are smooth and easy to sit on. They are wet, but Marrella's coat protects her. I watch until she says, "You may sit." She motions to a rock a good distance from her. As I sit on it, I notice this rock also glows. Why? A rock is not alive. I look more carefully and see patterns that are not rock, but tiny, flat plants. Some are black, some are green, and some are gray. I've never seen them before. Suddenly I know these are the plants Marrella must bring back. I am certain. But I also know I cannot simply tell her this. "Have you noticed these rocks?" I say.

She looks at me as if I am insane. "Noticed them? We're sitting on them."

"I mean, did you see the patterns on them?"

She gives me another unbelieving stare. "No," she says. "I am not in the habit of studying rocks. In any case, I am not looking for rocks. Apparently, that comes later."

I try once more. "I think there are little plants growing on these rocks. Maybe that's what you're supposed to find." I say "maybe" but I know it's true.

Marrella rises. "You are a very stupid girl. I'm looking for a plant. If I bring back a rock, they will think I'm as stupid as you." Her words don't even sting. I know I must take these plants back. The rock is split by frosts of past winters, and some small chips are covered in these little plants. As Marrella strides away, I quickly pry one out and take it with me.

We climb past the sign that points to Ski Slope and Lem Howl's house. We climb and climb. I have never wandered this far from the grand hotel, but there's no danger of getting lost because the path goes straight up. The trees thin, then disappear. Finally we crest the hill at a broad plateau. For the first time, I turn to face downhill, and when I do, I catch my breath. It's daylight now, gray but full, and the wispy fog has lifted. Down the hill lies the small valley that shelters the grand hotel. To the right, the rusting towers of Ski Slope rise. In the other direction, I see the landfill, the road to Kildevil, and the town itself, tucked against the shore. The bay looks like little more than a wide river. Across it, green and gray hills seem to roll forever. The land spreads before us like a beautiful cloth. A poem comes to me, unbidden:

> *"Had I the heavens' embroidered cloths,*
> *Enwrought with golden and silver light,*
> *The blue and the dim and the dark cloths*
> *Of night and light and the half-light,*
> *I would spread the cloths under your feet. . . ."*

Marrella looks startled. "What's that?"

I feel myself blush. "Nothing. Just a poem. The view reminded me. It looks like the cloths of heaven."

"Whatever that means," Marrella mutters, but she doesn't move and I'm glad. I can't take my eyes off the land. I have lived here for four years and never suspected such beauty.

"What is that river down there?" Marrella asks.

I hesitate to contradict her. "It's not a river, it's the sea."

"How can that be the sea? You are wrong."

I try to explain. "This is a backwater of a long sound that reaches far inland. We are a day's journey from the open sea by foot. The water is shallow and calm, but it is salt, and there are tides."

"How do you know this?" she asks.

I'm relieved she does not argue. "They brought us here from St. Pearl by ship, but a large ship cannot navigate this far inland.

The water is too shallow. We walked the last day of the journey. The road follows the shore, so I have seen the water from the open sea."

"And that's Kildevil?" she says, pointing to town.

"Yes, it is."

"I can't go there until the day of my investiture. Have you ever been?"

"Once. We passed through on the way to the work camp."

"And what was it like?"

I want to say I can't remember, but I do. The memory is all too clear. "We didn't see much. We are not welcome in town. Those people would be happier if we were somewhere else." I shudder inwardly at the memory of those closed faces, the people wordlessly lining the street, making a human fence to ensure that none of us slipped into their world. "Of course," I add, "they will not feel that way about you."

Her laughter is harsh. "They certainly won't. I am very important to them." She turns away, and I'm forced to follow. The plateau at the top of the hill is barren, too rocky and exposed for most living things. But in the shelter of a boulder by a small, boggy pond, Marrella finally finds a clump of small, purple flowers. In this unpromising place they have only managed to bloom now, when everything else is finished. "This must be what they want. Uproot it." I know it isn't, but I pry the straggling plant from the gravel. Then we turn and retrace our path. A wind follows us down the hill. How lucky we are, I think, to be going to a place that is warm and sheltered, a place I am coming to think of, in spite of myself, as home.

The Lesson

When we enter the house, Erica shoos us past her kitchen, which is now filled with the most amazing smells. "Straight to William's study. He's waiting," she says. She looks pinched, and I realize she is anxious too. As we enter the study, I feel the rock chip in my hand. Marrella plunks the clump of flowers, wilting now, down on William's desk. Most of the earth shook off the roots on the walk home, but bits of dirt and rock chips still scatter across the polished wooden surface. I am horrified. William ignores the mess but looks horrified as well. "Asters?" he says. The disappointment is naked on his face. "This is what you found?"

To my surprise, Marrella responds to his disappointment, and not with anger. She looks down. "They were the only flowers I saw," she says softly. "I thought they were pretty."

William turns away from us to the window. He sighs. "Marrella, I can teach you nothing. I'm afraid the process must stop here. If you'd brought me something else. . . ."

I thrust the rock chip into Marrella's hand. She reacts right away. "Well, I did, but it seemed so insignificant. . . ." She holds the fragment out to him.

As William lifts it from her hand, he is transformed. "Lichen.

Yes. This is what I hoped for. The best thing possible. Why did you not show it to me first?"

Marrella flounders. "I . . . I—"

"She had given it to me to hold, Master," I say.

He looks confused, but to my relief says, "No matter. I had thought you might not have read the book or that the lessons were lost to you. It would have meant—but that doesn't matter. Now we can get to work." He pulls a disk toward him. "Look through the magnifying glass," he tells Marrella, and he begins to explain. "Lichens look like plants, but they are actually communities, or a marriage of plants if you will. A fungus and an alga live together in the lichen. The fungus provides the alga with water and anchors it. The alga uses the light of the sun to make food for the fungus. You see? They work together and both benefit. Do you remember what photosynthesis is?" he asks. She nods, although I'm sure she is lying.

He's so happy. It means so much to him that I find I am listening intently. And, of course, because I have read the book, I understand what he says. I vow then that I will learn, even if Marrella is unwilling. I will read what needs to be read and try to make sure she learns too, just as they hoped I would. If it is this important to them, I must.

". . . lichen live in some of the harshest climates on this planet," William continues, "where other plants die. In burning deserts and arctic regions. But like you, Marrella, they react to the environment." With this, he catches her interest for the first time.

"Like me?"

"Yes. They cannot grow where there is too much pollution.

They also retain heavy metals, such as lead and cadmium. Scientists can use lichen to determine the levels of heavy metals in the environment."

At the word "scientists" Marrella pulls back. Inwardly, I do too. If techies were bad, scientists were worse, the source of all earth-destroying technology. Yet William speaks this word with reverence. I remember what Erica said last night, about things not being as I was told.

When we finally leave the study, the Master smiles. "Change now. Erica has made a special meal." It's hard to believe that Marrella stormed from this room only yesterday. As we leave, the Master adds, "Join us too, Blay. This is a celebration."

I'm too stunned to speak, partly delighted that he thought to remember me, partly appalled. I need more time to learn how to eat without embarrassing myself. But he's already gone. "Come, help me prepare," Marrella says.

As soon as she closes the door to her room, she turns on me. "How did you know what to choose! How could you?" She's furious.

"I don't know; I just did," I say. I cannot explain how I felt this morning. The feeling has faded now. Perhaps it was only my imagination.

She gives me a cold look. "Well, you did the right thing, pretending I had picked it up. Don't get any ideas about trying to impress the Master. I am the one doing these tests."

I wish I could make her understand that I would be her friend. I lower my eyes. "You are the only reason I'm here. I would never betray you."

"Make sure that's so," she says. I can't tell if she believes me.

I am scrubbed clean when we enter the dining room a few minutes later, but I feel as if I've sprouted extra arms. I hardly know what to do with myself. But the soup smells delicious. I am just about to lift the bowl when Erica picks up her spoon. So do the others. Soup, I see, is to be eaten with a spoon. I've never tried this. I pick up my spoon and fill it carefully. It isn't as hard as it looks. After the first few spoonfuls, I relax.

"Take some time off, Marrella," William says. "I've done your noon UV readings. Blay can help us with the late-afternoon observation set."

"If this is to be a holiday, Blay and I will go for a walk," Erica says. She smiles, and I know where she means to take me. My spoon falters, splashing red soup across the white tablecloth. "I'm sorry," I say, grabbing the spoon, reaching toward the stain to pat it. "I'm sorry."

Marrella sighs noisily.

"Think nothing of it," Erica says. "The tablecloth will wash. Marrella, would you like to come with us?"

"No, thank you, I would rather read," Marrella says.

I don't believe this for a moment, but William is delighted. "That's wonderful."

My face still burns from my clumsiness. My heart pounds, too, but that has nothing to do with shame. Today, I meet Lem Howl.

The House on Ski Slope

In the kitchen I work as slowly as possible. Too soon, everything is tidy.

"Ready?" Erica says. She has prepared another basket of food. I don't have to ask where we are going. My knees feel weak, but I nod. She smiles. "Good girl." She hands me the sunscreen. "Put this on."

"You were going to explain why I don't need protective clothing," I remind her as we step outside.

"Well, we're beginning to believe the hole in the ozone layer might be repairing itself."

"Can it do that?" The idea of a world without UV visors makes me forget where we are going.

"That's exactly what the Way wants to know," Erica says. "Marrella is careless about her work, but she's part of a network of bio-indicators, and we hope the readings they do will tell us what's happening to the ozone layer."

"That's what the Master said yesterday. Does the Commission know about this?"

"They might. We haven't told them, but we know they're watching us."

"Aren't you afraid?"

"Blay, all the governments across North America have been in power far too long. They are old, corrupt, and weak. We're hoping they haven't got the energy to challenge us."

"But . . ." I hesitate, remembering how I've upset her before.

"But you think the Commission should control these things," she says. She doesn't seem angry today, which makes it easier to agree.

"I only know what I've been told."

"Yes, but Blay, what if the Commission knew the earth was healing itself, but decided not to tell anyone?"

"Why would they do that?"

"Remember what I told you yesterday about the eco-warnings?"

"You said they aren't real. That the Commission uses them to control people."

"Can you believe that?"

"I know we were controlled at the work camp. In more ways than we understood, I think." I want to tell her about the apple drink at the Memory Day ceremony, then I remember who we're about to visit and stop myself. "But protective clothing isn't the same as eco-warnings. It doesn't keep people in. It lets them go out."

"Yes, but think what the fear of UV radiation does. Here, that UV clothing makes sure no one mistakes the work camp children for ordinary people. In St. Pearl the only people who live daytime are the ones who are allied with the Commission. The others live nighttime. It's a way of making sure that the rich and poor are kept as far apart as possible. That suits the Commission. Here, in Kildevil, people don't live nighttime because we've told them they no longer have to. If poorer people in the cities didn't have to live nighttime, what do you think might happen?"

I think about St. Pearl. "I lived with a Tribe for about a year before I came here. Do you know about the Tribes?"

She nods. "Well-organized groups of homeless children," she says, "with rules and social structure of their own."

It sounds like she's reading a description from a book. "Well, I've never thought of the Tribes that way before, but I guess that's right," I say. "The Tribe that took me . . . that I lived with," I correct myself to keep the story as far away from Hilary as I can, "they had taken over one of the sunken towers in the harbor. You know, one of the buildings abandoned when the waters rose." Erica nods again, so I continue. "We had a perfect view of the Core. Daytime and nighttime. The leaders watched for anything they could make use of. If there was a fire, they'd send out kids to see what could be lifted in the confusion. And it was like two different cities. The daytime people lived in the gated communities. Most of them never came to the Core, but if they did, they were completely protected with UV suits, heavy vehicles, even body guards. The nighttime people lived a whole different life. They stole and gambled, sold themselves." A shadow crosses her face, so I quickly add, "Most of those daytime people had nothing to do with us."

"Exactly." We have reached the path that branches off to Ski Slope. Erica pauses, panting a little. "This hill gets steeper every year," she jokes. As we begin to walk again, she says, "Blay, do you believe the Commission cares about people like us?"

What happened to Hilary flickers across my mind. "More than they did before they set up places like the work camp."

"But there was a reason for that. The technocaust put a lot more children on the streets. Then, suddenly, there were death squads to 'retire' them. That sickened ordinary people. The Commission was faced with a protest movement for the first time in many years."

Somehow she has read my mind. Death squad. The blackness opens a hole, my knees buckle. . . .

"Goodness, Blay, are you all right?" Erica catches me against her shoulder as I fall. She is warm and soft and smells like bread.

The black hole shrinks and disappears. "I'll be okay," I manage to say.

"Do you need to sit down?"

I shake my head. "It's just . . . I just . . . there are things I can't talk about." My voice falls to a whisper.

Erica squeezes my shoulder. "I think I understand." I appreciate her kindness, but how could she? Safe in this protected life of hers, how could she ever? Lem Howl's house looms ahead. Just yesterday I ducked off this path to sneak up without being seen. Now Erica knocks on the door and opens it without waiting for a reply, as if this were the most natural thing in the world. "Lem," she says, "Lem, are you here?"

A shaggy head bobs up from behind a barrier in one corner of the room. Lem Howl's head. When he sees me, he ducks back down. Erica coaxes him like a child. "Now, Lem," she says, "don't be like that. This is the girl I told you about yesterday. This is Blay."

"Like wheat?" The head pops back up again.

I'm so surprised I forget to be scared. "What do you mean?" I ask.

"*Blé, la graine de blé.* It's French for wheat." He speaks in a quick, distracted way, like half his mind is elsewhere.

"Is it? I didn't know that." Could my parents have spoken another language?

"There," Erica soothes, "she's harmless, see? Come and meet her."

With this, he stands and walks around the barrier. He's a big man, but he moves like someone who expects to be struck down at any moment. He comes closer, but not close enough to touch. This suits me fine. I liked him better behind the barrier. Erica holds out the basket. "Look, Lem, I brought you more food. Why don't you put it away?"

Lem takes the basket without getting any closer than necessary. He disappears into a side room. The kitchen, I guess. When he's gone, I look around. Like the outside, this isn't like anyplace I've ever seen. The corner where we found him seems to be some kind of workstation. Strange panels and modules climb the walls, some with blinking diodes. I have no idea what they are. Three identical objects stand in one corner. Long, narrow things on stands with white and black levers across them. The white levers are all the same, but the black ones are arranged in patterns of twos and threes. They look like some kind of simple inputting device.

Lem Howl pokes his head around the doorway. "Tea?"

"That would be very nice," Erica says. She moves a stack of

print books, lastbooks, and papers from an ancient-looking wooden bench and motions for me to sit with her. The house is very quiet. Ordinary noises come from the kitchen. I am sitting in Lem Howl's house, waiting for him to bring tea. I must be dreaming.

But I'm not. Lem Howl soon returns carrying a tray. He sweeps a small table clear with his elbow, sending papers cascading to the floor. Then he places the tray on the table and turns to us. He is huge and shaggy and terrifying at such close range. "Milk?" he asks. I nod numbly, my aversion to milk overridden by my fear. "Yes, thank you," Erica says, as if we were visiting any normal person. After he pours our tea, Lem Howl takes a mug in his own huge hands and folds himself onto a stool in a far corner, facing us. An awkward silence settles with him. All the questions I should not ask rush into my head. Do you really glow orange in the dark? Did your wife drink poison? Question after impossible question until I think I will burst. I steal a glance at him. At the same moment, his eyes come up from his mug and meet mine. I look away quickly.

After what seems like years, Erica says, "Would you like to play some music after we finish our tea?"

"I'd rather show you the garden."

"This time of year?" Erica is as surprised as I am.

"Been working out there," he says. "I'd like some feedback."

I should know I am safe with Erica, but this is Lem Howl, the man they used to terrorize us in the work camp. Into my head pops a vision of newly dug graves. Lem Howl means to lure us outside, kill us, and throw our bodies into those graves.

"That sounds wonderful," Erica says.

I don't know what to do. Kids like me are human garbage. In St. Pearl you never knew when one of us would disappear, only that sooner or later someone would. Even when I lived with the Tribe. One day a kid would simply not come back. What happened? No one even asked. All my life I've known that strangers are likely to be killers. If this is some kind of trick, I'm finished.

"Finished?" Erica asks.

"What?" The mug slips.

"Careful, dear. Have you finished your tea?" Erica puts her hand out to steady me.

"I'm finished," I say. I put the untouched mug back on the tray.

Lem Howl smiles, showing his big, yellow teeth. "Wait till you see this, Erica," he says. "It'll blow you away."

I hang back, trying to decide if I should bolt down the path when he opens the door.

He notices. "You too, Little Wheat."

Little Wheat. No one but Hilary has ever given me a nickname. I look at him, and the sadness in his eyes makes me remember what Erica told me last night. His massive shoulders stoop when he leaves the house as if he has been carrying a heavy weight for too long. And I know I have let my imagination carry me away. This is a new life. The old rules are meaningless now. Lem Howl isn't going to hurt me. I take a deep breath and follow him.

We walk around the house to the same path we arrived on and follow it up the hill. But after just a few meters, Lem turns sharply into the trees. This new path is deeply shaded and well worn, rocks and tree roots showing. Could this really lead to a garden? I see light ahead. The path opens onto a big, grassy clearing, completely hidden from the house. A fenced garden fills the middle, the bare beds already raked for winter. But it's not the garden that catches my attention. There are strange devices on the fence, in the trees, and staked to the ground. Some are made of plastic bottles (taken from the landfill, I guess), others are made of tree branches and flat ribbons, metal bars and rope. Dozens of them. It isn't pretty. Lem Howl must be insane to decorate a garden like this.

Then, as if to answer me, a strong wind howls down the hill. It rattles the dry leaves in the maples, sings through the spruce, and swoops down on the clearing, lifting my hair and touching my cheek. And the things begin to sing. Some hum and some whistle, some clang together but in the most beautiful ways, as if the wind itself were singing. It sounds like the music of the earth. Lem raises his arms to the sky and cries above the song:

"Make me thy lyre, even as the forest is:
What if my leaves are falling like its own!"

I join in,

"The tumult of thy mighty harmonies
Will take from both a deep, autumnal tone,
Sweet though in sadness. . . ."

But I stop, appalled, because just as I spoke the wind fell and my words have echoed across the clearing. Both Lem and Erica stare at me. Lem smiles. "Good for you, Little Wheat," he says. "'Ode to the West Wind.'"

But Erica looks shaken. "You're supposed to be a street kid," she says. "Where would you learn nineteenth-century English poetry?" She looks as if I have somehow betrayed her.

"From the lastbook scripts. I love poetry." I tell her about the biblio-tech and how I found poetry after I'd read everything else. She listens carefully.

When I finish, she says, "I see." But it seems she does not. Something has changed between us, something even our conversations about the Commission and the technocost could not. My chest aches in a strange way.

I've forgotten about the garden. Lem is disappointed. "I wanted to show you this," he says. "Come on, look." I follow him gratefully. My eyes sting as if I might cry. I can't remember the last time I cried. Could knowing poetry be wrong?

Plastic bottles are mounted on the fence posts. Each one is slit. "This is my wind-organ," he says. "See? The different size slits make different sounds. But each one has to be cut just so. It's tuned to a pentatonic scale." I have no idea what this means. I glance back at Erica. "I thought you were interested," Lem says. "Look." He takes me to some wooden frames mounted in the trees. "My aeolian lyres, just like in the poem."

A breeze catches them and they sing again softly as if to say, "Look at me!" So I do. The frames are strung with flat, narrow ribbon, brown and shiny. I've seen this stuff before. I've been looking at it all my life. "What are they made of?" I ask.

Lem catches the note of interest in my voice. "Audiotape," he says. "It was used to record sound. Useless now, but it lasts forever. It's just the thing to string an aeolian lyre."

"What do you mean, record sound?"

"It was a precomputer technology. The tapes were placed in a mechanical device. Magnetic patterns copied the sound waves. The earliest ones went from one big reel to another. The last ones were fixed into little plastic boxes."

"Little, flat boxes?" I can't believe this.

"Yeah. About this big"—he brings his hands together—"called cassettes."

My Object. We are talking about my Object. "Have you ever seen one?"

"Sure. There was a revival about thirty years ago. Cassettes are easy to find. I took some apart to make these." He motions to the aeolian lyres.

The wind gusts again, and I have to wait before I can speak. "Can you hear the sounds? Do you have a way to do that?"

Lem shakes his head. "It was a fad. The technology was too awkward to work with. Cassettes are just junk now. No one has that sort of machinery anymore." But Someone must have. I put my head down to hide my disappointment.

"Little Wheat, why all the questions?"

I can't give up. "Couldn't you? Couldn't you make a machine to hear the sounds on one of these, what did you call them, cassettes?"

"It would be a real challenge, even for me. The mechanical and magnetic components have to work together. Those primitive

73

machines are really complex. Anyway, all the music recorded on them was digitalized a long time ago."

"Oh," I say.

"Of course," he continues, "I'm not saying it couldn't be done."

"You aren't?"

Erica comes over to us. "What are you talking about?" she asks.

"My Object. Remember, you saw it the other night. Lem knows what it is."

"An audiocassette," he explains, "a throwback to the dark ages of sound recording."

"But why would you have something like that?" Erica asks me.

"I don't know. It was the only thing left. Hilary traded away everything else I had when she found me for stuff we needed. But she could never get anyone to take my Object." In my excitement Hilary's name tumbles out. I don't bother to stop myself or explain.

"They're totally useless unless you want the tape to make something." Lem gestures back to his wind lyres. "Worthless junk to most people."

"And you were a baby when you hit the streets?" Erica asks me.

"A little older. I could talk. You don't suppose—" I am almost afraid to continue. "You don't suppose it might have a message? For me? From my parents?" My voice rises with each word.

"But why use an extinct technology?" Erica asks.

Lem chuckles. "If you wanted to hide something priceless,

you'd be smart to put it in a worthless box. If she still has the message, it worked, didn't it?" He turns to Erica. "Only someone really clever would think of a trick like that. Someone with access to the technology. Maybe she's one of the Disappeared. Maybe her parents were trying to get to the Beothuks."

What does that mean! I want to ask, but Erica shakes her head. "We don't know there's anything on that tape, Lem. And look at her. She's too young. She can't be more than twelve or thirteen. That means she was born around 2354. If she could talk when she landed on the streets, it would have been '56 or '57. The technocaust was over then."

"What are you talking about, please." It isn't a question. I'm begging to know.

Erica looks as if she just remembered I was there. "Oh, sorry. The Disappeared are the children who vanished when their parents were rounded up in the technocaust. Some of them were taken away and adopted. Some died—"

"And some could be street kids like me!"

When Erica speaks, her voice is kind. "Yes, but Blay, it was over by the time you were born."

I am disappointed beyond words.

"Don't feel bad, Little Wheat," Lem says. "Tell you what. I'll try to make a working audiocassette player for you. Maybe there's something important on the tape anyway."

"Would you really?"

"I'll give it a try."

"Thank you." I can't believe he'd try to help me. Can this be the man I was terrified of?

"Now," Erica says, "we should get back." She smiles. "I have a feeling Blay will come to see you again, Lem."

Erica's right. I will be back. But as we leave, I remember how upset Erica was with me, for reasons I still don't understand. "That story about your Object is true, isn't it, Blay?" she asks suddenly.

"Of course."

"You really don't know who you are?"

It seems like such a cruel question. "If I knew who I was," I tell her, "what would I be doing here?"

She turns to me. "That's what I need to know. Look at me," she says, gripping my shoulders. "I have to know I can trust you. Did anyone send you here?"

I can't understand why she's suddenly treating me like this. The tears I managed to forget in the garden fill my eyes. "What do you mean? I thought you liked me." My voice drops to a whisper.

She softens a little. "I want to, Blay, but I have to be sure you are what you say. What kind of street kid knows nineteenth-century Romantic poetry? What was that, Keats?"

"Shelley. 'Ode to the West Wind.' Lem knew it too," I say, defending myself.

"Lem went to university. No street kid has that kind of education. It makes me wonder if you were sent to find out things about us."

"Who would send me?"

"The Commission. Remember what I said about the power struggle? The Commission would put someone in our house to spy on us if they could. For a minute, back there in the garden,

I was convinced you couldn't be what you seemed. Then you started telling Lem about your Object. Everything you say about your past is so consistent. Now I'm totally confused."

I choose my words carefully. "Marrella picked me. How could she pick a spy out of fifteen kids?"

She nods. "You're right. We hoped there wouldn't be time to recruit you. That's why William arrived early and why he wouldn't let you out of his sight after you were chosen. The warders don't like us, but they don't dare disobey. Not yet."

Now I understand the struggle between Warder November and the Master. I'm terrified Erica might send me back. "But you've told me all these things. If you don't trust me, don't tell me anything I shouldn't know. That would work, wouldn't it?"

She smiles. "It might. I'll have to think about it. I was hoping you would be someone I can trust." I wonder what she means, but it's not a good time to be too curious. "Blay," Erica adds, "you do seem to be telling the truth."

I let out a breath I hadn't even known I was holding. As we walk on, I think back to what Erica and Lem said about my past. I have to ask. "Who were the Beothuks?"

"That's what they called the techies who came to Terra Nova to hide," Erica says. "At first everyone believed the technocaust was necessary, and they let it happen. But soon they set up safe houses to get techies out of St. Pearl and into camps hidden in the bush. No one looked very hard for techies outside the city. Not like in the Industrial Zones. So word spread, and people came from all over, or died trying. The ones who made it into the bush to hide were called Beothuks, after the native people who lived here hundreds of years ago."

"But Lem Howl was already here?"

"Yes. He was born here. He went away to university, but he came back with Michelle and they built the house up on the ski slope."

"Was he a Beothuk?"

"No, he didn't have to leave here. People from Kildevil hid him."

"After his wife drank the poison?"

Erica stares at me. "What are you talking about?"

Truth

By the time we reach the house, I've told Erica the story of Memory Day and she has grown pale. She stops me at the door. "Don't go in yet. There's a bench in the garden. We can talk there." She sits with a sigh. "I knew the Commission was distorting the truth, but I never imagined it was this bad. No wonder you were afraid to meet Lem. He isn't dangerous. You understand that, don't you?" I nod, and she continues.

"Lem Howell was a brilliant musician. People all over the world heard his music. His wife, Michelle Blanchette, made breathtaking soundscapes with Lem's compositions. She was a technological wizard and that made her a target in the technocaust. Lem was teaching music in Kildevil when the Commission officers came for her. It took five or six men to stop him from going to her. Otherwise he would have gone to the concentration camp too. He might have died. Sometimes I wonder if they did the right thing." Erica's shoulders sag.

"There was no plot by the techies to sell technology to some evil power, Blay. They didn't cause the degradation of the environment. That happened centuries ago. All through the twenty-first century, governments tried to cope with the floods and forest fires, the rise of the oceans, the waves of refugees, the hurricanes, the ice storms, the droughts and famines. The world settled into a permanent state of emergency. There used to be a form of government called democracy that gave ordinary people some power. That disappeared. Governments took more and more power, and people allowed that because it was necessary. We call the twenty-second century the Dark Times. That was when the crises completely overwhelmed everyone, and civilization faltered.

"Gradually new institutions emerged. The Weavers' Guilds formed to provide women with a way to clothe their families and later to support themselves. The Way came about as people struggled to preserve knowledge. But everyone feared technology. A whole system of beliefs developed around bio-indicators and eco-warnings that was based on guesswork and superstition. Scientific knowledge wasn't recovered until near the end of the twenty-second century, when universities opened and old knowledge was rediscovered. Civilization was rebuilt, but governments still wanted total control, and most people couldn't imagine things any other way.

"Then the technocaust happened, just before you were born. At the time we had no way of knowing what caused it. Looking back now, it's clear it was organized by the Commission and governments like it around the world to allow them to keep power. If the people who understand advanced technology are evil, if the world is still in an environmental crisis, the state of emergency can be prolonged indefinitely."

"You mean all those things they said about the techies were lies?"

"Yes. Thousands, maybe hundreds of thousands, died or were left broken like Lem. Technology and science are strictly controlled today to make sure people like us don't know that the worldwide eco-emergency is ending."

I put my hand on the back of the bench to steady myself. "If this is true, everything I was taught is wrong."

"If you can believe me," Erica says. She pats my shoulder. "But I can't ask you to accept this right away. Think about it. We'll talk again when you're ready." She turns to the house.

"Erica, just one more thing."

"Yes?"

"What's a concentration camp? Is that where the Beothuks went?"

She shakes her head. "No. They were the prisons where techies were sent if they were caught. Not only techies. Anyone the Commission regarded as a threat. There were concentration camps in every prefecture during the technocaust, maybe all over the world. But there was only one on the island. At Markland. That's where Michelle died."

After she leaves, I sit in the garden alone for a long time. When I finally go to my room, I'm still trying to absorb what I've heard. In St. Pearl there was a black-and-white hologram on the streets for a while, advertising something. The black part looked like the outline of some kind of vessel, but if you looked long enough, the white part looked like the outline of two faces almost touching. Reality now seems like that hologram. The truth could be what the warders told me, or it could be what Erica says, but, unlike the hologram, it can't be both.

Marrella's tuneless chanting drifts in from her room. I had almost forgotten her. I knock on her door, and she stops chanting immediately. "It's about time you got back. We have to do the observation set before the sun goes down," she says. "Did you enjoy your trip?" Her question is a challenge but, in spite of everything, the memory of Lem Howell's garden makes me smile. This does not please Marrella. "You get along with that woman better than I do."

"That's not true," I say, but Erica does seem more interested in me than Marrella, for reasons neither Marrella nor I can understand.

"Well, you'll be too busy to go off with her again." She sighs. "William is so pleased with 'my progress,' as he puts it, that the next test will happen in just two days. This one will be about animals. I suppose you'll want to bring back some kind of plant." She gestures to a lastbook beside her bed. "I have no interest in reading this. You are supposed to help me. Read it." The book is called *Biodiversity for Bio-indicators*. I try not to fall upon it like someone starved for words. Marrella would prefer this to be a kind of punishment. I hug the book and turn to leave, but she stops me. "I still think it very odd that you knew just what was needed this morning."

My heart beats faster. "It was only luck."

She snorts. "I don't believe that for a nanosecond. You are too stupid to know what was needed. Is that not so?"

I lower my eyes. "Of course."

"So there must be another explanation." She smiles. "That is all for now. I won't need you until it's time to do the observation set."

I leave, clutching the book to my pounding heart. I am glad she asked nothing more. How could I tell her what happened? She would be angry if she thought I was lying, but maybe even angrier if she knew I wasn't. What really happened this morning, I wonder? I put the book aside, my mind too full of unanswered questions for reading.

Lem Howell is harmless. What we were taught about him is a lie. I think about his wife dying in the technocaust. Not because she was bad. Only because of her knowledge. I multiply her story by thousands, by hundreds of thousands. The idea is unbearable, but not unbelievable.

Erica is telling the truth.

The Eye of Heaven Shines

"There. That completes the mercury lamp test. Now the spectrophotometer is calibrated, and we can begin the actual observation set." The Master works to keep the annoyance out of his
voice, but he's not completely successful. After weeks of training,
Marrella should know how to measure the ozone in the strato-
sphere and the UV radiation, but we have spent almost an hour
just helping her prepare the equipment. I wish I was somewhere
else. Her refusal to learn is pushing the Master to the very limits
of his patience. I can't believe she is as stupid as she's pretending
to be. I've understood everything he's done so far, perfectly.

As we move outside, Marrella scowls at the small disk in her
hand, which I now know is called a Lewycka spectrophotometer.
"There must be an easier way to do this," she says.

"Oh, yes. Of course. Satellites could do readings from space
and transmit their data back. Or we could make sondes measurements using weather balloons. Or we could fix robotic spec-
trophotometers to the rooftops of buildings." His voice drips with
sarcasm. "If we had unlimited funds and if we didn't mind the
whole world knowing. Marrella, by learning this you are becoming part of a living system of knowledge. The bio-indicators in

this program will be able to monitor the ozone layer no matter what political disruption occurs. Now tell me again what you're going to do." We stand in the enclosed garden behind the house that shields us from prying eyes. I remember everything Erica told me about the Commission and wonder how dangerous it is to be doing this.

"Two readings, one aimed directly at the sun, the other at the zenith," Marrella drones.

"Two *sets* of readings for each," the Master corrects her. "Why?"

"Because you want to drive me crazy!" Marrella says.

I intervene as quickly as I can. "Two readings help to ensure accuracy."

The Master smiles. "Very good, Blay. At least someone understands what we're doing." I spoke only to shield Marrella, but her look tells me she thinks I am trying to impress the Master. I quickly lower my eyes, concentrating on the palm-held computer, recording numbers as she makes the readings. When she's finished, William smiles again. "That was much better. Those numbers are entirely in line with what I recorded earlier. Just make sure you follow the same procedure tomorrow. All right? I can't stress how important this is."

Marrella nods, and I relax a little. Now that I know how the readings are done, I can ensure hers will be accurate. Maybe that will win her friendship.

Chief Warder November

The next morning the Master enters the kitchen scowling. At first I think he's been fighting with Marrella again. Then I see the warders behind him. "They have come for Blay," he says to Erica.

She must have decided to send me back after all.

But she cries "No!" and I know this is not her choice. "No," she says more calmly. "We are happy with the child and find her useful. Why do you want her back?"

"Mistress, Chief Warder November wishes to speak with her. That is all."

This is like a bad dream. "I will go with them," I say. If I can keep them from becoming angry, I must.

Mistrust flickers across Erica's face. She has told me enough to make me a danger to everyone she loves. Now she misunderstands my quick surrender. "I will come with you," she says.

The taller warder steps forward, blocking Erica from me. "That is not necessary."

The smaller one speaks calmly. "The child will be back soon, mistress. We do not wish to disrupt your day." Erica bites her lip and nods, acknowledging defeat. Her eyes meet mine again just briefly, and I know she is begging me to say nothing. The look tears my heart.

William follows us to the door. "Please return the child to us soon," he says. "We do find her useful." For once he's not giving an order.

The warders walk on each side of me as if they think I might try to run away. As if I could. While we walk down the hill, I try to compose a plausible story of my work in the Master's house. In the Rotunda my palms begin to sweat. What if I never leave here again? I try to stay the tide of panic rising in me. Erica and the Master would come for me. Wouldn't they? I am in Warder November's office before I can answer my own question.

I have never been here. It would have been unthinkable before. The office is plain and bare. Warder November sits at a metal desk. The daylight behind her turns her cropped hair into a white halo. She smiles only with her mouth. "Ah, Lobelia September." She motions to a metal chair. "We cannot offer you the comfort of the Master's house, but please, sit down." I obey. "You are still a ward of the Commission, Lobelia, and we must ensure that you are taken care of. You are not mistreated at the Master's house, are you?"

"Oh, no, Chief Warder November." I try to make myself sound as stupid as possible.

"And suppose you tell me what your duties are."

"I help the bio-indicator with her lessons and care for her." The trick is to lie as little as possible. Lies are the snares. The more you lie, the easier it is for them to catch you.

"I wonder why the bio-indicator needs help? This has never happened before."

I nod. "The bio-indicator is not well, Chief Warder. She requires special attention."

"She seemed healthy enough when she came here."

I explain about Marrella's scalp. It isn't necessary to exaggerate. My description impresses her.

"I see," she says when I finish. "And have you noticed problems with the power supply in the house?"

I almost smile with relief. I don't have to lie about this. "Oh, yes. It's unreliable."

Warder November leans forward on her desk. "And suppose you tell me what you have learned?"

My heart jumps. "Learned?" I think fast. "Only the responses for the investiture." This is a risk, because I know nothing about the investiture.

"And do they talk to you about the Commission?"

"Yes, of course. They are grateful for the support of the Commission."

The disappointment in Warder November's eyes is encouraging. She sighs. "Lobelia, I wonder if you could collect information for us?"

With enormous effort, I will my face to remain blank, my voice empty. "What do you mean?"

Her disappointment turns to annoyance. "This conversation is getting us nowhere. I thought you were an intelligent girl, but when I reviewed your records from the biblio-tech, I found you were reading the same books over and over. What is the meaning of that?"

She knows nothing of poetry. I can use this to my advantage.

"I thought, if I carried a lastbook, I would seem to be learning and the others would leave me alone."

"And can you read, child?" she asks me.

"Hardly at all," I mumble, lowering my eyes to hide behind pretend shame.

"Well," she says a little more kindly, "you can do little good, but it seems your capacity for harm is not great, either. You are content to return to the Master's house?"

"Oh, yes," I say, truthfully.

"Then you may go."

The warders do not escort me back. I have been deemed harmless. I make myself walk up the hill slowly to hide my joy in case they are watching. I bound to Erica in the kitchen to tell her what happened, but she clamps her hand firmly over my mouth. "Oh, Blay," she says, "you clumsy child. You spilled flour all over yourself. Please go change." Her eyes beg me not to argue as she removes her hand.

"I'm sorry," I say, trying to hide my surprise. Erica motions for me to change my clothes

When I return, she goes to the control panel and presses a key. "There," she says. "You changed everything?" I nod. She scans my face with anxious eyes. "Did anyone touch your hair?"

"No. Why?"

"They might have planted a listening device on you. I will no longer pretend there are problems with the power. We have cloaking devices in these panels. The one in William's study is always on. They make it seem as if there are problems with the power supply. In fact, they create a screen impossible to hear beyond. It's our only means of privacy now."

"It's good I didn't know," I say. "That was one less lie to tell."
Then I tell Erica everything. When I finish, I say, "I'm sure they
think I'm too stupid to be a spy. The poetry did it. Warder
November noticed I was reading the same scripts over and over.
She didn't look back far enough to realize I'd read everything else
first. But why did they come for me now?"

"Warder November must have asked advice from her superi-
ors within the Commission. She can't challenge us directly. The
people would never tolerate it. I thought she would try to recruit
you as a spy, but as soon as I saw your face, I could see you had
nothing to hide. So you really are what you seem. Oh, Blay, I
have need of someone like you. Tomorrow night you will come
to the town with me. There are so many things you have to learn.
But now we must pretend this is an ordinary day. It's time for you
to help Marrella with the noon observation set." She restores the
control panel and the conversation is over. I am pleased I've
earned her trust, but what is she talking about? I leave the kitchen
burning with unanswered questions.

The spectrophotometer is a fussy little device, but I seem to
have a talent for working with it, and Marrella is content to
accept my help. After lunch we go to her room to prepare for the
second test. The book she needs is still in my room. "I should get
the book the Master asked you to read," I say.

Her look withers the words in my throat. "Sit down. I have
no intention of learning anything from books." She spits out the
last word as if it is hateful to her. Then she smiles. "There is a different way, something I learned in the divining parlors at home.

I've never really tried it myself, but I think it will work. And you will help me." Using the control panel, she dims the windows and the room grows dark. "There," she says. "I need these blue crystals, and I have the right earrings—lapis set in silver." She sweeps around the room gathering objects. She dips the earrings into disinfectant and slides them into her ears.

The stones are a lovely blue. "They're very pretty," I tell her.

She laughs. "They're more than pretty. The lapis will focus the appropriate energy. The silver will strengthen my faith in my higher self." I wonder what she is talking about. This must be a way of learning that I have never been exposed to. "One more thing," she says, picking up two scarves. "Put this over your shoulders." She hands me a lovely scarf, blue, shot with silver thread. She settles a darker one around her own shoulders. "Now we will begin. I have been trying to open up a channel to communicate with the Ancients. This is called channeling. If I can contact these discarnate beings, they will provide me with the knowledge I need."

I can hardly take this in. "Discarnate?" I ask

"Dead," she snaps, then she recovers herself. "Beings who have escaped the wheel of life. The cycle of incarnation. They can help me make the right decision tomorrow."

This is what she intends to do instead of reading? "But if these . . . discarnate beings come from ancient times, how can they help you with factual knowledge?"

"As usual, you fail to understand. The Ancients know everything. Cross your legs and place your hands on your knees, palms upward to let the energy flow outward." I do as she instructs. "We will begin." She guides me through a series of breathing exercises. "Now," she says, "you must try to join your energy to mine while I ask for guidance." And she begins the tuneless song I have heard from my room every evening. "Guide me, oh, ancient ones, oh, sisters of the earth. . . ." Marrella drones on and on. I cannot tell how much time has passed when the lights come on again. It's dark outside. I sit there blinking, like someone dragged into the light from underground. For once, her smile seems sincere. "I thought you might be restless and distract me, but you did not. Erica called us for supper and you didn't even hear."

I must have fallen asleep. "Did the Ancients come to you?" I ask.

She shrugs. "Not that I'm aware of, but who can say? If I've succeeded, I will know just what to do tomorrow. I am going to wash for supper. I will not require you this evening," she calls over her shoulder.

"But the book—" I begin.

She cuts me off. "If this works, it won't be necessary." As she sweeps from the room, I think about what she said. If she has been successful, she will know what to do. But that's the way I felt yesterday, and I did not ask for spirit guidance. I shake my head. It's too confusing.

When I enter the kitchen, Erica and the Master suddenly fall silent as if they have been talking about me. "Can I carry anything to the table?" I ask, pretending not to notice.

"Certainly, here." Erica loads me down with dishes. She follows with a tray of food. They seem to take it for granted I will join them at the table now.

"Did you have a good afternoon studying?" William asks.

While I fumble blankly for something to say, Marrella arrives. "Yes, certainly. It was exhausting and, if no one minds, I'd rather speak of other things."

The satisfaction that lights the Master's face makes me look down at my plate. Surely it is wrong to deceive him like this.

Biodiversity for Bio-indicators

I return to my room later, still longing to know what Erica plans for me. I had hoped for some clue while we tidied the kitchen after supper, but she only chatted about ordinary things. I was so impatient, I would have enabled the cloaking device myself if I knew how. Finally, as I was leaving the kitchen, she threw me one small hint. "Tomorrow evening I'm going to Kildevil to visit the First Weaver, the most skilled craftswoman in the village. She is making the cloth for Marrella's investiture robe. I would like you to come with me." Her voice sounds quite ordinary, but her smile betrays her.

I smile back. "As you wish," I say in the flattest tone I can.

I wonder what new mysteries tomorrow will bring. *Biodiversity for Bio-indicators* is waiting. There is no sound from Marrella's room. She seems content to put her faith in discarnate beings, but I cannot. I open the book, and it absorbs me. As I learned about plants two nights before, now I learn about animals. I learn that every crevasse and corner of this planet teems with life. Tiny creatures, even some as big as spiders, can be carried on the wind, sometimes for thousands of miles. Life that travels in this way is called *aeolian plankton*. I remember Lem Howell's aeolian lyres and smile.

Then I learn about biodiversity. Life is not aimlessly varied but follows complex rules. Animals fill different roles within each community and, if the species that takes a role is lacking, another will change, over hundreds of generations, to fill the empty place. This was recognized long ago when a man named Charles Darwin studied finches, small birds, on Pacific islands. Because there were few birds on the islands, the finches gradually took on roles played by other birds in other places. In hologram pictures I watch the finches of the Galápagos Islands, birds that should eat seeds, acting like woodpeckers and warblers and even stealing eggs like gulls do.

When I fall asleep, the diversity of life comes with me. I find myself riding the wind with aeolian plankton on my way to a newly formed volcanic island. Other life-forms drift across the waves. Not everything survives but, gradually, as tide after tide of wind and water sweep the island, a new web of life establishes itself until the once-barren bed of black ash teems with living things. I wake with that familiar, unexplained happiness. I have no idea what today will bring, but I am ready.

Marrella looks sleepy and annoyed when I wake her with green tea. "Oh, yes. The second test. Do you suppose I'll have to drag some animal home?" I shake my head. It doesn't seem likely. "Go down without me," she says. "I want to ask the Ancients for guidance." I am oddly touched by this. Her approach to knowledge is so strange, but I know she wants to succeed. If only I could persuade her to read the books or even listen to what I've learned. This wonderful knowledge fills me like a strange music, and she will not even open her ears.

When Marrella joins us in the kitchen, her bio-indicator's robes are left behind. She is dressed in clothing like my own, black leggings and a tunic. Her head is covered in the plain dark-blue scarf she wore yesterday. The Master can hardly contain his excitement while we eat. "William, please sit down," Erica finally says. "You're hovering." Powerful though he is, the Master obeys like a small boy, but his barely controlled energy still fills the room.

Marrella pushes her plate away. "How is this test to be accomplished?"

"Quite simply. Take this." William hands her a bound notebook. "Go for a walk. Record any animals you see—birds, mammals, insects, anything. Make notes about anything that interests you. When you return, tell me which you think is the most significant."

"That is all?" Marrella frowns. "What if I don't know the names of these animals?"

"Just write a description. That will do. As with the last test, what you choose will tell me a great deal about what you have learned."

Marrella takes the notebook. "This book is paper? I use a pencil? These are such primitive implements. Where do I go?" Marrella's voice rises anxiously. She has no idea how to begin.

"Allow your instincts to guide you as you did with the first test," William says. "I'm sure you will be fine." He leaves us.

Erica busies herself with the dishes. "The shore is a good place to look for wildlife," she says. Her tone is casual, but she's giving Marrella good advice. "Wear waterproof boots."

We find boots on the porch. Stepping outside, I am disappointed to see the world does not glow golden as it did on the morning of the first test. As I think this, a sparrow flies by. It is outlined in a light that is not white, not blue, but somehow both. Marrella ignores it. "Write it down," I say, grabbing her arm. "Write it down in your book."

"What did you say?" Her voice is stone cold.

I quickly drop her arm. "The bird. Do you want to record it in your book?"

"Yes, I do," she says as if it were her idea. "How do we get to the water from here?" she asks when she's finished.

I point down the path. "The road that leads to Kildevil follows the bay. It's a steep incline to the water, but there are paths."

"Then I suppose that's where we should go," she says.

I force myself not to look at the work camp as we pass. I must pretend I have no idea the warders might be watching us. Marrella hardly glances at the place. The road to Kildevil is no more than a gravel track. Land vehicles are rare in this part of the prefecture. We walk about halfway to the landfill before I find a path. "Here," I say, pointing to a barely visible parting of the trees. The treetops quickly close above us. The incline is so steep that the path slants diagonally at a gentle slope, then turns sharply and goes down in the opposite direction. The bay is perhaps twenty meters across, reaching out of sight in either direction. It is flat as glass but carries the sharp scent of the sea. Across the water the massive bulk of Kildevil Mountain towers. I feel unexpectedly protected here. A narrow strip of gravel follows the bay. As we step onto it, something moves.

"Look," Marrella whispers. On the strand ahead of us, a bull moose grazes. A man would barely reach his shoulder, and his rack of antlers must be wider than I am tall. He catches our scent, raises his head, and sees us. His eyes roll to panicked white and he is gone. Only a crashing in the bush tells us we were not dreaming. "That, I must record," Marrella says. She sits on a fallen tree and writes.

I crouch near her. "See his tracks." I point to the depressions in the gravel, filling with water. "How deep they are. He was huge."

Marrella smiles. "Surely that will be the most significant thing we see today."

Over the water, high in the sky, a lone bird glides. "Look," I say.

"What is it?"

"A fish hawk."

The bird folds its wings and plummets, disappearing under the smooth water without a ripple. An instant later it breaks the surface, a large fish fighting in its talons.

Marrella gasps. "I've never seen anything like that."

I nod. "I never saw fish hawks in St. Pearl, but we see them often here. Bald eagles catch fish with their feet too, but only fish hawks dive beneath the water."

Marrella opens her notebook again. "I may not have to move from this spot," she says. She is pleased.

I see flashes of blue-white light in the water, small creatures that would not be noticed otherwise. I must draw them to her attention. "Perhaps we should look in the water," I suggest.

"Perhaps," she says, leaving the notebook on the log. Marrella is suddenly cheerful. She's so unlike herself, I wonder if the person I've come to know is just a product of unhappiness.

The tide is low. A few kelp-covered rocks stick out above the surface. When Marrella wades in, the water barely reaches her ankles. I follow, thankful for the waterproof footwear. Even in the shallows, it's cold this time of year. At first it's hard to see below the mirror surface, but soon we do. Marrella gives a little shriek. "What was that?" she asks.

I follow the outline of a swimming creature. "A flat fish. Look at these rocks. They're covered in small shellfish." She retrieves her notebook, and I point out different animals. Some look like snails, some like little hats clinging to the rocks. "These white ones are barnacles; the purple ones are mussels." I describe those I cannot name while she scribbles in her notebook. We're so absorbed in this work, I almost fall over when I look up to find someone watching us.

He is tall, but hardly older than Marrella. He carries a cross-bow and is dressed in the skins of animals. A mocking smile shapes his face. The expression is not pleasant, but that doesn't hide how handsome he is with his fine, regular features and serious blue eyes. His straight brown hair is held in place by a head-band. He speaks with the broad accent of Kildevil. "Ye two will be in for trouble when you're caught slacking off like this," he says. His voice is as confident and mocking as his smile. "Why are you out here when there's work to be done?"

He has mistaken us for girls from Kildevil. Marrella raises one eyebrow, then draws herself up regally. "Perhaps this is our work," she says.

The mocking smile wavers. Marrella has the smooth, rounded tone of a city dweller. The twang of local speech is entirely absent from her voice. "Then pardon me," he falters. "I took you to be two of our girls." He touches his own bare head. "Your scarf is like those of our weavers."

I would forgive this mistake, but Marrella is determined to enjoy herself. She leaves the rocks and wades to shore. I follow. She stands directly in front of the young man, who now looks uneasy. When Marrella speaks again her voice is angry. "And are you so stupid that you cannot tell an apprentice weaver from your bio-indicator?"

He lowers his eyes and groans. "Stupid," he says without looking up, "would be exactly what I am, honored one. I should not even look on you before your investiture. Stupid I am this day and cursed as well." The mockery has vanished. He is abject.

Marrella literally swells with pride. "Your mistake was an honest one," she says. "I left my robes aside today." The young man does not raise his eyes, but he relaxes slightly. "And what is your name?" Marrella asks, not quite hiding the eagerness in her voice.

"Carson," the young man says. "Carson Walsh." He offers this information reluctantly.

"Well, Carson Walsh, what brings you to this place when others are working?" Marrella asks. She's mocking him now.

He lifts the crossbow slightly, keeping his eyes on the ground. "I am a hunter, honored one. I'm tracking a moose." A killer of animals, I think. No wonder he is dressed in skins.

"We saw your moose," Marrella says. "It went into the bush by that clump of trees a few minutes ago."

"Thank you, honored one," he says, turning to go, still miserable with shame.

"One more thing, Carson Walsh." Marrella halts him with her commanding tone.

"Yes, honored one?" He looks like someone awaiting a blow.

"It will not be necessary to speak of this meeting to anyone," she says. "I will have forgotten it myself by this afternoon."

He raises his eyes, forgetting himself in his gratitude. The smile that lights his face is an honest one now. Without the mocking swagger, he is too handsome to be believed. "Thank you, honored one," he says. "I am touched by your kindness. If my mistake were known, I would lose my right to hunt for the season and many would go hungry this winter."

"I understand," Marrella says, although I'm sure she did not know any of that until now. A small bird flies out of the bush, lights on a log, looks at us, and is gone.

"What kind of bird was that?" Marrella asks.

"A black-capped chickadee, honored one," Carson says, his eyes on the ground again. "Now I must go."

Marrella writes in her notebook while he disappears after the moose. "Black-capped chickadee," she says. She smiles at me. Her cheeks are a healthy pink. Her eyes sparkle. "He is beautiful," she whispers. To my surprise, we giggle like friends.

"Yes, he is."

"My power over these people will be great," she says with satisfaction. She gestures to the notebook. "Is this enough?"

I can't believe she's asking my advice. I shake my head. "Not yet. Let's look over there." I point to where the moose was. She follows my suggestion without question. Where the moose stood, a spit of fine gravel points into the water. The land is gently sloped and grassy before rising even more steeply to the road. Marrella sees none of this. She is looking up the hill, where Carson Walsh disappeared. He has taken her attention with him. Somehow I must draw her interest back. In the pit of my gut I know we have not yet found what the Master wants. I notice some flat stones by the water, about the size of books. "Let's turn those over."

Her nose wrinkles with distaste, but she flips one with the tip of her boot. She springs back with a small shriek. "It's crawling with bugs."

"Good." I squat opposite her. "These ones are called carpenters. The rest, we will have to describe." By the time we are finished, the creatures have scurried away. Marrella sits on a small boulder to finish her descriptions. I look around, nagged by the feeling there is something yet to discover. But Marrella seems happier than she has since I have known her, and that's something in itself. A feather of dead goldenrod sticks up beside her. It wiggles abruptly. There is no wind. "Marrella," I whisper. Too late I realize I have called her by her name but when she looks up her face is unclouded by anger. "Look down, beside that goldenrod. What's there?"

She quietly closes her book, draws herself onto the flat top of the boulder, and looks down. "A little animal," she whispers. "Come see."

I circle, approaching from the opposite side. There is barely room for both of us on top of the boulder. At first I see nothing in the sparse autumn grass. Then my eyes are drawn to the slightest movement. I see a creature hardly bigger than the tip of my thumb. It looks like a tiny gray mouse with very small ears, pinpoint eyes, and a long, pointed snout. It forages busily through the grass, unaware of the giants hovering not a meter above. We watch for several minutes. "What is it?" Marrella asks.

"A shrew. I've only seen dead ones before. We used to find them outside sometimes." When she closes her notebook, the nagging feeling is gone. "That's enough," I tell her. "We can go home." I'm certain, although I don't know why.

Taming the Shrew

". . . carpenters, earthworms, small black spiders without webs, and a shrew." Marrella finishes reading her list of creatures and smiles.

William smiles back. "Well done. The bird you call a fish hawk is also called an osprey. Long ago it was threatened with extinction because of the chemicals men put on their crops. Carpenters are also called sow bugs or pill bugs. They're common, but they are not insects. They are crustaceans, more closely related to crabs and lobsters than flies or beetles. They left the seas eons ago, but they still need dampness to survive. When they dry out, they die. Now, Marrella, here's your second test. Of the animals you saw today, which seems the most interesting?"

"The moose," Marrella says. "I have never seen one before, and it was the largest creature. Surely it must be the most interesting."

I know it isn't the right answer, but how can I tell her?

The Master shakes his head. "Perhaps you would like to reconsider?"

Marrella nods. "Could I have a few minutes to review my notes?"

"Of course. I'll go speak with Erica." William leaves the study.

Marrella turns to me and lifts one eyebrow like a silent question mark. I take the notebook from her hand, open it to the last page, point to the word, and hand it back to her.

"The shrew," she says when William reenters the room. "I think, upon reflection, that the shrew is a more interesting creature."

"That's right." There's approval and relief in William's smile. "The shrew is much more interesting than the moose. Shrews are not rodents like mice. They are insectivores."

"But they look like mice," Marrella says. Somehow her interruption pleases him.

"Looks can be deceiving. Shrews are among the oldest of mammals. They appeared about thirty-eight million years ago. Some details of their anatomy make them more like birds and reptiles than mammals. For example, they have a common opening for both urinary and reproductive systems called a cloaca, whereas most mammals have quite separate openings." Marrella blushes. I probably do too. He stops and looks at us, amazed. "Come now, girls, this is biology. Nothing to be embarrassed about," he says, but not unkindly. Once again, he's delighted to be teaching. "Another thing, some shrews use echolocation. Do you know what that is?"

Marrella shakes her head.

"Whales and dolphins use it. Bats, too. They send out a stream of high-pitched sounds that bounce back and allow them to create pictures of the world around them. It's like seeing without sight. The type of shrew found here on the island, *Sorex cinereus*, also uses echolocation but only in unfamiliar surround-ings. Shrews are not intelligent like whales and dolphins." William smiles as he finishes. "I don't suppose you thought you could learn so many interesting things about such a small creature."

"No," Marrella says. "I never even imagined there was so much life around us." She actually sounds interested.

"You have done well, Marrella. You've earned your trip to the Tablelands. Rest for a few days and enjoy yourself. Perhaps you would like to read about shrews?" he adds as we rise to go.

Marrella nods and takes the book he offers. She hesitates, then asks, "You wouldn't have any information about moose, would you?"

"No books specifically, but you can use the reference disks. You certainly were charmed by that moose, weren't you?" He leaves before he sees Marrella's deep blush.

Remembering her fury after the first test, I dread the thought of talking to Marrella alone. "I'll go see if Erica needs help in the kitchen if you don't mind."

"What?" she says. "Oh, fine. As you wish." Her thoughts are far from here, and it was not the moose that charmed her.

I manage to keep busy until it's time for the noon observa-tion set. I brace myself as I enter her bedroom. At first it seems empty.

"Blay, is that you?" I look into the kitchenette. Marrella is sit-ting at the table with some reference disks. "I was wondering how long it would take you to run out of things to do downstairs," she says, but she smiles. "Once again, you knew exactly what I should be doing." She leans toward me. "But how?"

There is no point in lying. "I don't know. Somehow I know the answers, but I can't say how or why."

To my surprise she is not angry. "I'm glad you're willing to talk to me at least. Did anything like this ever happen before you came here?"

I shake my head. "Never."

"I see. Tell me exactly what happens." So honestly and without holding anything back, I tell her about the happy feeling, the glowing lights, the way I feel connected with everything. When I finish, she is still calm. "This is interesting," she says. "It seems the Ancient Ones have chosen you as their medium."

"Oh, I hardly think so—" I begin, but she cuts me off.

"No, it all makes sense. I created a welcoming atmosphere and drew the Ancient Ones to this plane of consciousness. But they have chosen to speak to me through you. I understand perfectly. The Ancient Ones often choose humble, even simpleminded people. My role as bio-indicator removes me from direct access to these spirit guides."

This cannot be the right explanation, but I say nothing, hoping she will mistake my silence for agreement. She continues in a more serious tone. "Even though the Ancients chose to work through you, it is clear their messages are intended for me. Is that not so?"

"Yes, of course."

She relaxes. "Good. Then there is no reason to discuss this with anyone else. Is there?"

"Not at all." I can understand why she wishes to keep this a secret. She is winning the thing she wants most—the right to her investiture.

She smiles again. "You have made me very happy," she says.

Perhaps now Marrella will finally like me.

The Weavers' Guild

Stars glitter like green ice crystals. I shiver even though Erica bundled me into a thick cloak before we left the house. She notices. "Hard to get used to the cold when it comes," she says. "Looks like a frost tonight." We are on a path that branches off behind the Master's house before the path to Ski Slope and in the opposite direction. Through a break in the trees, I see the land-fill. This path is steeper and more difficult to navigate in the dark than the road below, but it takes us to Kildevil without passing the grand hotel. We are going to the house of the First Weaver, apparently to view the cloth for Marrella's investiture robe. Perhaps for something more. As we descend, my stomach churns. I remember the hostile faces of the people in Kildevil on my first journey to the work camp. It's hard to believe I will walk their streets without challenge now. As the path slopes down, the sur-rounding hills retreat to reveal the only flat plain on this side of the water for many miles. The houses of Kildevil lie on this fan of land.

The path ends abruptly in some yards scattered with half-cut firewood. The wooden houses look as if they were built by their owners but not in the ramshackle way of the barrio in St. Pearl.

They are tidy and well made. Light shines from the windows. Inside, families are eating, children are playing together or fighting. It's nothing like the sprawling danger of the city or the controlled, confined life of the work camp. We are in a world I have never known. "How long have these people lived here?" I ask.

"All their lives, most of them. The families have been here for centuries. Jones, Morgan, McGrath, Linegar, Clarke, Howell, Walsh—just a few family names down through the years. It's such an out-of-the-way place that it survived the Dark Times without much disruption. As technology became available again, the Weavers' Guilds encouraged people to avoid all but the most necessary innovations. These people had always lived close to the land, so they didn't mind. Now Kildevil is famous for its weaving, and the guild is very important in this region. But they don't welcome outsiders here. I often feel they've only begun to accept me."

I look at her in amazement. "Didn't you always live here?"

"No. William brought me here when we were married, about ten years ago."

Ten years! I thought they'd been married forever. They must have been quite old, and that explains why they have no children. I'd wondered. But where was Erica before? I don't know how to ask. My thoughts occupy me until we stop in front of a house, no bigger than those around it, but conspicuously well kept. The empty flower beds form a carefully laid-out garden.

"Here we are," she says. "This is the First Weaver's house. Now just relax. I'm sure everyone will like you."

Everyone? When the door opens, a wave of noisy chatter

floods out. A woman wearing the dark blue headscarf of a weaver takes our coats and ushers us into a main room lit only by oil lamps. About twenty women of every possible age circle the room. Some are seated on cushions on the floor. A girl about Marrella's age holds a baby. Many have pieces of cloth. A few are making things with long sticks and yarn. They dress differently, but every one wears a blue headscarf. When they see us, silence falls. Whether out of respect for Erica or hostility to me, I cannot say.

The woman who crosses the room to greet Erica must be the First Weaver. She is about Erica's age, I guess, and heavy, but she carries herself like a queen. "Welcome, Erica Townsend, your presence honors my home." She greets Erica formally, but her eyes shine with laughter and her voice is warm, as if this formality is a kind of joke between them.

"We welcome you," all the women in the room echo together.

"I thank you, Clara Linegar," Erica responds. "Thank you, all." Then she puts her arm around me and propels me forward slightly. "I've brought someone I'm sure you will all wish to meet. This is Blay Raytee." I burn with embarrassment. The women's faces are blank, closed. Why would they wish to meet me? "Blay has been helping your bio-indicator," Erica adds. The effect is immediate. The women smile. Two move apart to indicate I should sit between them, and a big cushion is produced for me to sit on. "Go ahead," Erica whispers, and I realize she has helped these women to accept me. Erica takes her place in a chair beside Clara Linegar, the First Weaver.

"Well, that's everyone," Clara says. "Who's going to chair

tonight?" A thin, older woman raises her hand. "Good, Madonna," Clara says. Turning to Erica she adds, "When Donna chairs, we know we'll get our tea before midnight." Everyone laughs. The tension in my shoulders eases. These women are so relaxed and friendly. A woman beside the baby holds a cloth to her face and pulls it down suddenly, to the baby's delight.

The woman named Donna clears her throat loudly. "Attention, please. As Clara said, I've no wish to be here all night. Has everyone signed the book?"

"Oh, I forgot," the girl with the baby says. A bound book is passed to her as several women argue good-naturedly about who should hold the baby.

"If we could proceed," Donna says. Her tone is mock stern, but the women quickly fall silent. "How many have brought pieces to be critiqued?" About ten women raise their hands. "That's a night's work. I'll take you in the order you signed up, and we'll see how far we get. Some of you may have to save your work over for next meeting."

"Next meeting is canceled because of the investiture," Clara notes.

"So it is," Donna says. Several women smile at me. Donna continues. "And Clara's presenting the cloth for the robe tonight, of course. We'll do that last. All the more reason to get at it. Who's first?" She consults the book. "Merna Bursey, what have you got for us tonight?"

A pale young woman holds up her cloth. "This is a new pattern for me, the *m*'s and *o*'s weave?" she says, making her statement into a question. "I'm looking for some feedback.

There might be something wrong with the tension."

The cloth goes from hand to hand around the room. Some women pass it with no comment, while others, especially the older women, spread the sample on their knees or hold it to the light, reading it as carefully as I would read a book, commenting on the technical aspects of the weaving. While Merna's cloth is examined she makes notes, and some others do too. When the cloth has made its way around the circle, Merna thanks them.

The next piece is brought forward. The vocabulary is strange to me: "floats," "weft," "huckaback," "warp," and "hettles." Understanding none of it, I am free to observe. Even the women who have little to say listen carefully. Some nod or shake their heads in response to the ideas of others, but no one interrupts. Finally it is time to bring out the cloth for the investiture robe. While Clara disappears into a back room, the women buzz with excitement. One leans over to me. "It's been decades since we've made an investiture robe for a girl, my dear. You can't imagine what a delight this has been. Clara wove it, of course, but many of us had a hand in producing the yarn."

"A year's worth of linen and cotton fiber went into it," another adds with a note of pride. "We only spin wool here, so that was our complete allotment of trade goods. No girl in her right mind will marry this year unless she can borrow a dress made before."

"Now, Helen, don't be talking. If the bio-indicator hears, she'll think us ungrateful."

Helen looks so appalled, I quickly say, "No, no, the bio-indicator appreciates your work." The women beam at me.

When Clara returns with a heavy bolt of cloth, the room falls silent. She sets the bolt down and flips it, unfolding her best work with deliberate carelessness. The women murmur as fine white cloth spills onto her spotless floor. A few touch it with reverential fingertips. "I'm glad to show you this tonight," Clara says. "Tomorrow, it's off to the seamstress."

"Almost a crime to cut such beautiful cloth," Donna says.

Clara smiles. "Cloth is woven to be cut. That's the way of it." Then she raises her voice slightly to include everyone. "This is an overshot weave, a cotton-linen blend with a small amount of fine lamb's wool in the warp. Woven on my five-shaft loom with yarn contributed by many of you. The pattern is a new design, created by senior weavers at special meetings held last spring after our new bio-indicator was chosen. And the name of the pattern is . . ."

"*Marrella splendens*," the women say together, laughing. The cloth is white, but when the light hits it in the right way I can see the pattern woven into it, a repeated pattern of tiny crablike creatures with pronged plates and delicate legs. *Marrella splendens*. So much thought and work has gone into the making of this cloth. I wonder if Marrella will appreciate that.

"Well done, Clara," Donna says. "It's even more beautiful than we imagined. I'm sure no one has any criticism." When a brief silence confirms this, Donna adds, "Then we can have our tea." The formal part of the meeting breaks up, and some women go to congratulate Clara. Others disappear, returning with plates of food. For the first time, I remember why I thought I was coming here, and I am disappointed. Erica said there were things I should learn. We were so careful to travel in secret. Surely this cannot be all.

But it seems to be. The women bring plates and cups and pots of tea. They pass food around and chat. A good-natured argument breaks out over one piece of weaving. A plate is thrust into my hands, but I am so wracked with disappointment the cake tastes like sawdust. The baby begins to cry, and his mother takes him home. Gradually, in twos and threes, the women leave until only Donna, Clara, Erica, and I remain. Donna and Clara collect the dirty plates. I wait for Erica to tell me it's time for us to leave as well.

But suddenly everyone is very serious. Four chairs are drawn together, and I am invited to sit. Clara says, "Erica tells us we can trust you, child, and I'm glad. We need someone who can travel between the Master's house and Kildevil without being noticed. You must speak to no one about what you hear tonight, not even the bio-indicator. Do you understand?" I nod, almost afraid to speak in my eagerness to show how well I will keep their secrets. "Good," Clara says.

"Now, Erica, we'll tell you the news. Something unusual is happening in St Pearl. The Commission is building a new fortification on Signal Hill. We don't know why. There's also news from within the Commission. . . ." She hesitates, glances at me, then continues. "Even the small freedoms we have won appear to be more than the Commission can tolerate."

"But I thought General Ryan favored reform." Erica sounds alarmed.

"So he does," Donna says. "And the troops are on his side if our information is correct. But the Commission may be more powerful than we supposed. Erica, the others need your guidance.

You must talk with them soon."

"Lem is working on a new encryption code. When it's ready, I will send a copy to you with Blay. It must be carried by hand to the communications center so its origin cannot be traced. Then we can communicate for a few weeks if we vary the points of transmission."

The other women look relieved. "Wonderful," Clara says. She turns to me. "Erica is probably the most important strategist in the whole prefecture."

Erica smiles sadly. "I hoped when I came here those skills could be set aside. I sometimes wonder why I survived the technocaust or even if I did. I seem to spend my life just dealing with the aftereffects."

Donna grips Erica's wrist with her strong hand. "The technocaust was staged to make sure we would always believe that science and technology are evil. Instead, it brought us all together. When our principles forced us to protect the techies from violence, we learned that their knowledge can be used to protect the earth. If we succeed now, the technocaust will no longer be just a shameful slaughter. It will be remembered as a force for great change."

"And if we succeed, imagine," Clara says. Her eyes shine. She turns to me. "Democracy. These many years we've preserved the idea in Weavers' Guilds across the continent. Like a flame passed from one generation of women to the next. When the degradation of the environment drew us to the brink of chaos, the forms of freedom were cast aside like a ripped garment. But all through the Dark Times, we remembered. We structure our groups on democratic lines. We teach our daughters the rules that will enable us, one day, to govern ourselves again. And now it seems the time draws near. Erica, do not lose heart."

Even I am drawn by the passion of Clara's words. The worry disappears from Erica's face. "Clara, your faith never wavers. When you speak of freedom, I can believe it will be ours. But it's late. We must get home."

"You will not travel alone," Donna says, rising also. "My young fellow will see you safe."

Erica tries to protest, but the other women will not hear her. "We believe you traveled here unseen, but who can say? Carson knows he's needed. I'll just fetch him."

I wonder if Carson is a common name for boys in Kildevil. I would like to ask Donna's last name, but then I remember what Carson Walsh would suffer if his secret were known. A few moments later I see Donna through the window returning with a young man. Even in the dark I know Carson Walsh, hunter of moose. At least I have a few seconds to compose myself.

"Carson," his mother says, "this young lady's been helping our bio-indicator."

He is guarded, but not surprised. He must have known he would be meeting me. We both do a good job of hiding our feelings. "Put your hood up," Erica tells me as we leave. "People here are faithful to the cause, but it's best if we are not seen."

Carson is dressed in ordinary clothes tonight, but anyone would know him by the way he carries himself. He reminds me of the fish hawk—what was the Master's name for it? The osprey—the way he glides silently, seeming never to touch the ground. We do not speak walking back through the village, but Erica relaxes a little on the path. "Thank you, Carson," she says, "for giving up your night's rest to see us home."

"It's little enough to do for you," he replies. His words are nothing, but he manages to convey his gratitude. He knows what Erica and the other women are doing.

"When is the next shipment of cloth going down the coast?" Erica asks.

"In two days. I was over watching the boys pack the first of the crates tonight."

"And will you go with them?"

Carson raises his hands in a gesture of frustration. "I should get that bull moose first, missus. He's devilish clever, or I'm losing my skill. The way this hunt is going, anyone would think I'd violated a taboo." He gives me a self-mocking smile. I'm glad the night hides my shock.

Erica notices none of this. "Well, moose or no, I think you should take that trip. Your mother will say the same, I believe."

"Then the moose gets some breathing space," Carson says. I remember what Erica said about carrying the encryption code by hand and realize that Carson is what I am about to become—a messenger for those who are trying to do the impossible.

The Secret Under My Skin

When I wake the next morning, the sun is already up. Marrella's bed is empty. I dress in a panic and rush downstairs, but Erica greets me with a smile. "I reset your panel from the main control so you could sleep in. Marrella and William did the observation set this morning. They're preparing for her investiture ceremony now, but they're getting along well enough to work alone. After you've eaten, we'll take a basket up the ski slope. Later you can take Marrella's measurements to Kildevil." I nod, remembering the encryption code. Now my work is to help Erica.

After breakfast I clear the table while she fills the basket for Lem. When I raise my arm to the cupboard, the scanner beeps. "That's the strangest thing," Erica says.

"Why do you think it does that?" I ask her. Since last night I've wondered if Erica was a techie. Why else would she have suffered in the technocaust?

But she shrugs. "I have no idea. Ask Lem." She picks up the basket. "Ready?"

I can hardly wait to go outside so we can talk. There are so many things I want to know.

"Erica, why does the Commission tolerate the Weavers' Guilds?"

"The Commission always encouraged the Weavers' Guilds because the weavers mistrusted technology. In the technocaust the Commission tried to use those feelings to stir up hate against the techies, but the weavers are too humane. They remember the history of the Dark Times, when violence ruled. Instead of hurting techies, the guilds became an important part of the underground. The Commission might regret the power the weavers have now, but they cannot be harmed. Like the bio-indicators, they command too much respect."

Talking about the technocaust makes me wonder about Erica's past again. But how can I ask? It would be like asking me to talk about Hilary. And then I realize that's where I should begin. "When I was little, on the street, someone looked after me," I say. "Another kid, but she was older than me. Her name was Hilary. . . ." And, for the first time, I speak of the one person I know loved me. My Hilary. I tell Erica how she cared for me, how she stole everything we needed, how she sang to me and taught me to read. Finally, choking on the words, I tell her how Hilary died, going willingly to the death squad so I could remain hidden. Erica puts her arms around me as I sob the words out, then holds me for a long time while I cry. When I stop, I feel as if the blackness inside me has finally been opened to the light.

"I knew there was something," she says when we begin to walk again. "I thought you'd tell me when you trusted me enough."

I sniff and dry my eyes. "Until last night I assumed you'd never understand. I thought you'd always lived here, safe."

"Well, now you know I didn't. I came to Terra Nova in the technocaust, looking for the Beothuks. I didn't get past St. Pearl, though. The cell I was to contact had been infiltrated by Commission spies. When I went to the safe house, soldiers were waiting for me. I spent almost a year in Markland."

"Did you know Lem Howell's wife?"

She shakes her head. "The technocaust lasted about three years, Blay. Michelle was taken near the beginning when most people thought the Commission was telling the truth. She died about a year later. Governments didn't come after people like me until near the end."

"But if you weren't a techie, why did they want you?"

"When it was almost over, governments like the Commission realized they couldn't stay in power simply by controlling the future. The official version of what happened in the technocaust is, as you know, very different from the truth. I suddenly became an enemy of the state, just as dangerous as any techie, and not nearly as necessary."

"But what were you?"

"A historian at a university. If people like me told the truth, everyone would know that the degradation of the environment goes back centuries. I know about the growing hole in the ozone layer, the gradual rise in the earth's temperature. I've seen the treaties signed at the end of the twentieth century, supposedly to limit CFCs and CO_2 emissions. I saw how those people, our ancestors, refused to take responsibility for the future, for our lives and the world we would live in." She sighs. "And I know what the world was like when there was democracy. Near the end of the technocaust, history was outlawed. Libraries and archives were destroyed, and I ran. I left Toronto Prefecture with the help of friends, made contact with the resistance, and tried to find the Beothuks."

"But you never did."

Erica smiles. "But you see, there's more to the story. Near the end of the technocaust, there were raids on Markland. Some of us were rescued one night by a band of Beothuks." Her voice grows happy with the memory. "They were led by a handsome captain, fearless and daring. We fell in love. And married."

It takes a while for this to sink in. "Not William?" I finally say.

She laughs. "I know. It must seem impossible to you, old and sedate as we are. But William was brave and brilliant. He could have renounced his profession and remained unharmed. But he joined the Beothuks on principle. He went underground the first year and rescued scores of people from the technocaust."

"What was he before?"

"A science teacher in a garrison town. Only at the pre-university level. Not a serious threat, or so the Commission thought. Little did they know." She gives a contented chuckle.

I'm so bewildered I stop walking. "But how . . ." I can't even finish the sentence.

"How did a daring leader of the resistance come to be a Master of the Way? That must be confusing. Remember I told you that the technocaust caused the split between the Way and governments like the Commission? Masters of the Way had always been nervous of science. Like everyone else, they blamed technology for the Dark Times. We had only a few Masters at the university, and they taught things like Latin and philosophy. The

Way seemed to be dying out. But during the technocaust, the Masters of the Way began to understand that they had been manipulated into fearing science. Like the weavers, they were sickened by the violence. When the technocaust ended, the High Elders of the Way demanded a general amnesty for surviving scientists, techies, and the resistance. When governments refused, the Way took thousands of us in. This forced government officials to negotiate. We finally got our amnesty, but at a price. We had to promise not to contradict the official history of the technocaust. We bought our lives with our silence.

"But that took two years. In the meantime, we lived under the protection of the Way, and William learned to respect their teachings. He wasn't alone. Many techies remained within the Way, becoming Masters or even High Elders. They've changed the Way dramatically. Now scientific research is respected and encouraged, though not openly yet. Together, the Weavers' Guilds and the Way have created a powerful new opposition. Perhaps powerful enough to bring about real change."

I have been blind and deaf to everything but Erica's strange story, so I'm surprised to find we are in front of Lem's house. The music, which must have been playing for some time, catches me unaware. It's like poetry without words. Erica opens the door and we step inside—into the music itself, it seems. Lem is standing with his back to us at one of those black-and-white inputting devices. His fingers fly across the levers and the music comes from it—or from him through it. A joyous tumble of sound washes over me, satisfying a longing I did not even know existed. Erica and I stand motionless as long as the music lasts, however long that may be. When the last notes die away, the silence that fills the room is a sound I have never heard before.

"That was lovely, Lem." Erica speaks as softly as she can, but Lem turns around startled, knocking the inputting device off its stand. "Your keyboard!" Erica cries, rushing to help him.

He looks shaken. "I wasn't expecting anyone," he mumbles as they right the keyboard.

"I said I'd come for the encryption code, remember?" Erica prompts. "You have it done, don't you?" She sounds worried.

Lem runs a hand through his wild hair. "Yeah, I do. It's just, well, Bach will do that to you first thing in the morning."

"Bock?" I ask. "Is that what you call that kind of music?"

"It's the name of the man who composed it, Little Wheat." He shows me a sheet of paper. "Johann Sebastian Bach. He was born almost seven hundred years ago. I don't think he even knew what he was—probably the greatest musical genius that ever lived. This is what I was playing." The paper is covered in little black blobs. "'Little Prelude in C Minor,' BWV 999. Originally written for the lute, an old string instrument, but it translates nicely to keyboard."

"You can read that?" I ask.

He looks puzzled. "Sure. It's music."

"Lem," Erica interrupts gently, "the encryption code."

"Oh, yeah." He hands her a micro-disk, which she pockets. "You'd better erase the original," she says.

I remember my Object. "Did you have time to work on that cassette machine?"

Lem nods. "I tried a few things. Isn't going to be easy. I might have something in a few more weeks."

I can hardly hide my disappointment. That won't be until after we go to the Tablelands.

"Why don't you ask him about the scanner?" Erica says.

So I do. When I finish, Lem smiles. "Now that's easy. You must have a subcutaneous microdot. You know. For ID. Implanted in your arm. Kitchen scanners use the same technology with different codes."

"ID?" My voice is very small.

"Yeah, identification. Lots of techies had them implanted in their kids' arms at birth in case they ever . . ." His voice trails off as the meaning of his words sink in.

". . . in case they ever went missing," Erica finishes his sentence. "You mean we can find out who she is?" Her voice is unbelieving. "Really, Lem?"

"Really. It would be in UIDC—Universal Identification Code. The idea is to make them as easy to read as possible. I could program a kitchen scanner to read UIDC in just a few hours if I had one." He turns to me. "Or you could go to the work camp. They'd be able to read it now."

"I could?" The idea is so compelling I have to stop myself from going there right away.

"That would be a very bad idea, Blay." I hear the fear in Erica's voice. "Our kitchen scanner is built right into the wall, but we'll find a spare somewhere. Talk to Clara this afternoon when you go to Kildevil. I'll give you a note."

The urgency in her voice makes me remember there are other things at stake. "I've waited all my life. I guess I can wait a few more days."

Erica hugs me. "Good girl," she says.

"What will it tell me, Lem?"

"Basic stuff. Your birth date, place of birth, your name."

"I would have a real name? I would have an age and a birthday. Erica, I would know who I am." The idea makes me laugh but, strangely, when I do, tears run down my cheeks. I can't stop smiling but I can't stop the tears, either. "If I get a scanner this afternoon, can I bring it to you right away?" I ask Lem.

"Sure, Little Wheat. Any time." I wonder why he's so kind to me.

Not until we're walking back to Erica's house do I understand what this information might mean. More than I'd realized at first. "Erica, do you think I might"—I am almost afraid to say it, but I gather my courage—"find my parents?"

Erica looks serious. "Blay, don't hope for too much. When children go missing, people search for them. With that microdot in your arm, you could have been located if anyone was looking for you, dear." Her voice is gentle, but I know what she's saying.

"You mean I wasn't found because I wasn't wanted." I look down when I say this.

Erica lifts my chin gently so our eyes meet. "No, Blay. Lots of parents want their children but can't keep them. Adults who fail to support themselves are indentured. When you were little, there were no work camps. People had to set their children loose on the streets. It doesn't mean you were unwanted. But indentured workers can have short life spans."

"I understand," I say, but my voice is flat. The joy of the moment is gone.

Erica seems to know what I'm feeling. "I hate to ruin this for you, Blay. It will be wonderful to know who you are. But the odds against finding your family are astronomical."

"You're right," I say, but I'm lying. I clutch my left wrist and wish as I never have before. I wish the microdot would unlock the secrets of my past and lead me home.

At the house, the kitchen is filled with unexpected smells. William is cooking. He looks sheepish. "I had hoped to surprise you with lunch," he says to Erica.

"Omelettes," Erica says. "Just like our bush camp days." They both laugh, then Erica frowns. "Oh, but the girls will never eat omelettes."

"I was surprised, but Marrella said she would. She even said she'd like to try moose some time."

"My goodness! What's come over her? Blay, do you know?"

I hope I'm not blushing. "She was impressed with the moose we saw by the water," I say. Then, to smooth Marrella's way, I add, "I would try some omelette too."

"You would?" William looks pleased. As he works around the kitchen, I try to picture him as he must have been in the technocaust. It isn't hard. Determination and power still radiate from him. I remember the first time I really looked at him, in his study the first day I spent in this house. I thought he looked like a warrior. That was closer to the truth than I'd guessed. Erica puts her hand on his shoulder. I remember the warmth in her voice when she spoke of her love for him. I've never known anyone who was married before. I wonder what it's like to have a life's companion. It seems impossible for someone like me.

My Name

By late afternoon I'm on the path to Ski Slope again, a palm-sized scanner in my pocket. I passed the grand hotel both ways without event. Clara took Marrella's measurements for the seamstress and Lem's micro-disk with equal calm, as if both were part of everyday life. Then we set out to find the scanner. People in Kildevil don't use kitchen scanners for inventory, but Clara knew where to find a group of kids who play with gadgets. "That wasn't allowed when I was a child," she told me. "It's a sign of the times."

As Lem's house comes into sight, I wonder what I'll learn— my identity, my age, my name? Things I never imagined would be mine. I quicken my step until I am running and arrive breathless at Lem's door.

"Lem? Are you there?" I call.

He walks out of the kitchen and smiles at me. "Hello, Little Wheat," he says. "Did you get a scanner?" I take it from the bag and hold it out to him. His smile changes to a frown. "Whoa, ancient device. Where'd you get this?"

"In Kildevil."

"Does it work?"

"It seemed to when Clara tested it."

"It's three or four generations out of date. Kildevil folks aren't known for their devotion to technology." He turns the scanner. "Here's the problem. After the technocaust, devices like this were limited to perform a narrow range of functions. This little critter was made just after those rules began to relax. I can program it, but it's going to take time. Come back tomorrow—"

"Tomorrow!" The word rips from my throat before I can think, startling Lem so badly that he almost drops the scanner. "Couldn't I help?" I add to make up for the outburst.

"I don't see how. I have to connect this to an inputting device and type the UIDC in manually. It's a job for one set of eyes and one pair of hands. The code is simple, but it's long." He sighs. "If I work all night it should be ready for you in the morning."

"You shouldn't lose sleep for me."

He shrugs. "I don't sleep much most nights anyway. It's good to have something to work on. Keeps those demons at bay." He says this as if living with demons is the most natural thing in the world. I'd almost forgotten what he's been through.

"I don't know how to thank you for this, for trying to get sound from my Object, for everything. You don't even know me, and you've been so kind."

It isn't usual for Lem to look directly at me, but he does now and he smiles, although that doesn't change the sadness in his eyes. "Lost souls like us have got to stick together, Little Wheat. You lost your family, your identity even. I lost a lot myself. More than I can say. Erica's like that too. We do what we can to help each other out. That's all anyone can do." He looks away, as if embarrassed to have said so much. "I'll get to work on this right away. Come back in the morning, and we'll see what we've got."

I don't know if Lem sleeps that night, but I don't. I can barely sit still long enough to eat supper, and afterward I can't concentrate enough to read. I lie awake hour after hour rigid with tension, playing my few, poor memories over and over. The city, the fine stone buildings. The arms that held me. The other arms that reached out of the blackness, the howl that followed me into the dark. All I have ever known about my past. Will what I am about to learn piece these things together in any meaningful way? It's foolish to hope, but I cannot stop myself.

When the sky turns gray, I rise and dress as quietly as I can, slipping down the back stairs to the kitchen. The thought of eating makes my stomach heave, but I put water on the methane burner. Maybe a cup of something hot will stop me from shaking. The back door opens, and I startle. I had assumed everyone was in bed. Erica reacts the same way when she sees me.

"Oh, Blay, it's so early." She goes to the control panel and enables the cloaking device. "You're not going to Lem's at this hour, are you?"

I nod. "He said it would take him all night to program the scanner. If I get this over with, he can rest. If I wait, I might just wake him."

"I suppose that's true. Would you rather go alone?"

"No. Would you come with me?" I can't begin to tell her how grateful I am. The tea helps too. By the time we leave the house, my hands have stopped shaking. My breath makes clouds as we step into the cold morning. Everything is rimed in downy white frost. I start to shiver again.

"You're cold."

I shake my head. "No, I'm scared. I've waited so long and now—I'm afraid of what I might find out and what I might not."

Erica says nothing, but she takes my hand in her warm, work-roughened grip and we walk up the hill. We find Lem asleep, his head resting on his arm, which is flung across his desk, his face toward us. He looks tired and peaceful and, although he is big and solid, somehow fragile. The gray in his hair and beard remind me of the frost outside, how it will wither when the sun touches it. Lem seems just as insubstantial. Erica gently shakes his shoulder. "Lem."

"Michelle . . ." He opens his eyes and then says, "Oh, it's you. Are you ready?" We all pretend we didn't hear the name he spoke on waking.

I am shaking so badly now that Erica brings a stool for me to sit on. "Don't worry," Lem says, "it won't hurt." He runs the scanner past my wrist. It beeps just as the kitchen scanner has dozens of times. "That's it," Lem says. "You can put your arm down." The display goes wild, red characters scattering across it like leaves in the wind. Then it stops.

"What does it say?" Erica asks. I can say nothing.

"Let me write it down." Lem takes a paper and pencil and writes for what seems like forever. Then he hands it to me. "Read it out," he says.

I do. "Place of birth: Toronto Prefecture. Registration number: 2352051409384. Date: July 14, 2352. Sex: Female. Eye color:

Brown. Identifying marks: None. Name: Blake Raintree." I look from Erica to Lem and back again. "Blake Raintree. My name." Then I realize something. "Why doesn't it say who my parents are?"

"The number's a prefecture code," Lem says. "The records would say who they were."

"But what kind of a name is Blake Raintree?" I ask.

"Your parents probably created it," Erica says. "That was the fashion before the technocaust. Raintree sounds like it comes from 'rain forest.' Blake is an unusual name for a girl."

"She could be named for the poet," Lem says.

"Oh, I don't know about that," Erica says. "And your parents' last names were probably different," she continues. She looks at the paper. "2352. Blay . . . Blake, I mean, you're not thirteen, you're sixteen. If you were one or two when you hit the streets, that would have been '53 or '54, the height of the technocaust." She turns to Lem. "You were right. It all makes sense. The message on a cassette. The microdot. The fashionable name. Her family was educated. She must be one of the Disappeared."

"Then I can probably trace her."

"You can? What does that mean?" I ask.

"The resistance posted lists of missing children on secret computer groups," Lem replies. "They're archived on the net. If someone was looking for you during the technocaust, I'll be able to find the postings."

I can hardly believe this. "How long would that take?"

Lem yawns and stands. "Long time, Little . . . Blake, I mean. The archives are encrypted. I've got the codes, but they weren't indexed, to make it hard for the Commission to trace people if they broke into the sites. Thousands of kids went missing. Even if I start at twenty-three fifty-four and work forward, it'll take weeks." He smiles. "It'd be useful if you disappeared early in the year."

"I don't think I did," I say, and I tell them my memories. The yellow bowl was outside. The trees had leaves. When I describe the stone buildings, Erica looks surprised. "A building with a round, green roof. You really remember that?" I nod. "There aren't many places that match that description," Erica says. "It sounds like the university in Toronto Prefecture."

"Really? You know it?"

"I used to teach there."

"Could you have known my parents?"

"I don't think so, Bla . . . ke. Thousands of people passed through that university. I didn't have any friends with small children. Odd though, isn't it? I might have passed you on that campus when you were just a baby. Back before everything changed." Her eyes grow distant and, when she turns to me, they shine. "If you are one of the Disappeared, it doesn't end here. There are ways to find out who you are. But this must be a secret. If the Commission knew, they would take you away from me. Your reasons for hating them are too strong. And we can't draw attention to the work Lem is doing here."

"But can't I tell people my name?" There's a pleading tone in my voice I had not intended. I have waited so long for a name, I must be able to use it now.

"Yes, of course. It would be cruel to say otherwise. Use your name, Blake, tell people about the microdot, but don't mention Lem."

"All right," I say. "I can do that. But you won't know for weeks?"

"If that was summer," Lem says, "and you were still with your family, I'll skip the early part of the first year. That should speed things up a bit."

Again, I am overwhelmed with gratitude. For the first time I can remember, I would willingly put my arms around a man. Just to let him know what this means to me. But I don't think he would be able to accept my touch. "Thank you," I whisper. My eyes fill with tears. There are tears in his eyes too. He turns away.

After a long moment, Erica speaks. "Well, you won't be idle while you're waiting, Blake. I was in Kildevil making arrangements this morning. We leave for the Tablelands tomorrow."

Geology Lessons for Bio-indicators

We arrive home to find Marrella eating a breakfast she made for herself. She looks annoyed. "You must wonder where we've been," Erica says, smoothing the tension from the air while she enables the cloaking device.

"Well, yes."

"First of all, I'll tell you your good news. A boat is leaving Kildevil with a shipment of cloth. It was supposed to leave today, but I have arranged for it to wait until tomorrow. You will stay in the cabin so we can travel to the Tablelands without anyone seeing you. That way, you can complete your final test before the weather grows too cold and keep the date of your ceremony without difficulty." Erica looks proud of herself. That explains why she was in Kildevil before dawn, at least in part.

"Thank you," Marrella says, but grudgingly. She would rather not owe Erica anything.

If Marrella's reaction angers Erica, she does not show it. "We have other good news," she says, "as Blake will tell you herself." Not for the first time, I feel as if Erica has made me the center of attention without warning.

"Who is Blake?" Marrella asks.

The words catch, and I must clear my throat before I can speak. "I am," I say. "There was a microdot implanted in my arm. Now I know who I am."

"The secret was in the kitchen scanner all the time." Erica tells Marrella the truth without saying more than she should know.

"But if you know who you are, does that mean you'll be leaving me?" Marrella turns pale.

The alarm in her voice is so sincere, I can't help responding with warmth. "Oh, no. I have a name, but that's all. My past is lost. Of course I'll remain here with you." The color returns to Marrella's cheeks.

"Go to William now, Marrella," Erica says, but kindly. "Tell him I was able to arrange this trip. He will prepare you. Blake and I will spend the day packing." When she leaves, Erica says, "I had no idea she had grown so fond of you." She sounds as pleased as I feel. Perhaps Marrella cannot bear to part with me because I provide the answers she needs, but I can't help hoping she has come to like me just a little.

After the morning observation set, we begin to pack. I always imagined that knowing my name would change my life completely. Outwardly it changes nothing, but while I work, ideas begin to knit themselves together to form a new picture of myself. Not an unwanted child, cast aside. Not set adrift because my parents couldn't keep me. The Someone who held me was not just a product of my imagination. "Mother." I test the word on my tongue, quietly, to see what it feels like. And I can almost see her, at the edge of my vision. When we make lunch, I ask Erica some questions, hoping to bring that Someone into focus. "What did

Lem mean this morning when he said Blake was a poet's name?"

"William Blake. A poet in late eighteenth, early nineteenth-century England. He lived around the same time as your Shelley, though Shelley was born later and died young. Blake was either a madman or a genius. Filled with passion and ideas. If you were named for him, your parents were probably idealistic. And they were almost certainly educated. To me, that explains a lot. You never seemed like a street kid. Not that street kids can't be intelligent. Of course they can. But your interest in poetry, your kindness, suggest that someone took good care of you the first few years of your life."

"I remember feeling happy until the last memory," I say. "The one of being snatched away into the night."

Erica nods. "That might have been when the troops found your parents if they came here looking for the Beothuks. They'd do that, take you away and leave you somewhere to be found. They didn't have children at Markland."

"And then Hilary found me. Do you think that's what happened?"

"It seems likely. Hilary was good to you, wasn't she?"

"Yes. She loved me."

"How old was she?"

"I don't know. I don't think she knew. She couldn't have been much older than I am now. She was still growing. She needed new shoes and clothes sometimes, and when she outgrew her clothes, she gave them to me." I smile, remembering. "They were big, but I loved them because they were hers."

"That explains a lot, too. All through your childhood

someone loved you." Erica jerks her head toward the work camp. "It isn't like that for most of them down there."

I haven't given those other kids a thought since I left. Now my conscience jabs me. "I guess I've been lucky."

Erica looks troubled. "Most people wouldn't say so, but in a way I suppose you have."

By the end of the day, my back is sore from bending over boxes and sacks. It was like a day in the landfill. But everything is neatly packed. Two of some things, because Marrella and I will go to the Tablelands alone while Erica and the Master wait where the boat lands. The sleep that would not come last night sings sweetly to me. I want only to surrender to it but I cannot. While Marrella is bathing, I find the right book in her room, *Geology for Bio-indicators*.

The chapter on the Burgess Shale captures my imagination. I am taken back 530 million years, to an underwater world inhabited by strange animals with musical names. I mean, the names came later, only a few hundred years ago. But pretty names—*Opabinia, Aysheia, Amiskwia,* and *Marrella.* And funny-sounding names—*Yohoia* and *Hallucigenia.* Some are graceful, some so odd it's hard to imagine they existed. I learn the shapes of their bodies and how they moved, reconstructing them in my head. I dive into the holograms and swim with these animals in a time long before man.

When I finally fall asleep, the creatures of the Burgess Shale come with me, filling my dreams with their silent dance. They aren't afraid of me. They treat me like a friend. I wake before dawn, filled with that now-familiar feeling of joy. "*Opabinia,*" I whisper to myself. "*Opabinia, Yohoia.*" My secret words. But why should I feel this way? It's not the morning of a test. What do these mornings have in common? Only the books I read the night before. The idea snaps into place with an almost audible click. On the floor by the bed, a small pack is waiting. I slip the book in, hiding it among my clothes. Maybe Marrella can read it on the boat.

As I make green tea in the kitchenette, I look around. I have lived here such a short time, but it's my home now. I don't like to think of leaving, even for a few days. I wake Marrella as gently as I can. She looks troubled. "Sit while I drink my tea," she commands. She sips silently, brooding. I thought she would be happy to be going to the Tablelands. "This is the last test," she says. "William explained it. It's very simple. They will leave us at the Tablelands with food and shelter until a dream comes to me. That is all." I don't know what to say. I can't assure her she will succeed, can I? I can hardly meet her eyes. "Blay—"

I interrupt her without thinking. "Blake. My name is Blake." My voice is kind, but firm. My name is the only thing I own. Whether this angers her or not, I want to hear my name.

But she only nods. "Blake. You will not betray me, will you?"

I look up, surprised. "Of course not."

"But why? You could be the one they honor. Why don't you want that?" The anguish in her voice startles me.

This never even occurred to me. Even now, so bluntly put, it makes no sense. "You are the bio-indicator. The one who suffers. The one they want. I am . . . nothing. Nobody. I didn't even have a name until yesterday. No one would accept me in your place.

I'm only here to help you."

"How can you feel that way?"

I shrug. "Why should I feel any other way? I'm grateful you brought me here."

After a long pause, she says, "Do you know why I chose you?" Her voice is hard.

To befriend me. I know that isn't the answer. I just wish it were. "No," I say. "Why?"

"Because you looked like someone who could never compete with me. Ironic, isn't it?" She laughs, bitterly. "Make my bed now. I have things to do." She rises and leaves the room.

I feel the numbness of a heavy blow, a hollow place that pain will eventually fill. But pain does not come. I'm trapped in a vacuum of feeling. I make her bed and tidy the room seeing nothing, all my thoughts imploded inward. I am back in my own room before feeling returns to me, but when it does, it isn't what I expected. Not pain, not grief, but a white-hot bolt of anger. Why did she have to tell me that? I thought she chose me for my value, not my lack of it.

But she is wrong. The thought surprises me, but it's true. I have been wrong, too. I am not nothing. I will never be nothing again. I stand in the middle of the room, frozen by the idea. Then I tuck it away, like a key that is unneeded now but may unlock something in the future. I go downstairs, and the chaos in the kitchen swallows me at once.

"You've packed too much," the Master says. "We can never carry it all."

"William, we might be gone a week. The weather is colder. Show me what we can do without." Erica is flushed, annoyed.

The Master throws up his hands. "Show me how we carry it." I've never seen them argue like this.

"The boys from the boat are coming to take it. At Green Gardens, we need only carry it from the landing to the top of the stairs. I'll repack for the girls, and we'll help them to the Tablelands. I'm not stupid, you know."

He pauses. "Erica, my dear, I do know."

She smiles. "Today is bound to be stressful. We shouldn't take ourselves too seriously." There is a knock at the door. "The boys." Erica turns to William. "Blake and I will help them. Please tell Marrella to keep out of sight."

Carson Walsh is at the door. "Missus," he says, "we've come for your things." As Carson and the others enter the kitchen, I realize what this means. We will travel on the boat that Erica and Carson spoke of on the path a few nights ago. And Carson will be with us, carrying the encrypted code. My feelings scatter in all directions. Marrella will be so close to Carson but unable to see him. Until this morning, I would have felt sorry for her. Not now.

But my heart pounds when I think about traveling with the encrypted code. Is Erica crazy or very clever? No one would suspect anything this daring.

Carson has brought two boys, one about his age and a younger one, closer to my age, small and dark. The two older boys set to work at once, but the younger one stares at me, his mouth slightly open until I redden under his gaze. Carson elbows him. "Tuck your eyes back into their sockets, Fraser, and get to work. Where's your manners, my son?" Carson is not unkind, but the third boy laughs at the one called Fraser, who sets to work like a whipped dog. He doesn't look at me again, and I'm glad. There must be something wrong with him. When the kitchen is emptied, Carson returns. "We'll get your things stowed on board now. Everyone will leave after that so you can get the bio-indicator tucked away. When I see the rowboat tied to the boat, someone will bring us across. We should be under way in no time."

Carson leaves, and Erica enables the cloaking device. I'm glad, because I want to know why we're doing things this way. "Couldn't you have used a vehicle?"

"Not without offending the townspeople. Attitudes toward technology relaxed after the technocaust, but the change has been gradual. Fuel cells are tolerated in boats but avoided on land unless long voyages make them necessary."

"That's confusing," I say.

She smiles. "Human behavior generally is. Now it's time to leave. Would you tell Marrella and William they can come down?"

Just before we go, I make one last trip to my room. Closing my pack, I see the book, *Geology Lessons for Bio-indicators*. Are the books really the key? I wonder. I take it out. I could leave it here and let Marrella fail her test. But I won't. No matter how I feel about her, I can't disappoint the Master. I slip the book back into the pack and go get William and Marrella.

Half an hour later, we leave the house. Marrella is dressed in an uncomfortable suit that covers her completely to protect the townspeople from seeing her. But we don't get far without being noticed. In front of the work camp, Warder November waits with four other warders. When William sees them, he tenses. His hand goes to his side involuntarily, as if reaching for a weapon that is not there.

"Good morning, honored one. We will escort you to Kildevil, to see your journey off to a good start." Warder November's greeting is civil, but firm. This is not an offer.

"As you wish," the Master says coldly. Nothing will be gained by arguing. As they fall into step beside us, the air around Erica almost shimmers with anger.

"How long will the quest take?" Warder November asks. She does not explain how she knows what we are doing.

"The bio-indicator must wait for the earth to speak to her. This is not a matter to be measured in hours or days," William replies.

Warder November does not seem to notice the hostility in his voice. "I've always wanted to know more about the Way," she says. "On the streets and in the work camps, I had no opportunity to learn." There is an awkward pause when the Master makes no reply. With all the hostility between them, Warder November should understand, but when I catch a glimpse of her face, I am amazed to see she looks hurt. Until this moment I had not suspected she was capable of ordinary human feelings. Suddenly I see the thread that binds us—both homeless kids longing for something more. She is like me.

But this spark of sympathy is smothered by the oppressive feeling of being under guard. Walking like this, I realize how much of my life has been controlled and twisted by the Commission. And the same anger that Erica feels puts energy into my step.

We finally arrive at the wharf, which is empty, as Carson promised it would be. A rowboat waits to take us to the larger vessel moored on the deeper side of the bay. The village looks abandoned.

"We will take our leave of you here," William states firmly.

Warder November looks confused. Perhaps she hoped to learn who would travel with us. She gives a curt nod. "I hope the girl finds what she's looking for." Calling Marrella "the girl" is a deliberate insult. No one else would. She turns, and the other warders follow.

I do not like boats. This one bobs on the water like a cork. William scrambles down with an agility that surprises me and helps Marrella into a seat in the bow. When he reaches for my hand, I hesitate. I have reason to fear men. But William's hands are not cruel. Even in anger, he does not raise them to do harm. So I force myself to put my hand in his and he helps me into the boat. The warmth of his touch stays with me long after he has turned to Erica. I tell myself it is not always necessary to fear the touch of men and, for the first time, I know this is true.

Erica faces William as he rows with his back to Marrella and me. She speaks in an angry whisper so her voice does not carry over the water. "Intimidation. That's what that was. Letting us know our movements are known to them. What an insult!"

"Erica, you know the game as well as I do. It's best to pretend nothing is wrong."

She wrings her hands. "But William, how much longer can this standoff continue? What are we to do?"

"Let's not waste time worrying," William says, but he puts

more power into the oars than is necessary.

The boat that will carry us to the ocean is smaller than I'd expected. The cabin Erica promised is nothing more than a neatly cleared space in the hold. After a long struggle, Marrella finally emerges from her heavy suit sweaty and grumbling. "I spend the entire voyage here? This is unfair!"

"Marrella, keep your voice down," William says. "This behavior is unbecoming."

Erica glances upward to the deck as the engine hums to life. "Yes, Carson and the others are aboard now."

Marrella's eyes widen. Her mouth falls open, then snaps shut before she can betray herself. Now she knows. Carson Walsh is just meters away. She turns to me. "Make yourself useful. You've done nothing for me today. Make up my bed."

On my way to the boxes, I slip *Geology Lessons for Bio-indicators* out of my pack so I can place it beside her bed. Whether this is kindness or malice I can no longer say. Then I settle a sleeping bag on a self-inflating pad.

"Not like that. You're useless." Marrella pushes me aside and grabs the bedding.

William rises as if he intends to do something, then stops, defeated by the situation.

"Blake," Erica says calmly, "it isn't necessary for you to remain shut in down here. Why don't you explore the boat, dear? Get some air."

Marrella flings the bedding down and stares first at Erica, then at me, tears of frustration in her eyes. She is being punished for treating me badly, but more than Erica suspects. Until today I might have remained with her out of loyalty or kindness. Not now.

"Thank you, Erica, I will."

The hills that wall the bay move slowly past us. No, we are moving past them. The water is so calm I feel no motion. An older man stands in a shed on the deck, steering. The entire crew is composed of the three boys who came to our door this morning. The small, odd boy named Fraser sits on a barrel with long sticks and yarn in his hands. Apparently he was using them, but now he only stares at me as he did this morning. Again I wonder what's wrong with him. Suddenly I realize I am in the company of strange boys. I want to return to the safety of the stuffy hold below, but Carson approaches before I can.

"Settled in now, is she?" he asks without threat or mockery.

I swallow unkind words about Marrella. I cannot disillusion him. "She's fine," I say.

He smiles. "We had some time cleaning up the hold. You should have seen her before we started. Made everything neat and tidy, we did."

I'm glad he didn't see Marrella's gratitude for his hard work. "It's lovely," I say, "very comfortable."

He beams at me. "Mark and his father are proud to be taking you." He nods toward the captain of the boat and the other boy. When he hears his name, Mark comes and stands beside us. "Warm for this time of year," he says without apparent reason. I grasp for a topic.

"Have you seen the Tablelands?" I ask.

Carson nods. "Went there myself for my initiation rites when

I became a hunter. It's a place of great power."

This sounds so odd to me. "What did you do?"

"Pretty much the same as she'll be doing, I expect. I listened to the earth, waited for a vision, and, of course, I asked forgiveness, too."

"Forgiveness? For what?"

"A hunter kills," Carson says. "He takes from the earth. It's important to thank the earth, to atone for the damage we do by being on it."

"Oh. I thought. . . ." I stop, not knowing how to continue.

". . . that we're a crowd of barbarians with blood on our hands," Carson says. "We know what city people think. Civilized people don't eat meat. Well, civilized people know squat. There's balance between us and the earth. We don't just drain off resources like the cities do. We take what nature gives, but we thank her as well. When a hunter does his job, the balance is not upset. That moose I've been after this fall, you think he'll live forever if I don't get him?"

"I never thought about it."

"No, I know you never. My arrow's sure. I kill clean. I take pride in that. Dying of disease or hunger is no treat for any living creature. City folks, their imaginations don't stretch that far. So my life is some sort of crime against nature." He gives a short laugh. "My life is devoted to nature. Think about that." Carson's anger frightens me.

"Leave her be, Carson. She's no enemy to you." The voice behind us is as soft as a girl's. Fraser's dark eyes are fearful, but he stands his ground.

Carson laughs. "You're right, youngster." He turns to me. "I never meant to speak so strongly." This rough apology embarrasses both of us, and he goes to Mark on the other side of the boat.

"What's your name, anyway?" Fraser asks. I'm beginning to realize this abrupt way of speaking has more to do with shyness of strangers than lack of manners.

"Blake Raintree."

He stares. "What kind of name is that? And where do you belong to?"

I should feel hurt or embarrassed, but his bluntness makes me laugh. "I can't answer either of those questions." So I find myself sitting on deck telling this strange boy the fragmented story of my life, only leaving out Lem as Erica asked me to. While I talk, Fraser plies the wool purposefully with the sticks, making a length of beautiful gray cloth.

"That's a good story," he says when I finish, as if I'd made up my entire life just to amuse him. "And you never knew your real name until yesterday?" He shakes his head. "You wouldn't be joking me, would you?"

"Of course not." The idea annoys me.

Fraser notices my reaction. "I had to ask, you see. Everyone's always after tricking me 'cause I'm just the goat boy."

Carson hears this as he passes by. He reaches down and fluffs Fraser's silky black hair. "That's right. Fraser's our goat boy. All the sheep we keep aren't half as much trouble as those dozen goats. Are they, Fraser, my son?"

Fraser shakes his head. "Goats is trouble. Always want their own way. And these goats don't suit the climate. Can only stand the cold if they're dry. But when is the winter dry? It's my job to keep them safe and healthy. Got them all penned in today," he says with satisfaction.

"Why do you keep them if the climate's wrong?"

"These goats is special. Angora. They give a fiber called mohair. The weavers value that. Value the goats. I wish someone valued me as much." Fraser sighs and gives the yarn a tug.

"How do you do that, Fraser?" I ask, pointing to the wool.

"Knitting? Don't tell me you never seen knitting before."

"Only at the Weavers' Guild meeting the other night."

"Well, now, you're the one who's a barbarian, I'd say." Fraser laughs without malice. He calls across the deck. "Imagine, Carson, a girl her age who can't knit. All of us knits. Every one. See Carson's sweater? Made it hisself, he did. Didn't you, my son?"

The sweater is lovely. Thick navy blue wool about the color of Carson's eyes, the pattern complex. "This is the first design I made myself." Carson lowers his voice, though no one could possibly overhear. "We knit to honor the weavers, you see, to show our respect for them and the democracy they keep alive."

"That we do," Fraser says. He spreads his knitting out to show me what he's done. "What do you think of that, then?" He has made a pattern that looks like interwoven ropes.

"It's hard to believe you can do that just with two sticks," I say.

"Needles, not sticks," Fraser says, but he glows with pride. "Lately we've started using knitting machines, but you can't take those to work with you. So mostly the men use needles."

Time slips by like the land around us, without me noticing. The boys laugh and talk more easily as they begin to accept me. I wonder how Marrella is faring down in the hold but not too often. After a while Fraser puts his knitting away and takes out a strange object, two small octagons joined by pleated leather. He pumps it between his hands and sweet, sad music carries over the water. It lulls me until I must close my eyes, leaning against the side of the boat. I don't realize I'm asleep until the music stops. When I open my eyes, Fraser is staring again.

"That was beautiful. What is that thing?" I say to divert his attention.

He looks pleased. "It's a concertina."

"Where did you learn to play like that?" I ask.

"Oh, Fraser can play any old thing," Carson says. "Comes by his talent honestly, don't you?" But Carson stops abruptly as if he suddenly knows he's said the wrong thing. Fraser reddens with an anger I have not seen in all the teasing he's taken. Carson looks apologetic but says nothing. Then Fraser turns away, playing a fast tune that ends all possibility of conversation.

Soon after the boat is moored at Woody Point and Carson takes me aside. "I'm leaving now," he says. "I'll be back here tomorrow to help unload the crates and take the boat home after she's dropped ye lot at Green Gardens." He pauses awkwardly, then reaches into a pocket. "Could you give her this? When you're alone, I mean." He presses a small envelope into my hand. I mumble something as I take it, I hardly know what. The eagerness in his voice, his eyes, brings an almost overpowering wave of jealousy. Will any boy ever feel that way for me?

"What are ye two doing with your heads together?" Fraser demands.

"Nothing, Fraser. Just taking my leave and now I'll do the same with you." Carson swings over the side of the boat with his usual grace. No one would suspect he's on a secret mission. Wherever the communication center is, it's less than a day's travel from here.

After so much fresh air and freedom, I hate to return to the inevitable tension of the stuffy hold. But to my surprise, everything is calm. Erica is spreading a cold meal on some boxes. Marrella is reading the book I left for her. She must have read steadily because she's almost finished. Maybe the book will work its magic on her. Maybe she will be the one who knows. Carson's note is like a live coal in my pocket. I haven't decided what to do with it.

The Tablelands

We are on the beach at Green Gardens a few hours before nightfall. While William takes Marrella to the campsite, Erica and I
deal with the baggage that is scattered on a strip of gravel backed
by rocky cliffs. Landing here was tricky. In rougher seas, it might
have been impossible. For Mark's father, Captain Daniel Jones,
the danger lay not in the sea but somewhere deep inside him.
Although we kept Marrella out of his line of vision as much as
possible, he had to break the taboo to land us here. The strain of
this showed in his pale face as he rowed us ashore. Mark and
Fraser avoided us, then went below to protect themselves from
the sight of the bio-indicator, even though she was encased in
that heavy protective suit. Only now do I realize how dangerous
this was. "Erica, what if the rowboat had capsized? Fraser and
Mark wouldn't have known."

Erica looks up from a pack. "That's right. But that wouldn't
occur to them. They expect the earth to care for us."

This annoys me. "We might have drowned. Where do they
get all these stupid ideas?"

Erica smiles. "They only seem stupid out of context, Blake.
You have to imagine the Dark Times. People were left in a

degraded world without science or technology, without government or social structure. They had no control, so they developed customs and beliefs to help them cope."

"But the beliefs are silly, and they don't need them now."

"People don't stop believing just because they can. It's part of their way of thinking."

"They have such funny ideas about danger. Look at Carson. He walked off with that secret code like he was going to a party but . . ." I stop myself just in time.

Erica looks puzzled. "But what?"

"But he chases after that big bull moose without any thought for his safety." I improvise. I almost told her about his reaction to meeting Marrella by the water that day.

"Well, Carson is consecrated as a hunter. The role is considered sacred because people were forced to hunt for food in the Dark Times. They felt it was wrong to kill animals, but they had to eat, so they created rituals to reconcile the conflict."

"I know. He told me about coming to the Tablelands." Looking up, I see William climbing down the steps from the campground where he has left Marrella. I talk quickly, hoping to find out more before he comes. "Will Marrella do the same thing Carson did?"

"Not exactly," Erica begins, but she looks up too. "Oh, good. Here's William. Now we can get to work." My question is forgotten. "How's Marrella?" she asks.

He frowns. "Physically, better than I'd hoped. No sign of her asthma. I was worried about allergies to mold this time of year."

"But?" Erica says.

153

"Her mood is troubling. She did so well on the other tests; she shouldn't be this anxious."

For a moment I wonder if I shouldn't just tell the truth. It doesn't feel right to deceive them. But something stops me. Marrella finished the book before we came ashore. If I'm right, there's a possibility she will be able to pass this last test on her own and accept the role of bio-indicator with some honesty. I'm also afraid for myself. If the truth were known, the role might fall to me. The idea of being trapped by beliefs I cannot share fills me with dread. Something important is happening in the world I understand. The Commission's stranglehold may be broken, and I want to be part of that struggle. My invisibility makes me useful in ways that a bio-indicator never could be. So I say nothing as we load up like pack animals and prepare to make the first of many trips up to the camp. But the secret I carry is heavier than any pack I'll lift today. Maybe when these tests are over, this deception will finally stop.

The camp is surprisingly pretty—sheltered and grassy, backed by heavy woods overlooking the ocean. The Master shows me how to activate the tent we will take to the Tablelands. It is a complex interfacing of semipermeable membranes that slowly assembles itself when opened. Marrella watches us fretfully, saying very little. I think about the note Carson gave me. We haven't been alone since I got it, but I'm not sure she deserves it anyway. The sky grows grayer, the air colder. By nightfall thick flakes of snow begin to fall, melting when they touch the ground, our tents, or us.

"Into the tents with you," Erica says. "You'll be warm enough as long as you stay dry." She cooks supper without regard for her own comfort.

"This is miserable," Marrella says, but I can never remember food tasting so good. It warms me like happiness. That night I fall asleep in the deep, rich darkness of the flapping tent. The snow turns to cold rain, but I am dry and, except for the tip of my nose, warm. Brilliant dreams dance before me all night long. In the morning they recede beyond the edges of my memory. But I know they were there.

We eat breakfast in the remaining tent after ours has been packed for the final journey, then prepare to leave in wet confusion. The driving rain slants almost sideways. While I rinse the dishes in some heated water, Erica grumbles. "I don't like carrying the tent wet when it's not dormant," she says. "What if it catches a virus?"

William comes up behind her and kisses the top of her head. "It won't be packed for long. And the Tablelands will give it a good airing."

Marrella has eaten little and said less. When we are finally ready to leave, she sits on a boulder and bursts into tears. "I'm cold and wet," she wails. "I didn't close my eyes last night, wondering if we'd be blown into the sea. Why couldn't this have waited until spring? I want to go home." She buries her face in her hands and sobs.

The worried looks William and Erica give me show they regard me as an equal here. I appreciate that, but I have no words of comfort for Marrella this morning. So Erica steps forward. "Child," she says, lifting Marrella's face gently, "so much is happening in the world right now. By spring this journey might be impossible. We have done this for you." Marrella looks confused, but Erica's kindness seems to soothe her in a way that facts could not. She rises and shoulders her small pack. Her eyes are blotchy and her nose is bright red. She looks so pathetic, even I manage to feel sorry for her.

The inland path slopes upward, sometimes gently, sometimes steeply, through a thick forest of spruce that shelters us from the worst of the weather. At one point I see what looks like asphalt or tar running along the side of the path. "Was this place paved?" I ask Erica.

She laughs. "This area is volcanic."

William eagerly cuts in. "Four hundred and ninety million years ago, volcanoes bubbled up on the floor of the Iapetus Ocean, a sea between two continents, Laurentia and Gondwana. These are the remnants of the vents. The continents and the sea are gone now."

This reaches Marrella. "Gone? How could they be gone?"

"The sea closed in. The continents came together, then broke apart again to make new continents. This island is a history of that event. The west coast, where we are now, was once part of a shelf in the tropical sea off Laurentia. The central part of the island was once the seabed, and the eastern zone was part of Gondwana. There are rocks in St. Pearl that were connected to what is now northern Africa. Land seems solid to us, but the continents glide on giant plates. Gradually, over millions of years, they shift to create earthquakes, mountains, volcanoes, new landmasses."

The joy in William's voice tugs at something left over in me from last night's dreams. The next time we pass one, I bend and touch the tarry surface of the asphalt outcrop. William says, "Imagine, the dance of continents happens all around us but at a pace too slow to comprehend, our lives passing in less than an eye blink of geological time. Even our time on this earth as a species is mere moments." And I try, but his ideas are too vast to hold. They slip from my grasp and are gone.

As the land rises, the landscape thins. The path flattens and the ground grows stony. The rain lets up and a thick fog rises off the land. Now the path is nothing more than a bare line of stony earth snaking across a plain that is studded with orange rocks and sparse vegetation, enshrouded. Suddenly we face the massive rise of a long loaf of stone that runs off into the fog on both sides. Nothing grows on it. "The Tablelands." William sweeps his arm toward the hill above us.

"Why is it so empty?" I ask.

"Good question," William replies, "but we've done enough geology for one day."

His sudden refusal to teach upsets me. I want to learn. Erica notices my disappointment and says, "The Tablelands must remain a mystery for now, Blake. This journey is to discover their secrets." Abruptly I remember that I am not the one brought here for this purpose. As we walk on, I wonder again what's behind these tests. Is it science or magic? It isn't supposed to be my concern, but it is. Everything has happened, not to Marrella, but to me. And it seemed more like magic than anything I have ever known or heard of. Maybe not the channeled wisdom of discarnate beings, but magic all the same. I wish I knew. We cross a road that runs along the base of the Tablelands, stretching out of sight in either direction. "A road?" I say. I thought we were in the middle of a wilderness.

"There was settlement a few kilometers from here until the sea level rose. Trout River." William explains. Then he points straight ahead. "A fjord meets the sea there. Once it was land-locked. It comes right in on the other side of the Tablelands, but there's no place to land a boat there. Now we must push on. Erica and I will travel back to camp and you," he says, turning to Marrella, "have work to do. Cheer up, child. You've done better than I thought possible. It will all be over soon." The gloom Marrella casts over the day is thicker than the fog.

The Tablelands are steep. The few plants clinging to the slopes rapidly fall away until we are climbing a broken pavement of powdery orange rock. It is like nothing I have ever seen before. The exertion makes Marrella pant and then begin to wheeze. We stop so she can take medicine. "Just a bit farther," the Master says. "I wouldn't push you, Marrella, but there is a campsite." Soon after we reach a place where some boulders make a natural windbreak for the tent. Erica and William set up camp quickly, falling into the rhythms established in their days as outlaws, I'm sure. Then William hands Marrella a small homing beacon. "When you are ready, activate this."

"But how will I know?" Marrella asks, her voice desperate.

William smiles. "You'll know." He turns to me. "Blake, take good care of her."

Care for her and do her work, as well. I try to return his smile but cannot. Erica gives me a swift, questioning look. I am glad there won't be time for her to talk to me alone.

William and Erica are swallowed by the fog almost immediately. Then we have only the howl of the wind for company. I lay out our bedding. The tent is damp, our clothes are damp, the bedding we slept in last night is damp. The fog swirls by until I feel light-headed. I retrace our path to a small brook that runs through the naked stone, get some water, run it through the purifier, and heat it for tea.

"This is miserable," Marrella says by way of thanks when I hand her a steaming mug. "It's so uncivilized."

"Yes, it is," I say, for who could disagree? What we can see of the landscape looks as it might have millions of years before man. But once more, unexpected joy leaps up like a small, warm flame in my heart. No wind will blow it out. No dampness can dull it.

After we eat our evening meal, I clean the dishes and tidy the camp. Then, although it's early, there's nothing left to do but crawl into the tent. Outside and busy I could ignore Marrella's bad mood, but it fills this small space until I feel I will suffocate. I must say something. "You did read the book, didn't you?" I ask her. "I saw you reading on the boat."

"Most of it. Boring, but the trip was worse. When I am bio-indicator, no one will ever hide me away like that again."

It's difficult to have a conversation with someone who will only talk about herself, but I try once more. "I think the answer lies in the books," I say.

Finally I have Marrella's attention. In the gathering darkness, the light through the tent casts strange colors over her face.

159

"What do you mean?"

"I read the books the Master wanted you to read. *Plant Life: A Natural History for Bio-indicators* before the first test; *Biodiversity for Bio-indicators* before the second test. Both times I knew what to do. As if someone had already told me the answers. I don't think there's anything special about me. I think it's the books. And now you've read the right book. Maybe the dream will come to you."

Marrella brightens. "Do you think so? I just wish this were over. It isn't what I imagined at all. Ordeal after ordeal. It's not fair. Do you have any idea why they're doing this? I used to think they were trying to get rid of me, but they've gone to so much trouble, I don't know what to think anymore."

I wonder how much I should tell her. Maybe it's okay to let her know. "I think some of it has to do with politics," I begin, my heart pounding.

She waves my words away. "Oh, politics. The Commission hates us. Who needs to know more than that?" She lies down with her back to me. The conversation is over. So she misses her chance to learn what I know. She did not sleep last night and today's hike was exhausting, even for me. I'm not surprised that she falls asleep right away. It's too dark to do anything but follow.

I wake abruptly in the middle of the night as if someone has called my name. Something has changed. At first I don't know what it is, but then I realize—the wind no longer howls and tugs the tent. Everything is still and cold. I want to go back to sleep, but I know I won't until I empty my bladder. Silently I slip out of my sleeping bag and out of the tent, grabbing my heavy coat.

I am totally unprepared for what I find. The fog is gone.

Above me, millions of stars press down as if I could reach up and catch a handful, the radiant spine of the Milky Way arching over my head. The beauty of this place fills me like water rushing into an empty space. I raise my arms to the sky and circle slowly, drinking in the dance of the universe. I could be the only living creature on this planet, and yet I feel surrounded by life. As if the rocks beneath me could breathe. As if the sky above contained all the thoughts and feelings ever thought and felt, every breath ever taken, every wish ever made, every life ever lived. And I am part of all this, now, in my short life, and forever. I do not know how long I stand there, lost in wonder, caught in the web of being, but, finally, the moment passes and I remember why I'm outside.

In the tent again, I fall into a deeply peaceful sleep, and last night's dreams return like wild animals made tame by my happiness. The earth spreads before me like the cloths of heaven, and I dream in geological time. I see a single, great landmass on the planet, a flat, bland, featureless desert. The globe of the earth is transparent. Through seas that shine like clear, blue ice, I see the huge plates the landmass rides upon, and below even that, the molten red rock that floats them. As I watch, the plates break apart and crash together again. Sometimes there is one great continent, sometimes many small ones. Sometimes most of the land lies beneath the sea. Huge mountain ranges rise where plates fold into one another; volcanic chains spill out of the sea where the plates pull apart. Heaving waves of land flow like water in a great, monstrous dance, each figure taking millions of years. Then I am drawn to one area where an ancient tropical ocean expands, creating pretty volcanoes on its floor like a glowing necklace.

Gradually it contracts again and, in the pinch where plate meets plate, a small portion of the glowing rock beneath thrusts up and cools. Over eons it is worn away and exposed to the harsh, dry light, smoothed by glaciers and weathered into powdery orange rock. Forests spring up around it, but the rock remembers its molten self far below the earth and never accepts the gentling green of life. Even in the dream, I recognize the Tablelands.

I wake at first light to the raucous cawing of crows, knowing it is over. The dream hidden in this place has come, and it came to me. Beneath the churning doubts and confusion on the surface of my life, I feel a liquid mantle of contentment. It no longer matters whether I wanted this or not. This, whatever it is, has claimed me. I wonder if Marrella could have had the dream too, but when I see her sleeping face, I know she did not. From this day I will always know the ones who have dreamed as I have dreamed. This bit of information arrives fully formed. If someone had tossed it into my lap, it could not surprise me more. There must be more to this than the books, but I can't imagine what.

The Blake who walks out into this morning is not the girl who left the tent in the middle of the night and never will be. I breathe the cold air deeply. To one side, flat-topped hills reach away, row on row, green and gray toward distant horizons. On the other, I see the fjord and the open ocean, not too far away. If I did not look down, I would not suspect this barren rupture in the landscape. I take the kettle for water to give myself time to think.

I am the person William has been looking for, but I won't tell anyone. Marrella wants to be the bio-indicator. I do not. She wants the role for power and status, things that mean nothing to me. So I will give her my dream, not for her sake but my own. A purely selfish act, to allow me to keep my secret until I decide what to do. But not yet. I'll give her tonight to have a dream of her own. I tell myself this is kindness. But I know this isn't true. Marrella has used up all the goodwill I offered. I will not make life so easy for her now. The thought of giving and withholding brings me back to Carson's note, still safely tucked in my pocket. Unwilling to witness the pleasure that will light her eyes when I give it to her, once again I thrust it from my thoughts. I return to the campsite and heat water for Marrella's green tea. Oddly, the idea of serving her does not bother me. I do not serve her with my heart.

Broken Bonds

The fine weather holds and next morning, while we break camp, we watch Erica and William approach from far across the barrens, responding to the beacon we activated at dawn when I finally decided it was time to tell her the dream.

"What should I do next?" Marrella says. Until today I could not imagine her helping me.

"Empty the water purifier. You'd better recite the dream again," I tell her while we work, "just to make sure." Her memory of my dream is good. She learns quickly when she wants to. "That's fine," I say when she's finished. "You'll pass for certain."

"And you won't tell?" she asks. I shake my head, but I cannot say the words. I'm not doing this for her.

When William sees our half-packed campsite, he smiles. "You must be very certain of yourself, Marrella. Tell me your dream." When she finishes, he claps her on the shoulder. "Excellent. Perfect. The Tablelands were once part of the earth's mantle, just as you dreamed. You pass your final test. This is wonderful." Erica goes to congratulate her, and I am forgotten. I watch them celebrate, wondering if I have done the right thing. William pushes back his sleeve and touches a device on his wrist. "There," he says.

"That will activate the beacon at our campsite in Green Gardens. Someone will come from Woody Point in a few hours."

When the boat arrives, everything is packed and waiting on the beach. The sea is calm, and we board easily. This is a larger, faster boat crewed by a man from Woody Point named Chesley Barnes and his brother David. Their community is not led by a Weavers' Guild, so the taboo means nothing to them and Marrella doesn't have to hurry below.

The trip should be relaxed, but Captain Barnes looks worried. "We're going straight back to Kildevil," he says. "I want to see you home as quickly as possible."

"What's wrong?" Erica says.

"The Commission guard came without warning and took the youngsters. Most are gone."

My heart gives a lurch. "Even in Kildevil?"

"They hit Kildevil first. The story's told all up and down the coast. The weavers stood their ground, demanding their apprentices remain at home. The standoff lasted hours. Finally the Commission relented. I have to admire the Weavers' Guild. Even the Commission is reluctant to tangle with them." He chuckles, then adds more seriously, "Everyone looks to Kildevil for guidance now. I guess the Commission knew there'd be an uprising if the weavers were crossed. In the end, they left the apprentices. But they took all the young fellows, anyone over fifteen."

I think about the boys. Fraser, Carson, and Mark gone? How dangerous will this be for someone like Carson? I feel sick.

Marrella has gone pale. "I think I'd like to go below now," she says quietly.

"We both should. I'll see to her," William says to Erica. "Learn as much as you can."

Captain Barnes tells us everything he knows about the movements of the Commission, which is a great deal. I realize it's no accident he came for us. He's part of the resistance.

As we travel, we pass Commission vehicles moving up and down the shore. I am glad we don't have to stop. Late in the afternoon, a boat full of uniformed people comes toward us. But it sails right past. "I thought they were Commission guards," Erica says.

"No, that's the military," Captain Barnes replies. "We don't think the military is involved in this. But surely the Commission wouldn't interfere with you. The Way is like the Weavers' Guild, too powerful for the Commission to challenge."

Erica sighs. "I used to think so. I'm not sure now." She puts her hand on my head. "I'm so glad you were tucked away on the Tablelands when this happened."

The captain looks at me and laughs, but not unkindly. "She's small to be of use to them yet, Erica. I think you'll get to keep her." Still, her concern touches me.

It's late afternoon by the time we reach Kildevil. Captain Barnes sent word of our coming, so the town seems as deserted as when we left. Thankfully, no reception party of warders awaits. The thought of the warders brings a question to my mind.

"What about the work camp?" I ask Captain Barnes. "Did they go there, too?"

"Oh, yes. People are saying that the work camps were nothing more than holding tanks for Commission recruits. Everyone of age was taken, even some warders. The place is half empty.

And Warder November has been appointed chief representative of the Commission in these parts. The conscripts were taken to St. Pearl."

"Will we hear from them?" Erica asks. She must be thinking of Carson too.

Captain Barnes shakes his head. "I don't know. I'm glad I've no young ones of my own. You're sure I can't see you home?" he asks.

"It's best if you're not seen with us," William says.

"I'll keep in touch," Captain Barnes tells Erica. Who will pick up all the things at the wharf in the morning with the boys gone? We shoulder what we can and leave the rest. I half expect we'll take the back path to the house, but we set out along the road. The work camp is already shut down for the night. We only left the house three days ago, but I have never been so happy to be anywhere. After a quick meal, I help Marrella unpack, then fall into bed leaving my own bags unopened.

It's late when I wake in the morning, but Marrella's room is silent. I rise and quietly take the dirty clothes from my pack. Cleaning my pockets for the wash, I find Carson's note. Tears fill my eyes. I should have given it to her for his sake. We may never see him again. When I make Marrella's morning tea, I place the note on the tray.

"What's this?" she asks.

"Something I should have given you days ago," I say, leaving without another word.

I'm surprised to find Clara and Donna in the kitchen with Erica. This emergency must override their fear of the taboo. Donna's eyes are red from crying, and I know for certain Carson is gone.

"We were just talking about the investiture," Erica says. "Clara and Donna feel we must proceed as soon as possible to make a political statement." They shouldn't be talking like this here. My eyes travel involuntarily to the control panel. Erica reads the alarm in my face. "Don't worry, Blake. The cloaking device is enabled permanently now." She sits straighter in her chair. "Let the warders ask why if they dare."

"This is war," Clara says. "We hope it won't come to blood and bullets, but if it does, we will not back down. Erica, the others are frantic to hear from you."

"At least the new encryption code is in place," Erica says. "It's best to vary the transmission sites. Can you find a place for me to work this afternoon?" The women nod. "Good. Blake, will you take a basket of food up to Lem later?"

"I'd be happy to." It may be selfish, but this is all I really want to do.

"Thank you, dear." Erica rises and puts some food onto a tray for me.

"Have you heard from the boys yet?" I ask. The women shake their heads.

"I'm sure they will soon," Erica says. "Now we have to plan for the investiture. Just boring details. Why don't you take this into the dining room where you can eat in peace?"

It seems odd to eat breakfast alone in the dining room. The thought of seeing Lem, finding out what he knows, makes me too restless to sit. I walk over to the window, bread in hand. The big dining-room window looks down on the work camp where the land slopes gently to an almost-level lawn. What I see there this morning almost makes me drop my bread. The children, mostly little ones now, march in rows to Warder November's commands. They look like tiny soldiers. "What on earth . . ." I say to myself.

"Quite the sight, isn't it?" William says behind me.

This time, I do drop my bread. "I didn't hear you come in," I say, fumbling after it.

"Sorry, Blake, I didn't mean to startle you." William comes to stand beside me. "I was watching this lovely scene from my study when I heard you. I wanted to make sure you saw it. What do you make of her?"

"Warder November isn't like the last chief warder. This is more than a job to her. It's her life. Her name means she was a street kid, you know? Like the rest of us."

"Yes, I know. I've wondered why she embraced the Commission with such fervor."

"If you wanted power, maybe becoming a chief warder would be a start."

"Do you think that's what she wants?"

· I shake my head. "I can't imagine what she wants." Then I remember the look on her face when William rejected her the day we set out for the Tablelands. "Maybe she's just looking for a place to belong, like the rest of us."

There's a long silence after this, and I wonder if I've said the wrong thing. "Well," William finally says, "you've certainly found your place here." His voice is warm. "I thought Marrella was sure to fail her tests until you started helping her study. She is doing so well now."

We are on dangerous ground. I need to get away as quickly

as I can. "I'm always glad to be useful," I say. "And speaking of useful, Erica probably needs me." I don't look back. In the kitchen I gather the empty cups Donna and Clara left, happy to fall back into our usual routine.

When Marrella comes down for breakfast, I avoid meeting her eyes, working around her until she has gone to study with William. Only then do I remember the UV readings. "Don't worry," Erica says when I ask. "William set up a small robotic device to do the readings while we were away. He says Marrella's readings have improved so much, she doesn't need to do them while they prepare for the investiture. She only has a week. And you and I have lots of unpacking to do," she adds. It pleases me to finally put away the equipment we've packed and unpacked so many times. Erica gathers our dirty clothes and bedding. Mountains, it seems. The morning goes by quickly.

In the afternoon Erica fills the basket for Lem. "I'd come with you but I'm still waiting to hear from Donna and Clara," she says. The knock comes as she speaks.

"Fraser!" I cry when I open the door. My joy surprises even me. He blushes but looks pleased. "I—I wasn't sure you'd be safe," I say, trying to excuse the outburst.

"They stuck me in school with the little ones, guessing I'd be safe there," he says, looking a little rueful. "It worked."

"I hoped you would be, Fraser," Erica says. "You're only fifteen, aren't you?"

Fraser frowns. "Fifteen and a half."

"Of course. Come in. Tell us what happened."

But because he spent the day in the school, Fraser missed

most of it. "Carson, Mark, and the others were already rounded up by the time school let out in the afternoon," he says. "I saw the weavers stand their ground, though. Fierce as mother bears, they were. It would have done your heart good to see them." He smiles at the memory. "They insisted their apprentices be spared, and they'd put headscarves on every young woman in the place. So they were all released." Then he stands. "But I've come to see you back to town. We should be going."

"Just tell me where to go, Fraser. I don't need an escort in broad daylight," Erica says. "You can stay and visit with Blake."

This is kind of Erica, but I can't wait to climb Ski Slope now. "Maybe you'd come to Lem Howell's with me," I offer.

"Oh, what a good idea," Erica says.

Fraser stiffens. "No, thank you." His voice is tight.

"Oh, Fraser, are you sure?" Erica is coaxing. I'm not sure why, but if she wants him to come with me, maybe I can help.

"You're not afraid of Lem Howell, are you?" I ask, teasing him like Carson would.

Something behind Fraser's dark eyes goes dead. "That I am not," he says. "The subject is closed. Now, missus, if you're ready, I'll see you safe." And he leaves without another word. Erica gives me an apologetic glance and follows.

I feel as if I've been punched in the stomach. I wait until I know they're far ahead of me before I leave for Ski Slope. Why was Erica pushing Fraser to come with me? Why did he react so badly, and why do I hurt so much? I try to push the ache aside. If Lem has discovered something about my past, that will make up for any amount of hurt. At least, that's what I tell myself. When I pass the path that branches off to Kildevil, I relax a little. I can't imagine what Fraser and I will have to say to each other the next time I see him. I climb the path to Ski Slope as fast as I can.

But the house is empty. I leave the basket in the kitchen and poke around the small, cluttered rooms as if someone as big as Lem could be hidden. As I do, my disappointment gives way to alarm. What if the Commission came here? But the house doesn't look like it's been disturbed. Suddenly I know where Lem might be. I take the path that leads to the garden and there he is, taking his aeolian instruments down for the winter. I call to him from well across the garden, hoping not to startle him. He turns and smiles. "Little Wheat, you're home." He pauses. "I guess I should call you Blake now."

"No, Little Wheat is fine," I say, unwilling to give up his special name for me. "Can I help?"

"Sure. An extra pair of hands would be great."

We work in silence, untying the lyres from trees, putting them in a box at our feet. I know he would tell me if he'd found anything and he hasn't, so I try to make this moment before I'm disappointed last.

"All hell broke loose while you were gone," he says in a matter-of-fact way.

"How did you find out?"

"My brother came up from Kildevil to make sure I was okay."

"You have a brother in Kildevil?" Will this place ever stop surprising me?

Lem nods. "Not that we've ever seen eye to eye, but he does what he can for me. Now you'll want to know if I found anything.

The answer is no. But I've worked at it steady. All the way through June of 2354. I'm just starting on July. If you're there, I'll find you. And the tape machine's coming along. The cassette moves at the right speed now. I just have to get the magnetic playing device right." The determination in his voice reassures me.

"That's wonderful."

"Don't get too hopeful. What's left is the tricky part."

"This must be taking all your time. How can I ever thank you?"

He looks off into the distance. "So many children lost parents in the technocaust, one way or another. So many bonds were broken. I can't mend my own life. But helping you makes things better, somehow." He picks up the box at his feet. "That's all of them. Come on, I want to show you something."

In the house Lem hands me a book. "Here," he says. "You like poetry, and maybe you were named after Blake, so I thought you'd like this."

"Thank you," I say. It's a real book. An old one. I read the spine. *Complete Poems of Milton and Blake.* "I'm glad they didn't call me Milton."

Lem laughs, a big, barking laugh with no sorrow in it. "You don't look much like a Milton to me. I'll make some tea."

I almost open the book but decide to wait. Instead, I go to the music keyboard. It's easy to switch on but very disappointing. Single notes sound uninteresting, but when I press many notes at once, it sounds terrible. The harder I try, the worse it sounds. "Why can't I make it sound like you did?" I ask when Lem brings the tea.

He laughs. "That takes a long, long time. Lots of patience and years of practice."

"You make it look so easy."

"Well, it isn't. Not at first. Even people with natural talent have to work hard."

I think about Fraser and his concertina. "I know someone like that. A boy in Kildevil named Fraser."

A shadow passes over Lem's face. "So you know Fraser," he says, but quietly, as if speaking to himself.

"Do you know him, Lem?"

He shakes his head. "No. Only what Erica and my brother tell me. Now, Little Wheat, if you'll excuse me, there's things I have to do." I find myself out the door before I can ask another question, the tea untouched. Another of those Kildevil mysteries.

The afternoon is almost over, but Erica is not home. Marrella's probably in her room. I'll have to face her sometime. It might as well be now. She is sitting on her bed with the note in her hands. "Were you going to give this to me, ever?" she asks. I'm surprised she isn't angry.

I answer truthfully. "I don't know. I guess I would have some-time."

Her voice drops to a whisper. "You must despise me."

I don't seem to be able to lie to her now. "I don't like you very much, but I wouldn't go that far."

The note flaps in her hand like a bird with broken wings. "He wanted to see me. I was supposed to send you with a note. I'll probably never see him again." Tears spill down her face.

"His mother is upset too," I tell her.

Her eyes widened. "You know his mother?"

I nod. "Madonna Walsh. She's a weaver."

"Do you think she'll like me?" Marrella asks. She's pleading.

I can't imagine that Donna would want this spoiled brat for Carson, but I say, "I don't know." There are limits to my honesty. I leave her miserable. My thoughts churn as I go downstairs. Erica has been gone too long. Maybe I should look for her. But when I open the door to the kitchen, she is already cooking the evening meal.

"I'm glad you're back." I do not ask what she's been doing. It's better not to know.

"How was Lem?" she asks.

"Fine."

"Do you want me to explain about Fraser?"

I'm surprised. "I thought it was some kind of secret."

"No, it's not, though no one would talk about it without reason. But I think you should know. Maybe you'd better sit down." When I sit, she continues. "Lem went into a state of shock when he lost Michelle. I've told you that. He wasn't anything like himself for years. He needed treatment, but that wasn't possible during the technocaust. People here just hid him and did the best they could. His recovery was slow. Everyone who knew him before says he's just a shadow of the man he was. And there are, well, holes. In his memory. The months before Michelle was taken are just a blank for him."

I imagine how much easier things would have been for me if I didn't remember Hilary's death. "It's a blessing in a way, isn't it?"

Erica sighs. "It might be, but Lem can't remember one really important thing."

"What's that?"

"The birth of his son."

Slowly I realize what Erica is saying. "Fraser?"

She nods. "He was only six months old. Lem has no memory of him at all. The soldiers left him in his crib, crying. People from Kildevil got him as soon as they could, and the women cared for him until he was old enough to live with Lem's brother, Rob."

I remember what Lem said this afternoon about only knowing about Fraser from Erica and his brother. "But why haven't they met? This is crazy!"

"Rob's a difficult person. People in Kildevil say, if you call something white, Rob Howell will tell you it's black. Even before the technocaust, he and Lem were always at odds. He never accepted Lem's love of technology. And he refuses to believe Lem can't remember Fraser. He says Lem's only pretending to avoid responsibility. And Rob has managed to pass his bitterness along to Fraser. He hasn't met Lem because he won't. And Lem isn't strong enough to insist."

I recall how Lem looked when I mentioned Fraser. "But he wants to! I know he does. He talked about kids lost in the technocaust today. I didn't understand then."

"I think you're right, Blake. I think that's the reason he's trying so hard to help you. But most people feel it might be too much for Lem. They think it's best, for his sake, to leave things as they are."

"Do you?"

Erica shakes her head. "I don't know."

"Don't know what?" William says as he enters the room.

"I was telling Blake about Lem and Fraser."

William frowns. "Rob Howell is a bitter man. Always was. Poor Fraser. There's so much of Michelle in him. What's this?" William says, taking the book from the table. "*Complete Poems of Milton and Blake.*"

"Lem gave it to me. Because I like poetry. Because of Blake."

William opens the book. He looks surprised. "This was Michelle's," he says. "Look."

Her name, Michelle Blanchette, is written inside in a bold, firm hand.

The Sweater and the Dress

The week passes quickly. There's no word from the boys who were taken away. We watch the children perform military exercises in front of the grand hotel every morning, but otherwise life is disturbingly normal. There's a rumor that the Commission is not strong enough to maintain a presence outside St. Pearl, but it's hard to tell how much of that is wishful thinking.

Marrella spends her days with William preparing for the investiture and the Sacrifice. She's learning what she wants to now and needs no help from me. Erica disappears each afternoon and returns looking more troubled every day. Aside from household chores, my days are idle. For the first time in my life, I can read all I want. I take science books from William's study. I read the poetry of Milton and Blake. I lose myself in books. I visit Lem as often as I can, but he makes no progress with the tape player, and the archived computer lists yield nothing. But that doesn't bother me as much as it might because it's my future that occupies me now, not my past. No matter what happens after the investiture, I won't return to the work camp. Maybe Erica can find me a place in the resistance, working against the Commission. I will talk to her when the ceremony is over, even though the thought of leaving Erica and William makes my heart ache.

As the day of the investiture draws near, excitement spills up from Kildevil. It reminds me of the days before Memory Day, back in my distant past a few weeks ago.

"The dress will be here tonight," Erica says on the eve of the ceremony, "for Marrella to try on."

"Have you seen it?"

She nods. "It's beautiful. They even made a turban to go with it when I explained it was needed." Erica runs a hand through my hair. "Your hair could be lovely. Why don't you wash it and I'll cut it for you?"

I shrug. "Nothing about me is lovely and no one will look at me tomorrow night."

To my surprise, Erica looks hurt. "Blake, don't talk that way."

"I'm sorry. Of course you can cut my hair. I'll wash it."

When I return she's waiting with scissors and a mirror. As I watch, she carefully layers my hair so that it falls in curls around my face. Even I have to admit it looks better. But as I help Erica prepare supper, I find my heart won't stop hurting. I can't bear the thought of leaving, but I don't see how I can stay.

There's a knock at the door. I answer without thinking. If I had, I might have realized that Fraser would be the one to deliver the dress.

"Wonderful," Erica says. "I'll just take this upstairs. Blake, why don't you make Fraser a cup of tea?" And she is gone in what seems to me a highly deliberate move to leave us alone. I scarcely know where to look. I expect Fraser to be sullen, but he's not.

"You've done something with your hair," he says.

My hand flies up to my head as if this is news to me. "Erica cut it. For tomorrow. So I would look respectable."

"So you do," Fraser says. He's still holding the bag he carried the dress in. He glances around the kitchen. "Did someone say something about tea?"

"Sure. Of course. Sit down. Please, I mean." I seem to have forgotten how to talk. I feel like a complete fool. I turn my back while I put the kettle on.

"I'm sorry I was short with you the other day," Fraser says quietly.

"No. It was my fault. I didn't know about you and Lem. I wouldn't have asked you to come with me if I had."

"Missus Townsend told me so," he says. The kettle is on the burner, but I still stand with my back to him. It seems I literally cannot face him. I stay like that, knowing how awkward I must look, hoping the kettle might boil. It doesn't.

"Aren't you planning to turn around?" Fraser finally asks. So I do. There, on the table, is a knitted tunic of the finest, whitest wool I have ever seen. He holds it up. "I made this for you," he says. "Would you try it on?"

The tunic falls to just above my knee. It feels like a cloud. The pattern is incredibly intricate. "It's beautiful," I tell him. "I've never owned anything like this. How can I thank you?"

"Just wear it after the ceremony tomorrow night for me. That will be thanks enough."

William walks into the kitchen a few minutes later. "My goodness, Blake. You look—beautiful."

I feel myself blush. "Erica cut my hair and Fraser made me

this." I run my hands over the sweater, feeling the fine texture of the wool.

William frowns. "Fraser offered you the sweater and you accepted? Fraser, do you think she understands what this means?"

Fraser reddens as he stares into his tea. "I expect so. She's not uncivilized."

"You're right, she's not. But she's from St. Pearl, and our ways are unfamiliar to her." They are talking as if I'm somewhere else. "I'll tell you what, Fraser. Erica and I will speak to her tonight, and perhaps you can talk to her again tomorrow."

Fraser looks hurt, his face closed. "Will she be giving me back the sweater, do you think?"

"No!" I say, but William holds up his hand to stop me. "We'll have to see."

Fraser stands abruptly. "I'll take my leave then." And he is gone before I can stop him.

For the first time I can remember, I don't try to hide my anger. "What was that about? Why were you so mean to him?"

"My goodness, Blake, you look beautiful," Erica says when she comes back into the room, but she quickly adds, "What's wrong?"

William turns to her. "It's the sweater. Fraser made it for her."

"Oh, my."

"Won't someone tell me what's going on?"

Erica puts her arm around my shoulder. "In Kildevil," she explains, "when a boy designs a sweater for a girl, it's a token. If she takes it, it's a sign."

"What do you mean?"

"A token of love," William says. "If you accept the sweater, everyone in Kildevil will understand that."

The embarrassment is more than I can bear. I burst into tears and rush from the house. It's cold outside, but the heat of my shame and the running and Fraser's fine sweater keep me warm. I don't even know where I'm going until I catch sight of someone on the path ahead. I've caught up with Fraser. When he sees me, hope lights his eyes.

I am still crying. I can't stop. "Fraser, I didn't know," I pant. "I had no idea what the sweater meant. How could I?"

He puts his arms around me. Instead of pulling back, I lean into his frail, bird-boned body, somehow unafraid. "Hush, now," he says. "I never meant to make you cry. You seemed so happy when you saw the sweater, I thought you knew what I was about."

I shake my head and try to speak. Instead I sob and hiccup all at once. Fraser laughs softly. "Don't break your heart, Blake. The first time I saw you, right there in the Master's kitchen, I couldn't take my eyes off you. Remember how Carson tormented me? And then on the boat, when you told me about your life, it seemed to me that we were just the same. I decided to make you the sweater that very day."

"But William told me what the sweater means." My voice drops to a whisper. "I don't know if I can love you—or anyone. I've never tried."

He looks shocked. "You don't try. It either happens or it doesn't."

I can't look at him. I look down instead. "I'm not ready," I say. "It isn't you, Fraser. I just don't know how. I'll give you back the sweater." I start to peel it off, but he stops me.

"No," he says. "I won't give it to another. And you won't be taking one from anyone else, will you?" I shake my head. He smiles. "Keep it, then. Not to wear, just to have. We'll talk again later. It'll be easier after the investiture. Things will be more normal then." His dark eyes are gentle. In his place, another boy might have been angry or cruel. I feel a surge of warmth toward him. "Are you all right now?" he asks. I nod, then turn away. His kindness means more than I can say. I felt this way once before, overwhelmed by unexpected kindness. For a moment I cannot think when and then I remember. With his father. With Lem.

When I return, Erica and William are sitting at the table. They look stricken. "I'm sorry," I tell them. "I'm okay now."

"It isn't you, Blake," William says, "it's Marrella. She's refusing to wear the dress. Would you talk to her?"

I turn toward the door, but Erica stops me. "You're still wearing the sweater. I thought you went after Fraser to give it back."

"I did talk to him. We decided I'd keep it for now. Not to wear. Just to have."

William looks serious. "It's only natural a boy like Fraser would want to settle down as quickly as he can. He's never had enough love in his life—"

I interrupt him. "Then you can understand why I couldn't just turn him down, can't you?" I had no idea I felt that way until the words leave my mouth.

"Oh, Blake, be careful." Erica says. "You're too young to get locked into anything."

"Don't worry. I have some ideas about my future. Maybe after tomorrow we can talk. Now let me see what I can do with Marrella."

She is lying facedown on her bed. The ceremonial robe, made with such love, lies crumpled on the floor. For the second time tonight, I'm furious. I bend down to rescue the beautiful dress and to give myself time to check my temper. Marrella turns and looks at me. "What happened to you?" she says. I grope for a way to explain why I've been upset, but she continues. "I'd die for hair like that. And I suppose you'll wear that sweater tomorrow?"

I shake my head. "No. The sweater goes away for now. But that's not what I'm here to talk about. Do you have any idea how much care went into the making of this dress?"

"It's covered in tiny crabs," she wails. "It makes my skin crawl."

"*Marrella splendens.* The creature you were named for. They planned this dress for months. They used up all their best fibers. How can you be anything but grateful?" Marrella sniffs but says nothing. I'm encouraged. "If you reject this dress," I tell her, "Carson Walsh's mother will never, ever have anything to do with you." In fact, I'm not sure this is true. I think they will accept her no matter how badly she behaves. But I won't allow her to do that to them.

Marrella sits up. "Really?"

"Really." I've never been a good liar, but I want to believe what I'm saying so much that it sounds true even to me.

Marrella straightens her turban. "The dress will need to be ironed," she says.

"I'll see to it." As I leave the room, I press the dress to my heart and to Fraser's sweater, which was also made with love—made for me. Before, I would never have imagined myself worthy of such a fine garment. Now, I do.

The Investiture

Next morning, even before I open my eyes, I know something is wrong. The silence seems to be filled with a wailing pitched just beyond the range of my hearing. Instead of going to Marrella, I pull on my clothes and go downstairs, knowing somehow that the answer will be found in front of the grand hotel. And it is. Military vehicles of every description cover the lawn. They are empty and silent now, but the whine of their fuel cells must have woken me. Erica and William join me. Erica's mouth is a grim line. "So, it has come to this," she says.

I grab her arm with both hands. "Have they come for you?"

She gently releases my grip. "No, child. They are here because of the investiture."

"The ceremony gives the Commission an opportunity to show its dominance. We were afraid of this," William says.

"Will they try to stop us?"

When William speaks, I see the warrior in his face. "They may try, but nothing can. As long as any of us are left standing, the investiture will proceed."

"That's right. It will." Marrella is standing in the doorway. I would not have guessed courage to be one of her virtues, but she shines with it now.

The day that should have been filled with happy anticipation is colored with dread. We wait for the soldiers to come, but nothing happens. In fact, aside from the vehicles, we see no sign of them. William and Erica debate strategies over the noon meal.

"We could spirit Marrella away to Kildevil along the back path now," Erica suggests.

"You know the women must come for her at sunset. It's part of the ceremony. Change that and we admit defeat before we begin," William says. He takes her hand. "This isn't about the ceremony or even the Way. It's about everything that we value, everything you've worked for. You know that, Erica, don't you?" Erica agrees, though tears fill her eyes. The debate is over. Marrella stays.

The day creeps by. Finally, when the light begins to fade, Erica brings a case to Marrella's room. "Cosmetics," she says.

Marrella's hands fly up as if to protect her face. "I can't wear cosmetics."

Erica smiles. "These won't hurt you. They were very hard to find." And she sets to work, bringing color to Marrella's pale face. "Blake," Erica says while she works, "I've laid a dress out on your bed. Why don't you put it on now, then we'll help Marrella dress."

I gasp when I see the dress. From hem to neckline, it flames from dark red to orange. I had not thought to wear anything special tonight. I shuck off my everyday clothes. The silky cloth flows over me. It's the first dress I've ever worn. When I spin, it flashes like fire.

Anger flares in Marrella's face when she sees me, but then she must remember what lies ahead, for she drops her eyes and says nothing. Erica only smiles. That smile is worth more than any compliment to me. "Now we will dress you," she says to Marrella. When we're finished, Erica says, "Come, both of you. I want you to see yourselves." In her bedroom we stand before a full-length mirror. Marrella is like a delicate flower or a field of new snow. I remember how beautiful she seemed the first night I saw her, and I know, no matter what happens tonight, I would not give up these last few weeks for anything. Behind her, I am like a colored shadow. My dark hair and dress fade in the light of her beauty. "Downstairs now," Erica says. "And ask William to come up. We must dress as well."

Marrella and I enter the dining room in the gathering dusk, and I can hardly believe what I see—the military vehicles are gone, as if magic has restored the balance for this ceremony. Is it magic? I wonder. Has it always been? Will there be magic in the ceremony tonight? I can't ask Marrella. She is pacing, too excited to speak, for we can hear the song of the women from Kildevil. Then, through the bare trees, we see the flicker of torchlight.

"Marrella, keep back from the window," William says as he enters the room.

"I'm sorry, I forgot," Marrella replies. Her eyes shine, and for the moment everything is as it should be. William and Erica are resplendent. Her robe is yellow and green, and his shades from blue to deepest violet.

"Come." Erica takes my hand. We stand in front of the house, William, Erica, and I. The women crest the hill below us, a river of them singing, all joyful in the torchlight. I hold my breath when they come to the grand hotel but they pass unchallenged. Then they stand before us, clad in rainbow robes like ours, their faces shining.

Clara steps forward. "We come to welcome our bio-indicator," she says.

"How will you honor her?" William replies.

The women reply in unison. "We honor her with our voices and our song."

"That is not enough." William says. I look at Erica, startled, but she smiles.

"We honor her with our lives and our work," the women say. Their voices are louder.

"That is not enough."

"We honor her as we honor the earth itself!" they shout joyfully.

"Then she is yours," William says. The door swings open and Marrella comes forward on cue. Her white robe glows in the faint light as if lit from within. A hush falls.

She raises both hands. "My people," she says, "I will serve you as I serve the earth, with my life." A cheer goes up from the crowd as a few older women guide her to a chair that is decorated with ribbons and mounted on poles. When Marrella is seated, four boys come forward to carry her. Fraser is the oldest. They are too small for this burden. I remember with a pang that the older boys are gone. Somehow I know Carson Walsh would have been a bearer of this chair.

The boys take Marrella's weight bravely. Everyone pretends not to notice what a struggle it is for them, but the women's faces grow more worried even as they sing and dance. Walking directly behind the chair, I see how Fraser trembles with the strain. His fine black hair is plastered with sweat, even on this cool night. When it seems the boys might collapse, William moves forward. The rest of the journey is less difficult. Only those immediately near know that William has braced the back of the chair, taking most of the weight.

The ceremony is to be held in the largest edifice in Kildevil, the Hall. This is a meeting hall, but Erica explained it's also the place where they keep the biblio-tech and other technology the townspeople are willing to tolerate but don't want in their homes. As it comes into view, I realize how foolish I was to suppose that the military vehicles had simply disappeared. They are here, of course. I want to run away, but the women do not miss a beat of their song, weaving around the armored vehicles as if they were part of the celebration. They are not surprised. They knew the soldiers would be here and it did not stop them. Their courage fills me. Somehow I will face what lies ahead. The huge back doors of the Hall stand open, darker than the night. It's like walking into the jaws of some devouring monster. A narrow corridor leads us to a circular floor backed by a stage. Rows of chairs rise in a broad semicircle. Half the hall is filled with the townspeople and the other half with soldiers. I wonder how long they have waited like this, side by side. The boys finally lay the chair down before the brightly decorated stage, and the oldest weavers guide Marrella up the stairs. William, Erica, and I follow, as do other weavers and the four boys who carried the chair. Fraser looks sick, though whether from exhaustion or fear it is hard to say.

"People of Kildevil," William begins, but Warder November marches up to the stage with a small group of officers. Their drab uniforms are like a blot on our colorful ceremony. William's shimmering blue robe does not hide the anger in his bearing. "What is the meaning of this?" His voice echoes through the hall, which is as silent as if it were empty.

To my surprise, Warder November speaks. "The Commission wishes to welcome the new bio-indicator."

William's shoulders relax. "If that is the only reason you have come, you are welcome."

Warder November looks confused, then angry. "We also wish the bio-indicator to swear an oath of allegiance to the Commission before your ceremony begins. If you refuse, you will answer to the military." It seems she will settle for nothing less than confrontation.

William draws himself up like a storm gathering fury, but before he can speak, an officer steps forward. He speaks so quietly only we hear him. "Warder November, this is not what we discussed." He turns to us. "I am Captain March of the Corner Brook garrison. We are here only as observers. My orders do not permit me to act."

Warder November turns on him. "You would disobey the Commission?"

"I take my orders directly from General Ryan."

She hesitates, looking for some way to enforce her wishes. Suddenly we hear music. Gentle notes from a keyboard fall over us like peace itself. "'That Sheep May Safely Graze,'" Captain March says when the last notes fade away. "How appropriate.

Master, on behalf of General Ryan and the military, we welcome your new bio-indicator and wish her joy."

"Captain March, I thank you," William replies. "And, Warder November, we accept your welcome as well." The officers retreat, leaving Warder November no choice but to follow. The ceremony begins, but I hardly notice. While the music was playing, I located the source in a dark corner of the hall. So did Fraser. Lem's contribution to the ceremony must have been carefully planned, for his music blends beautifully. He sits deep in shadow when he is not playing and plays with his eyes closed, as if he were alone. For the rest of the evening, I watch Fraser pretend not to watch his father.

What's Lost

The party that follows the investiture goes on until the sky is bright, and then it's time for the bio-indicator's Sacrifice. They lead Marrella to a walled garden beside the Hall. She stands so that the sunlight falls on her naked face. She closes her eyes and breathes deeply. Then she is given an earthenware cup of water and a carrot that was grown here last summer. While she eats and drinks, people chant quietly. At first the words are too soft to understand, but, gradually, I hear what they are saying: "We thank you for your Sacrifice," over and over. When she has finished, William dips his thumb into the water and draws a line across Marrella's forehead. Then she smiles. People cheer, and the ceremony is over.

There's no risk in this ceremony now, but there's no magic, either, I'm sure. Bio-indicators must have died because the world was full of toxins, not because of this ritual exposure. And there would be no way of knowing what killed them. No wonder we call that part of the past the Dark Times. What pathetically poor protection the Sacrifice must have offered when the danger was real. I imagine people in a degraded world with only their superstitions to protect them. Finally I understand how important these rituals must have been and why, even now, people cling to them.

We make our way home in the full light of day, and I fall asleep almost before I'm in bed. Late in the afternoon, I rise to find William alone. Somehow he manages to look exhausted, satisfied, and anxious all at once.

"What happened to the soldiers?" I ask him.

"They're still in Kildevil. The Commission invited them and they came, but not to stop the investiture. They wanted to make sure it went ahead. I wish they could have told us that yesterday, but they wanted Warder November to think otherwise. Erica was called to a meeting between Captain March and the Weavers' Guild a few hours ago," he says. "She might be gone for the rest of the day. We've wondered where the military stands. It's all very promising."

"But why Erica and not you?"

"Erica's one of the most important resistance leaders on the island. I thought you knew that. My project isn't as political, although ultimately, I suppose it will be."

"Is that what you're training Marrella for? This project?" I busy myself with the kettle to avoid his eyes, trying to pretend my interest is casual.

"Yes, it is. While the Weavers' Guild leads the resistance, the Way is quietly trying to reverse the damage of the technocaust. We find those most capable of becoming scientists and educate them."

I swing around, knocking a canister off the counter. "*That's* what the tests were about?" William looks so surprised, I realize I must have shouted. "I mean—" I say, rapidly trying to think what

I might reasonably mean, "I thought they were magic."

William chuckles. "Not magic. Science. Though science may be the only magic we have. The Commission fears science the way the Church hated magic in the Middle Ages, and the people can't seem to give up those empty rituals you saw last night. But, no, the tests are not magic. The logic that led to the right answers was embedded in holograms in the books Marrella read. It's called enhanced learning—still very experimental. Good scientists don't work by reason alone. There's a creative factor in scientific discovery. Call it intuition. We still don't know how it works, but we've learned how to isolate those who have it. They make the best scientists and, these days, we can only train the best. Anyone could have read the books I've given Marrella, but only those with a talent for intuitive learning would know the right answers without conscious thought, pick the plant or animal that is most interesting from a scientific point of view, unravel the geology of the landscape we have chosen to place them in. I was sure Marrella didn't have that talent, but suddenly she did. If there was any magic, that was it."

I lift the canister from the floor and turn away, feeling sick. I thought what I gave Marrella was worthless. Now it seems I have given my future away. I fuss with the teapot, wondering how I will forgive myself for this. I don't want to know what happens to Marrella next, but I have to ask. I wait until the kettle boils so that my voice will not betray me.

"That depends," William says. "Until a few weeks ago she would certainly have stayed here. But if things change as we hope, we may be able to open a university again. Just imagine!"

I try not to. "I think I'll take my tea upstairs," I say.

William, lost in his vision of a university, only says, "Fine. Don't wake Marrella. She's earned the right to sleep."

I flop down on my bed, thankful that Erica was not present for that conversation. Or Marrella. I recall the tests and how effortlessly the answers came to me. Now I know why. On the Tablelands I was called to a new life. I threw that away without thinking. If I had known even yesterday, I might have been able to put things right. Now it's too late. The investiture is over. Marrella is the bio-indicator. She will have the life that belongs to me.

I need to see Lem. Grabbing my Object, I rush from the house and up the hill, as if this ache were something I could outrun. Halfway to Ski Slope, I find Fraser coming down the path. When he sees me, he smiles. "I was just coming to see you," he says. "The town's upside down today, everyone pretending the Weavers' Guild isn't meeting with the military, trying to act as if a town full of soldiers is the most natural thing in the world. I had to get away. Where are you rushing off to?"

I don't want to mention Lem, so I say, "Nowhere."

This doesn't seem to bother Fraser. "Suppose we go nowhere together then," he says, falling into step with me. "What's that you're carrying?"

"A cassette tape. It's something I've always had. It might have a message from my parents. Lem is going to—" I stop, cursing my clumsiness.

"Go on, then," Fraser says in a neutral tone. "What's he going to do?"

"He's trying to find a way to let me hear it. You saw him last night, didn't you?"

Fraser scowls. "I seen him. He never even looked at me. Doesn't know me from a hole in the ground."

"Fraser, that's not his fault. It's what he's been through. Don't you want to meet him?"

"My uncle says he doesn't care about me."

I pick my words carefully. "I don't think that's true. He can't remember you. He doesn't care about anything the way ordinary people do, but when I asked him about you . . ."

Fraser's mouth falls open. "You asked him about me? When?"

"The day you wouldn't come to see him. I was trying to figure out what was going on. It was before I knew."

"And what did he say?"

How can I say what I mean without giving Fraser false hope? "Not much," I begin truthfully.

"There, you see?" Fraser makes a gesture of annoyance. "You're as bad as Missus Townsend. Giving him the benefit of the doubt when he deserves none."

I grab his arm. "That's not true. Listen to me!" All the pent-up emotion of the morning pours into my voice.

Fraser responds to my urgency. "I'm listening."

My eyes fill with tears. I hold my Object up, my voice shaking. "If I knew someone who had known my mother, nothing could keep me from him."

"Does he remember her?" Fraser asks. It never occurred to me that he wouldn't know this.

"Of course he does. He thinks of her every day. He gave me

a book that belonged to her. Would you like to see it?"

"What kind of book?" he says, his voice small as if he's afraid to ask.

We turn back down the path. "Poetry. Because maybe I was named for one of the poets. William Blake." Then I remember what Lem said when he gave me the book, about the technocaust and what he'd lost. "Fraser, he spoke about you like you were someone he could never recover. I didn't understand then, but maybe he gave me the book because I remind him of you."

Fraser smiles. "Well, you remind me of me, so maybe that's so."

An easy silence settles between us. Suddenly I don't feel as if my life is ruined forever. When I give Fraser the book, he holds it like something incredibly fragile. I open the front cover, and he runs his fingers over the handwriting. "Her name," he breathes softly. "Do you suppose she read this?"

I have to laugh. "I would imagine so."

"Read to me, please? Just read anything," he says, thrusting the book at me.

"Fraser, can't you read?"

"Course I can," Fraser says, indignant. "I went to school same as everyone. I'm just out of practice, is all."

I decide I'd rather not know what that means. We sit on the garden bench in a patch of weak winter sun and I open the book at random. "This is by Milton. It's called 'XIX.'"

"What's that mean, then?" Fraser asks.

"I don't know."

"Well, read it anyway."

So I do:

"When I consider how my light is spent,
Ere half my days, in this dark world and wide,
And that one talent which is death to hide
Lodged with me useless . . ."

This catches my attention. I read on with more interest.

". . . though my soul more bent
To serve therewith my Maker, and present
My true account, lest he returning chide;
'Doth God exact day-labour, light denied?'
I fondly ask; But Patience, to prevent
That murmur, soon replies, 'God doth not need
Either man's work or his own gifts: who best
Bear his mild yoke, they serve him best. His state
Is kingly. Thousands at his bidding speed
And post o'er land and ocean without rest:
They also serve who only stand and wait.'"

"Read it again," Fraser says. When I finish, he asks, "Did you understand that?"

I shake my head. "Not much. I like the last line, though, 'They also serve who only stand and wait.' That sounds like me. And I liked the part about hidden talents, too."

I hope Fraser will ask what I mean, but instead he says, "She read that, do you think?"

"She must have."

He sighs. "I wish I could have known her."

"I know." I hesitate. "Do you think you'll ever want to meet Lem?"

His eyes grow troubled. "I'll think about it. Read me another."

But as I flip through the book, a shadow falls across the bench. "You two look comfortable."

"Erica! I thought you'd be gone longer."

Erica laughs. "A six-hour meeting is long enough. Come inside and hear the news."

We follow her into the house.

The Future and the Past

". . . and it's not just here," Erica says, finishing. "The military is willing to work with Weavers' Guilds across the continent."

"Then democracy could be restored without bloodshed. Erica, this is better than we dared hope." The joy in William's voice finally causes Marrella to take notice. While Erica described the meeting, she paid no attention at all. Now, no doubt, she wonders what she's supposed to understand. I'm not about to help her out, but Fraser has overlapping concerns. "What about the conscripts the Commission took away?" he asks.

Erica looks troubled. "We don't know. Captain March says the military hasn't seen them. Our sources say they're in that big new fortress on Signal Hill. We think they were taken to St. Pearl and not the garrison towns so the Commission could keep them away from the military. It's possible the Commission is going to use our children to fill out the Commission guard. I hate to think of them pitched against trained soldiers. We have to hope it won't come to that."

"But surely the military wouldn't fire on them, Erica," William says.

"Captain March said General Ryan could make no promises.

If the young ones fight along with the Commission guard, the military will have no choice."

"But that's terrible!" Marrella cries. "How could they fight their own people? Are they monsters?" She storms from the room without waiting for an answer.

Everyone looks at me, expecting I'll follow, but I want to know more. "Can't you contact them somehow, Erica? Your people are all over the island."

"Yes, but the conscripts have been isolated from all but the most loyal Commission followers. And other things are happening now. The Commission has started to scramble communication signals so that it's difficult for us to send or receive. They also seem to be sealing St. Pearl off from the rest of the island. The roads are closed."

"Why on earth would they do that?" William asks.

"Captain March says the Commission may think it can hold St. Pearl by force, even if it loses control over the rest of the island."

"Using our children as their army?" The happiness is gone from William's voice. Erica bites her lip.

"But Mark and Carson and the others would never fight for the Commission," Fraser says.

Erica smiles sadly and puts her hand over Fraser's. "People can be forced to do things they'd never imagine, Fraser. They won't betray us in their hearts, but they may have to fight for the Commission to save their lives." She shakes herself and rises. "But nothing bad has happened yet. Things are very hopeful, really. And this situation could take months to play out. In the meantime, let's not worry ourselves sick." But Erica sounds as if she doesn't believe what she's saying.

Fraser leaves when Erica decides we should eat. I'd rather help her than deal with Marrella. Erica hands me the poetry book as she clears the table. "You were reading to Fraser?"

"Yes. A poem by Milton. About serving and waiting."

"Oh, 'They also serve who only stand and wait.' That's the one about his blindness."

"He was blind?"

"He went blind in adulthood. Milton was a political rebel too. In fact, his blindness probably saved him from being executed for his beliefs."

"How long ago was that?"

"Let's see—about seven hundred years."

The forks I was holding clatter to the table. "Doesn't anything ever change?"

"Don't be discouraged, Blake. Everything changes. Except people and their desire to control one another."

My eyes fill with tears of frustration. "Then what's the point?"

"The point is the other thing that never changes. The desire of ordinary people to control their own lives. If anything is worth fighting for, that is."

The salad greens get a furious shredding while I think about Erica's words. By the time the bowl is full, I have to admit she's right. I didn't know what freedom was a few months ago. Now I'll never accept anything less. That brings me back to my own problems. "Erica, what did Milton mean about it being death to hide his talent?" I study the salad when I say this, afraid to meet her eyes.

202

"He didn't mean actual death, of course. He would have been safer not writing." She pauses to consider. "He probably felt as if the life would go out of him if he couldn't write, even though his blindness made it difficult. Even if it got him into trouble. That's what talent does, I think. You feel as if you have to do the thing you do best, or you'll just shrivel up inside. Why do you ask?"

"No reason," I manage to say. I pick up the salad bowl and carry it to the dining room so Erica will not notice when I start to shrivel up inside.

Fraser had said that things would be more normal after the investiture. Over the next few days, I realize I had no idea what normal was. Suddenly the house is filled with people I have never seen before. They come to talk to William and meet Marrella. Only Fraser comes to see me. Erica still leaves every afternoon, trying to contact other members of the resistance. I see Marrella only to help with her UV observations now that she's doing them again. We barely talk and that suits us both. I didn't realize what a strain it was to spend so much time together.

Then, one night, Erica comes home later than usual, looking exhausted and gray. "We haven't been able to reach anyone off the island for days. Now the whole system's scrambled. Unless someone finds a way around this, we won't be able to communicate at all."

"That's terrible," I say, easing her into a chair. "Was there any news from St. Pearl?"

"Only from the few who managed to get out. They say people aren't going to accept Commission rule even there. We know something is being planned, something big. But without information, we have no way of protecting the children." Erica puts her face in her hands. I reach out, tentatively, and rub her back. She pats my hand. "Thank you, Blake," she says. "You're such a help to me." And I realize that Erica is the friend I have been looking for.

I don't understand what all these changes mean to me until I'm in bed that night. The archives Lem has been searching are probably accessed through the network that is now scrambled. If that's true, he'll have to stop looking. It's a small thing compared to what's happening to Carson and Mark, but it matters to me. I lie awake long into the night hoping I'm wrong. In the morning I find Erica alone in the kitchen, strangely idle. She looks as if she hasn't slept at all. I wonder if I can get her mind off all of this. "I'm going to see Lem today," I tell her when I finish breakfast. "Will you come?"

"Yes," Erica says as I knew she would. "I've been neglecting Lem." As we climb the path, she asks, "Has he found out any more about your past?"

"No. I think he's wasting his time." I take a deep breath. "He won't have access to those archives now, will he?"

"Oh, dear. No, he won't. Not unless he thought to download them. He has the capacity."

"Would he have, do you think?"

"I can't imagine. You'll have to ask him." We lapse into silence, each occupied by our own worries.

Lem is busy with a small device at his workbench. "Good. You're here," he says, as if he's been expecting us.

"Have you tried to access the archives lately, Lem?" Erica asks so I won't have to.

"Can't get through," Lem says. "Are there solar storms or something?"

"It's the Commission, Lem." Erica explains what's happened.

When she's finished, I ask, "You didn't download the data, did you?"

Lem runs his hands through his wild hair. "I didn't bother. Could have, if I'd known. I'm sorry." My eyes fill with tears. Lem turns back to his workbench. "Such a shame," he adds, "especially now that I've got this tape machine running."

"You do?" Erica and I say together.

Lem smiles, half sheepish, half proud. "Meant to tell you. I got distracted."

"So I can hear what's on my Object—the cassette, I mean?"

"Sure can. Did you bring it with you?"

"No, but I can get it." I turn to Erica. "I can, can't I? Get it now?"

She laughs. "Of course you can. Go. I'll stay here—I'd only slow you down."

I tear down the steep path just as I did the first day I came here, all those weeks ago. Only now I'm not running away from anything, I'm running toward the secrets in my past. I run as fast as I can but the trip seems to take years. When I finally collapse into a chair beside Lem, my legs tremble and I'm panting too hard to talk. I hand my Object to Erica and bend over to catch my breath.

I hear a slow, deep moan. I look up, shocked. Could this be my mother? Lem makes an adjustment, the pitch rises, and suddenly we hear a woman's voice, just as plainly as if she were in the room with us.

". . . so it seems strange to be talking to you as if you were grown up and far away when, in fact, you're safe right here in my lap where you belong," the voice says. A small child gurgles in the background. Me. "But the journey we are about to undertake is so long and perilous that I may have to leave you safe with someone along the way. If I do, I want you to be able to hear my voice so you will know how much you are loved and what a blessing you are to me." My eyes fill with tears. Erica puts her hand on my shoulder.

"Your father was taken from his lab last night." The voice grows thick with emotion. "He knew this might happen, Blake. He made me promise I wouldn't wait for him. If I were alone I would stay, but I have you to think about. So, somehow, we will travel very far from here to a place I've heard we can hide. That's all I can tell you.

"One day, I hope we can listen to this together and talk about how frightening everything was in the dark and dangerous past. But I can't be sure. If you listen to this tape without me, just know that you were loved as much as you could be. I will never leave you unless I have to."

That's all. My eyes are blinded with tears, but I raise my face to Erica. "She didn't tell me her name." My voice is a wail. I can't help myself. "She didn't tell me anything!"

Erica presses my face to her side and holds me. After a while she says, "She thought she'd be able to leave you with someone who would know who she was, Blake. She couldn't imagine what lay ahead of her. None of us did."

Then Lem speaks. "Maybe she was afraid to leave clues. She

didn't say where you were going, either."

I wipe my eyes roughly on my sleeve. "I guess you're right," I say, but I can't overcome my disappointment.

Lem hands me a micro-disk. "I digitalized it for you. You can listen to it any time you want."

Erica strokes my hair. "There are some clues, though, Blake. Your father had a lab. He must have been a scientist. And your mother's vocabulary. Did you notice? She talked about the 'long and perilous' journey. She was well educated, too. Probably not a techie, but it fits with everything we already know."

"Would they have harmed her if we'd stayed?" I ask.

"Maybe not, but she did the right thing. Especially for you."

"What do you mean?"

"In Toronto Prefecture, children were taken from techies and adopted by childless government officials. They could have taken you."

"Then I'd be on the other side?"

"Yes, and you'd probably never even know."

Did my mother do the right thing? Erica is certain, but I'm not. Maybe we would have been okay where we were. What if I had been adopted? Walking back down the hill, I wonder what it would have been like to grow up privileged in some big city, unaware that anyone was living as I have lived. Thinking the right people had the power. Would that really have been worse?

In my room Erica shows me how to use the control panel to listen to the micro-disk. Then she leaves me. I spend the rest of the day alone. I listen to the micro-disk until I've memorized every word, every nuance of my mother's voice. I understand how frightened she was and that she was doing what she thought was best for me. Erica brings me a tray at noon, just as we would for Marrella. In the evening she says, "William and I would like to talk to you."

I half expect a lecture about sulking, but as soon as I enter the kitchen I know I'm wrong. Erica looks as if she has a secret. William is serious but seems pleased as well. "Please sit down, Blake," he says, almost formally. "Erica told me about the recording. We've been talking about your future. It's unthinkable to send you back to the work camp now. Even without this political upheaval, I don't think we could have done that."

Erica interrupts eagerly. "You see, Blake, knowing that you're one of the Disappeared makes you, well, almost like family. If your mother had reached the Beothuks, we would certainly have known her. And we were wondering if you'd consider staying here?"

"In Kildevil, you mean?"

Erica laughs. "No, here with us. We have no children. You have no family. It makes sense for you to stay here and be—ours."

I'm stunned. "You want me?"

"Yes, we do. You'd be like a daughter to us."

I can't speak. I nod my head numbly and smile. "I would like that," I finally say. William gravely shakes my hand. Erica hugs me. Then I think about the education Marrella is promised and take a deep breath. "But if I stay here, what will I do?"

Erica smiles. "You could be apprenticed to a weaver. I think Donna might take you." But the tone of her voice tells me she's certain Donna would. So that's my future. I'll stay in Kildevil for the rest of my life, apprentice as a weaver, maybe even learn to love Fraser if I can.

Alone in my room again, I wonder what's wrong with me. Finally I'll belong to someone. That's what I've always wanted. And I do love Erica. Why don't I feel happier? Before I go to sleep, I open Michelle's book to the poem by Milton again.

When I consider how my light is spent,
Ere half my days, in this dark world and wide,
And that one talent which is death to hide
Lodged with me useless . . .

I close the book. That's what's wrong.

The Battle of St. Pearl

"Blake, wake up." Erica is shaking my shoulder. It's dark, and her voice is urgent. I could be dreaming, but I've never felt this tired in a dream.

"What is it? What's wrong?"

"Something's happening in St. Pearl. Signals are getting out. Fraser came for us."

I'm on my feet and dressing before Erica has finished. "What do they see?"

"I don't know, exactly. I didn't wait to hear. Fraser can fill us in while we walk."

But Fraser doesn't know much, either. "Donna woke me up and told me to get you to the Hall fast as I could," he says. "I didn't stop to ask questions."

It must be two or three in the morning but Kildevil is wide awake. Children are playing in the streets and everyone is walking to the Hall.

When we get there, it's almost like a party. People have brought food. They eat and talk while they watch the HD, the holograph display, in the air in front of the stage. The signal fades in and out. What we see doesn't make much sense: people running along alleys, people throwing burning torches, then, after a break of about five minutes, a long shot of the city.

"That's from Signal Hill. They must be on the Hill," someone says. The signal fades, and everyone groans.

Erica works her way around to Donna. "What's happening?" she asks.

"They started picking up transmissions around midnight. Some kids were using the HD to play games, and they noticed signals getting through. Whatever this is, it's not official. People seem to be running around with cameras pinned to them, and someone is transmitting the signals through the jamming." Donna turns her eyes from the cylinder of static that now fills the center of the room. "It looks as if rebels are trying to take over St. Pearl."

The night is long and frustrating. Signals fade in and out, sometimes disappearing completely, only to resurface somewhere else along the bandwidth. The fragments we see tell us so little. Someone is fighting, but who? Is anyone winning? By dawn, when most people have fallen asleep, the signals stop.

It goes on like this for four days. In Kildevil everyday life is reversed. People do only what's necessary, sleeping in the daytime and spending their nights glued to a beam of static that gives us only occasional glimpses of a confusing struggle. After the first night, William joins us but Marrella won't. "How can I, knowing Carson is somewhere in there?" she asks when we're alone. Donna does, I almost say, but I swallow my words.

How much longer can this go on? I wonder. Here in Kildevil the suspense is terrible, but what must it be like in St. Pearl? I think about the Tribes. Where are they in all of this? And the ordinary street kids, like Hilary and me. Life must be unbearable for them. On the morning of the fifth day, I wake to find flowers dancing in the middle of the theater. It's a children's program. HD transmissions have returned to normal. I don't know how to change the display to find the news. I look for Erica, but she's asleep a few rows down, so I tug on William's sleeve. I point to the flowers, which have fallen into a giggling heap on the floor. William rises groggily and disappears into a control room. Suddenly, a man in uniform is sitting at a desk three times over, each image facing out to form a triangle. People wake at the sound of his voice and sit up, silent and alert.

". . . may resume normal activities," he says. "We will restore services as quickly as possible."

It's over. We've failed. But Erica looks up at me, her face shining. "That's General Ryan," she says. Everyone sits motionless, listening.

". . . the Commission will be dismantled. The military has no desire to rule, and councils will be established to discuss the transition to democracy as soon as possible. We anticipate full cooperation of the Weavers' Guilds. Indeed, we cannot hope to succeed without them. In other parts of the continent, the fighting continues and we may be called upon to send troops to restore order. "

A cheer goes up from the crowd. But he continues. "Those killed or wounded in the taking of Signal Hill will be returned to their families as soon as possible."

We spend the rest of the day trying to piece together what happened, watching programs filled with people who have never appeared on HD before: Tribe members with tattooed faces, shop owners, street cleaners, musicians. Gradually we learn how they took the city of St. Pearl, neighborhood by neighborhood, until the military arrived to help them. But our celebrations are muted because the list of the dead and wounded has not been released. On the second day, messages begin to come through. One by one, the boys who were taken away contact their families. No one from Kildevil was killed, they say, and everyone relaxes. But the day after, when the list of wounded is released, Carson Walsh's name is on it.

A week later Donna comes to our door carrying a personal message from General Ryan. "Carson's badly hurt," she says. "He's going to lose his foot and part of his leg."

A shocked silence follows her words. Finally Erica says, "Donna, I'm so sorry."

"Well, at least it was an accident. He was pinned behind a metal door when they brought armored vehicles into the fortress. He's going to be in the hospital awhile longer. General Ryan has offered me passage to St. Pearl." She bites her lip. "Of course I'll go, but such a long journey among strangers. I've never been so far from home." I'm used to thinking of Donna as fearless. Outside Kildevil, I realize, she would be a very different person.

Erica puts her hand on Donna's. "Would you like someone to go with you?" Erica turns to William. "You should go, William. Donna will feel safe with you, and Carson needs support. Your presence would mean a lot to him. What do you think?"

William looks surprised. "Of course, if that's what Donna wants."

"Oh, that would be wonderful," Donna says.

William warms to the idea. "There are people in St. Pearl I could talk to about the idea of opening a university." He looks very happy, then remembers himself. "Of course, I'd spend most of my time with Carson."

"Just having company on the trip will help," Donna says.

Donna and William begin to plan their journey. I look at Marrella, who has said nothing. She is trembling and pale. "I don't feel well," she says. This time I go with her. I sit on the bed beside her until she stops crying. In spite of everything, I cannot dislike her now. "A hunter needs both legs," she says finally.

I remember the first time we saw Carson, dressed in animal skins. His grace was like the flight of the osprey. Gone forever now. "It's terrible," I say.

Marrella sniffs, sits up, and looks at me with that strange strength she shows at the oddest times. "When he comes home, I will care for him," she declares. She is going to be fine.

Erica is alone when I return to the kitchen. "How is Marrella?" she asks.

"I think she'll be all right."

"I wonder why she's so upset?" Erica says.

I consider telling her, but the secret belongs to Marrella and Carson, not me. "Where's William?" I ask, changing the subject.

"Gone with Donna to see if passage can be arranged for both of them. They're hoping to leave tomorrow. And you missed the rest of the news. There's a meeting in Kildevil tomorrow night to discuss the return to democracy. Donna says Fraser has been helping to organize it." Erica smiles. "And there's good news for you, too. I thought you'd apprentice with Donna. Of course, that isn't possible now, but she says Clara will be happy to accept you. You start tomorrow afternoon. First Weavers almost never take beginners, Blake. You should feel honored."

"I do," I say, and I try. After a moment I think to ask Erica, "Will I wear a headscarf?"

"Not until you weave your first respectable piece of cloth," she says. "It's a badge of honor, given in a special ceremony."

I try to imagine myself as a weaver, but I can't. The future seems so blurry. "Erica," I say, "what happens now? Everyone seems to think things will be better. But will they?"

I feel guilty for asking, but Erica seems to understand. "That's a good question, Blake. I wish more people would think about it. Is everything going to be better? Not right away. In fact, some things may be worse at first."

"How do you mean?"

"People hated the Commission, and they had a right to, but the Commission gave us stability. Even our food moves through Commission-run lines of supply. I've been stockpiling, because this seemed inevitable. Even so, when the Commission is dismantled, our standard of living is going to go down."

"What's going to happen to the work camp?"

"Maybe it could be more like a school. Then, eventually, the children might be integrated into Kildevil."

I'm surprised. "It sounds like you've been thinking about this."

"Yes, I have. I guess that's one reason why I encouraged William to look there when Marrella needed help. I've always wanted to do something for those children. I hope we'll talk about it at the meeting tomorrow night. People have to take things slowly and not expect everything to suddenly be exactly the way they want. Even with the best of intentions, it may take the military a few years to set up elections. In the meantime, we'll lose a lot of the comforts we've taken for granted. It will help if people feel they're doing something positive when that happens."

"Do you think it will be that hard?"

"Yes. Remember, I know my history. There have been similar events, the French Revolution, the end of the Soviet Union in Europe. People long for freedom and they expect it to bring wonderful things overnight. But at first their lives are often worse. Most don't know that."

"Couldn't you tell them?"

"People won't listen to things they don't want to hear, Blake. It's better to keep them busy and lower their expectations gently." She stops and smiles. "Now, you've got quite a day ahead of you tomorrow. Just relax this afternoon."

I remember what Erica said as I pass the work camp on my way to Clara's the next day. It's so quiet, it almost seems empty. Warder November's military exercises stopped as soon as St. Pearl fell. I wonder what's happening inside now. Would people in Kildevil really accept the children? I remember the first time I passed through on the way to the work camp. Even now, the memory of their coldness chills me. But things are changing. Men at the wharf wave to me as I pass. Everyone seems cheerful. Maybe their attitudes will change, too.

Clara welcomes me at her door. "I'm right pleased to take

you under my wing, Blake," she says. "We'll make a fine weaver out of you." I glance nervously toward her loom, and she laughs. "Don't give that a thought, child. It'll be some time before you're ready for the loom. We'll start you off with something simple." What could be simple about weaving? I wonder. "Winding," Clara continues. "There's always lots of winding and unwinding to be done. Simple work but important and time-consuming. I'm not feeling well today, so that's where we'll start." She hands me a wooden rod with a peg at each end. "This is a hand reel." She starts it for me, holding the center bar, expertly dipping it back and forth, taking the loose yarn up into a tidy skein. "See? Work it like this, and in no time you'll have your skein. Now you try."

It's much harder than it looks. The yarn behaved so nicely for Clara, but in my hands it slips off the reel, sags when I wind it, or just tangles at my feet. After a few minutes, Clara says, "You're probably just nervous with me watching, Blake. I'll leave you to it."

But the harder I try, the more difficult it seems. Soon I'm close to tears. I've never been good with my hands. When Hilary tried to make a thief out of me, she gave up laughing. "Blay, you're all thumbs," she said. But now I've got to learn. Becoming a weaver is my only chance. I clench the bar until my knuckles turn white, but my work only gets worse.

"How you coming with that, then?" The voice behind me is gentle, but I jump and the reel flies out of my hands.

"Fraser, don't creep up on me like that!" All the anger I feel toward the wool and myself flies out at him. Poor Fraser blinks as if I've slapped him. "I'm sorry. I'm sorry," I cry. "It's just, I'm getting nowhere with this damned thing."

Fraser picks up the reel and sits on the bench beside me, unwinding the worst of my work. "You just need practice is all, Blake." There's no anger in his voice. I feel even worse about yelling. "Here," he says, "put your hand on mine and get the rhythm of it." I like the feel of his hand, warm and soft under mine. He dips the reel over and over, and I begin to get a sense of how it works. I smile. "There," he says. "Just don't try too hard. Tension is everything."

"How did you learn this?"

"The weavers raised me till I went to Uncle Rob when I was seven. First thing I can recall is crawling on the floor among some weavers' apprentices. They set me to work as soon as they could, to keep me out of mischief. Uncle Rob says if he'd known how much trouble I was going to be, he would have let them keep me." Fraser tries to laugh without success. Even I feel the sting of this insult. I squeeze his hand just slightly. My eyes stay on the reel, but I feel him relax.

When Clara comes to check on me, I'm winding an almost-respectable skein by myself. She looks relieved. "Well, Fraser," she says, "you know we don't encourage apprentices to receive gentlemen callers while they work, but in this case I think you've done some good." I blush deeply. I don't know what embarrasses me more—my clumsiness or Clara's joke.

Taking the hint, Fraser moves off a little. "Are you coming to the meeting tonight?"

"I wouldn't miss it," I say.

"Fraser," Clara says, "I've been fighting a migraine all day. If I don't rest tonight, I may not be able to work for the rest of the week."

Fraser looks upset. "But you and Donna are the senior weavers."

"Yes, but I've been in touch with her. We both think someone younger should chair the meeting tonight," Clara says. "We won't live forever, you know." She turns to me. "Eat supper here if you like, Blake, so you don't have to walk home and back. I'll let Erica know."

Fraser still looks dismayed, but Clara has made up her mind. When she leaves us alone, he suddenly looks shy. "I wondered if you'd sit with me tonight," he asks.

"Of course."

He smiles. "Good. I'll let you get back to work. See you this evening."

The rest of the afternoon is easier. Clara is too ill to teach so she puts me to work with dye vats in a shed behind her house, moving the wool to make sure the dyes are taken evenly. I'm much happier here. The job needs no skill. Now I know it will take real effort for me to become a weaver. I have no talent for the work at all.

The Meeting

Leaving Clara's house that evening, I try to put my worries about weaving aside. Who knows? If I work hard enough at it, I might eventually find I have some hidden ability. Besides, what's happening tonight is more important than my own concerns. When I reach the end of the street, Fraser steps out of the shadows.

"You were waiting for me?" I ask. "I thought you'd be getting ready."

"Plenty of hands to do that work," he says. "I wanted to make sure you found a seat with me."

Fraser's straightforward regard warms my heart, but I can't imagine telling him that. Instead, I say, "What's going to happen tonight?"

He smiles. "A real exercise in democracy. Everyone can speak on any issue. The weavers hope this might be the start of local government."

"You like this a lot, don't you?"

"I do. When you get this close to something you've always wanted, you can't just sit around and wait for someone else to do it. I'd like to run for office myself one day."

His enthusiasm makes me so happy, I laugh. "Fraser, I never

pictured you as a politician."

He stops walking. "That's what Uncle Rob says."

I've struck a nerve. "I didn't mean . . . Fraser, I wasn't laughing *at* you. I think what you're doing is wonderful. So does Erica. I don't care what your Uncle Rob says." I search for the words that will make him feel better. "I'm proud of you." The look on his face tells me I've said the right thing.

When we turn onto the main street, we're suddenly part of a crowd. It's like a festival. But just outside the entrance to the Hall, I notice a group of men watching everyone go in. An unspoken threat hangs about them like bad air. Fraser feels it too. He goes rigid with tension and places himself very firmly between the men and me. As we enter the door, I hear a laugh that startles me. It's Lem's laugh. But how could it be? I stop, confused.

"What's wrong?" Fraser asks.

"Nothing. I just—nothing," I say.

Inside the theater I can see the weavers have been busy. "Oh," I say. The stage is decorated with handwoven rugs and hangings. Two elevated platforms face the stage on either side. "What are those?" I ask Fraser as we sit.

"Speakers' corners. They're amplified. People who want to be heard can line up at them."

"It looks wonderful," I say. Fraser beams.

"It certainly does, Fraser. What a fine job," Erica says as she sits beside me. She is alone, but I'm not surprised. This isn't an event to interest Marrella at the best of times, and she's still upset about Carson. "I only wish William and Donna could be here," Erica continues, looking around. "Where's Clara?" When Fraser explains, Erica looks surprised. "Who's taking the chair?"

"Merna Bursey," Fraser says. I remember the slight, hesitant woman who presented her cloth at the Weavers' Guild meeting.

Erica frowns and lowers her voice. "I'm sure Clara knows what she's doing, but . . ." The critical words stick in her throat, so Fraser finishes.

"But Merna's soft-spoken and lets others have their way. You're not the only one who thinks so. There was a lot of talk this afternoon, but no one wanted to spoil things by challenging Clara. And the other weavers won't participate in the discussion tonight, so no one can say they're trying to control things." He sighs. "I wish Donna could be here."

"So do I," Erica whispers, but quickly because the meeting is about to begin.

Merna Bursey steps forward. "On behalf of the Weavers' Guild, I'd like to welcome . . ." she begins. But suddenly the men from outside pour in. Merna's quiet voice is lost in the commotion as they take over the back of the Hall. Donna or Clara would know what to do, but Merna stops, confused. I glance at Erica, who leans forward as if she would like to help. When the theater is finally quiet again, an undercurrent of hostility radiates from the back of the room.

Merna begins again. She finishes her welcome and explains the open discussion that will end the evening. "But first," she says, "I want to provide a retrospective of events." She begins with a history of Weavers' Guilds in North America over the past century. I can't believe it. People shuffle restlessly in their chairs as she drones on and on. The noise from the back of the room grows until finally a man shouts, "We'll be here all night if this keeps up!"

"That's right," says another. "Are you trying to keep us from having our say?"

Merna turns bright red. "Of course not. If that's how you feel, we'll go directly to the open meeting." And she sits down. "The meeting is now in session."

Fraser groans. "She forgot to introduce the agenda," he whispers. "We had an agenda, to keep the meeting on track."

A big man stands in the back. He wastes no time. "I want to know how long we're supposed to tolerate that place up the hill. When the Commission is gone, it'll be nothing but a drain on us." His voice is so much like Lem's that I realize he must be Rob Howell.

"That's right," another man shouts. "Send the scum of St. Pearl back to the streets."

I can't raise my eyes. Erica puts a protective arm around the back of my chair.

Merna struggles to regain control. "If you wish to speak, please line up at one of the speakers' corners."

"Don't you try to control free speech," Rob Howell says. "The Commission did that long enough." A murmur of agreement fills the room. Merna looks as if she will cry.

Erica rises, walks to one of the speakers' corners, and very deliberately waits to be recognized. She is a full head smaller than Rob Howell and stands the length of the room away, but she faces him down across that distance until he looks at his feet. I sit up straighter in my chair.

"I hoped this discussion would progress more slowly," she

says, "but I can see it isn't going to be a slow evening." People laugh, and the room warms by several degrees. "I'm concerned about the children in the work camp, too." Erica goes on to explain how the camp could become a school. While she talks, others begin to line up and order is restored.

I recognize the man who steps forward next, Mark's father, Daniel Jones. He speaks quietly but with conviction. "We all know where Madonna Walsh is tonight," he begins. "My son Mark was unharmed, but none of our youngsters is restored to us yet." People shift uncomfortably in their chairs. Captain Jones nods to Erica. "You mean well, missus, but you're an outsider still. You can't ask us to take in what dregs the Commission dumped on our doorstep. It's more than we can tolerate."

His quiet dignity shifts the weight of opinion very firmly to Rob Howell's side. People come forward, one after another. The work camp was never wanted. The history of their efforts to prevent it are bitterly recounted. Some are angry and some apologetic, but all agree. The children in the camp will have to go. Hours later, when Rob Howell comes to the microphone again, I realize Erica has expected these people to be better than they can be.

"We all feel the same," he says. "So what are we waiting for? The sooner we clear that place out, the better." Muttered approval comes from the back of the room.

Merna Bursey rises from her chair. "Tonight's meeting is only for discussion—" she begins, but Rob Howell cuts her off.

"No one elected you, Merna Bursey. Or the Weavers' Guild, for that matter. Women were good enough when no real power was at stake, but things are different now. It's time some men took charge. I'm going up that hill tonight and when I come down, the place will be empty. Who's coming with me?"

When he says this, a number of families gather their things and scurry away. I want to yell, Don't go, we need you! But it's useless. They don't care what happens as long as they aren't responsible. Fraser has gone pale. Erica rises. "You can't do this," she says.

This time Rob Howell will not be stared down. "Then stop me." He leaves with about twenty men, mostly ones he came with. It's only a fraction of the people in Kildevil, but enough to do harm. And no one but Erica has tried to stop them. I think of the kids who are left in the work camp, all little ones. Erica turns to Fraser. "Get Clara up to the grand hotel," she says. He's gone almost before she finishes. She turns to me. "I'm going to follow them. I have to."

I grab her sleeve. "Couldn't we contact Donna and William?"

Erica shakes her head. "There's no time." She thinks for a moment, then says, "Go to Lem. See if he'll come. If he won't, stay with him. Promise me, Blake. Don't come down alone."

I only nod, hoping this doesn't count as a lie. With or without Lem, I'll be back for Erica.

The back path is all uphill. After the first few minutes, I hear nothing but my own loud panting. But I can follow the progress of the men on the road below even through the trees because they have torches. I try not to wonder what else they've armed themselves with. From here, they look just like the torch-lit procession of the investiture. But this is the complete opposite. A procession of hate and destruction. I hope Erica keeps out of sight.

Running alone and frightened, it isn't hard to outdistance the men, but when I reach the main path I still have to get up Ski Slope. I haven't a hope of returning with Lem before they get to the grand hotel. I don't even know how Lem will react. If I pound on his door yelling in the dead of night, he might not open it at all. So, when I see his cabin, I slow and try to catch my breath. At least his lights are still on. I knock quietly and call as calmly as I can. "Lem, Lem, it's me, Blake. Please open the door."

After a painfully long pause, I hear a fearful "Blake?" How could Erica have imagined he'd be up to this?

"Yes, Lem. Please. Let me in. Something bad has happened."

The door swings open. "Are you all right?"

I nod, still trying to catch my breath. "It's your brother. He's got some men and they're heading for the work camp. They want the children out," I say between gasps.

Lem's face clouds. "He can't do that," he says.

I nod. "Erica is trying to stop them. She's alone."

"We'll go." He grabs his coat from a peg beside the door.

Halfway down the hill something streaks toward us, sobbing in the dark. It's a child, but she doesn't see us. I have to catch her by the shoulders to keep her from running by. She squeals with fright and I recognize her. "Poppy, Poppy, it's me, Blake—Blay. I gave you the gloves. Remember?"

Her eyes come into focus. "Men," she says, "at the work camp. With torches. I got out the back."

"We know, Poppy. We're going to stop them." Lem's voice is

quiet, conversational. He holds out his hand. "Come with me?" He could be asking her to take a pleasant walk. Poppy hesitates only a moment before slipping her hand into his. She must be too panicked to consider who he might be. Introductions can wait, I decide. She's scared enough already. When Poppy stumbles, Lem swings her into his arms and we continue down the hill. I can hear the mob now. Rounding the corner of the Master's house, we see a semicircle of men with torches at the front entrance of the grand hotel. Erica faces them like an animal at bay. Not a timid one. She looks like a wildcat.

By now my legs are like water. I stop uphill from the circle of light, unable to plunge past the crowd. They remind me of a death squad. Lem leaves me behind and races to Erica. I think he has forgotten he's carrying Poppy. The sudden appearance of this huge man with a child in his arms confuses the mob. They fall back, lowering their shovels and guns. Poppy freezes, blank-faced with terror. Lem speaks to his brother as if they were alone, but his voice carries over the night air. "It's not going to happen this way, Rob," he says. "Nobody hurts the children." I'm the only one who notices when Fraser and Clara arrive. Fraser frowns with the effort of trying to puzzle out what he sees.

Rob Howell's voice is filled with scorn. "Go home, Lem. You're just a crazy man. Everyone knows that. Go and let us do what needs doing."

Lem shakes his head. "Before you touch these children, Rob, you have to deal with me."

"And me." Erica speaks for the first time.

"And me." Clara pushes her way through the crowd.

A voice rings out behind me, almost scaring me out of my skin. "I am ashamed to witness this." Marrella's sense of drama serves her well. She has dressed in her investiture robe and carries herself like a queen. The men part respectfully to let her pass. And I am proud to follow, even though my heart pounds in my ears. It seems the warders have no intention of coming out.

Five of us face the mob, Lem still carrying Poppy. We are badly outnumbered, but Marrella has tipped the balance. No one would dare touch her. Then Fraser pushes past the crowd. He stands between his father and me, looking directly at his Uncle Rob. "You'll have to deal with me as well," he says. His voice wavers only a little. After a silence that seems to last forever, the men begin to drift away in twos and threes. Rob Howell curses and follows them.

Erica leans against the door. "Thank you all," she says. I can see she's trembling now. "We'd better keep watch tonight. There's a loud whistle in the house. We can use that to raise the alarm if they come back. Clara, you look ill. Go up to the house. I'll make up a bed for you." Clara looks grateful.

"Well, good night, everyone," Marrella says cheerfully. We stare at her.

"What?" she says. "You can't expect me to lose sleep for this place. I've done enough." She sails back to the house.

Erica takes Poppy's hand. "Did anyone else run away, dear?" she asks. Poppy nods, and Erica sighs. "We'd better find the warders then, before those children die of hypothermia." Which leaves me with Lem and Fraser.

If I'd expected some sort of reconciliation, I'm disappointed.

"I'll be back in four hours," Fraser says. He scoots up to the house without looking at his father.

I turn to Lem. "You were so brave," I say. "I couldn't have done that."

He chuckles. "Little Wheat, you're half my size. Besides, I know Rob. He's mean, but he's a coward. I figured he'd back down."

"What if he hadn't?"

"I thought about that coming down the hill. I really do think I'd rather die than let what happened before happen again." He runs a hand through his wild hair and smiles. "Next time, though, remind me to put the kid down first."

Recovering What's Lost

After Hilary died, I couldn't cry. If you showed any weakness in the Tribe, they beat it out of you. So I learned to cry in my dreams. I haven't done that in years, but tonight, after my watch, I do. All night I dream I'm crying, stumbling through the woods, looking for the little kids who are lost in the cold.

In the morning everything is quiet. I find Erica and Clara hunched over tea. "We found them all," Erica says before I can ask. "Most of them were hiding in the sorting sheds. But the warders are leaving. They've probably already gone."

"What happens now?"

"People have to take responsibility," Clara says.

Erica sighs. "I wish William were here so he could assert his moral authority."

"What's that?" I ask.

"That," Erica replies, "is what Marrella used to such good effect last night. That girl never ceases to surprise me."

Fraser enters the kitchen rumpled and yawning. "That couch in the study makes a fine bed," he says, then he frowns. "Something I'll be needing, come to think of it. Can't expect Uncle Rob to welcome me home after last night. I expect he'll find someone else to look after those goats."

"Don't worry, Fraser. We'll find a place for you," Clara says. "I never wanted that man to have you anyway."

"Where's Lem?" I say. This is unkind and I know it, but I can't stop myself. I'm furious with Fraser for turning his back on Lem last night.

"He went home after his turn at watch. I'll make you both something to eat." Erica's tone tells me the subject is closed.

After breakfast Clara hands me a list. "I want these people from town. Both of you go round them up for me now and bring them to us at the grand hotel. Those children need attention right away." This is not a request. Any hope of avoiding Fraser vanishes.

I decide I'll settle for an icy silence, but as soon as we step outside, Fraser says, "I know you think I should have spoken to him last night." I allow a nod. "One good thing doesn't undo a lifetime of bad," he says.

That's it for icy silence. "One good thing!" I explode. "He's all good. You don't know him."

Fraser sighs. "You're right, I don't. All this time I figured he'd be just like my Uncle Rob. I thought, One's trouble enough. What do I want with another?"

My anger melts away. "Is that true, Fraser? He's nothing like your Uncle Rob. He would have died last night protecting those children." I tell him what Lem told me, even his joke about reminding him to put Poppy down next time.

"He said that?" Fraser says.

"Yes, he did. Would you meet him, Fraser? Please?"

He hesitates, then says, "I guess I could use a relative about now." Before I know what I'm doing, I've thrown my arms around him. I push away, not knowing where to look, but Fraser says, "Anyone else you want me to meet?" When I look up, he's grinning.

"At least we know where you get your sense of humor," I say. Then I see something on the road ahead that makes me jab Fraser in the ribs harder than I intended. "Ow!" he says.

"Look, it's Warder November." She walks slowly under the weight of her baggage. At the sound of my voice, she looks back. "Let's catch up." I break into a slow run. This makes her try to hurry. The idea that she might be frightened of me makes me laugh, but the sound of that laughter shocks me. It belongs to someone I would rather not know. "Wait," I yell. Maybe she decides there's no point in trying to escape, because she stops walking and puts her bags down. "Where are you going?" I ask when I catch up.

"Away. I've arranged for a boat to meet me at the wharf." She looks younger without her uniform, and her face is drawn with fear.

"What about the children?"

"They're someone else's problem now. I haven't been paid since this trouble started. Special representative of the Commission. Ha! You know what happened last night. Am I supposed to sit here until someone else decides to take revenge?" Her voice is bitter. My hands clench into fists that feel like hammers. I want to make her pay for what she has done.

Fraser catches up. He picks up a bag without speaking and continues walking toward town. I stare after him for a moment, but then I understand. He is being someone who is not Rob Howell. My fists become hands again. I pick up another bag and follow him.

All the way to town, Warder November looks like she's struggling to say something she has no words for. In the end she settles for "thank you" when we leave her by the waiting boat. And that will have to do.

News travels fast in Kildevil. By now everyone knows what happened last night. And Clara knew exactly who would feel too guilty to refuse to help. We quickly collect the people on her list and head back to the grand hotel. We pass no other warders, but when we arrive they're all gone. Not that they appear to have done much over the past few weeks. The hydroponic plants have all died from neglect. The place is a mess. Clara and Erica have already organized the children into teams. We spend the day cleaning. By the time I fall into bed exhausted that night, I know that running the work camp is going to be a huge responsibility.

As I dress the next morning, I realize that all this could mean one good thing for me. I put the idea to Erica over breakfast as tactfully as I can. "It's going to take a lot of work to run that camp," I say. "I could give up my apprenticeship with Clara."

Erica looks pleased but says, "You can't make a sacrifice like that, Blake. The apprenticeship only takes half your day. You can spend mornings at the work camp. That will be enough." I curse myself for trying to be clever when I should have been honest. But if I told Erica how bad I am with the yarn, she would only tell me to give it time.

Fraser comes to the door before I've finished clearing the

dishes. "I'm ready," he announces. He looks so grim that it takes me a moment to understand.

"You are?"

Erica laughs. "What's going on?" When we explain, she stops laughing. "I'm glad," she says. "Lem is stronger than we imagined. You saw that for yourselves. And, Fraser, I think he wants to see you."

Fraser looks apprehensive. "Do you want to come with us?" he asks.

Erica shakes her head. "This is between Lem and you."

"Then maybe I should stay here too," I say.

"No!" Fraser shouts, then catches himself. "I mean, I won't go without you."

"All right then. Let's go." I'm afraid if we wait any longer, he may lose his courage.

We don't speak going up the hill, but when Fraser sees Lem's house he grabs my hand. He holds so tightly it hurts but I don't tell him. When the door opens, I start to say, "Lem, this is—" but Lem doesn't let me finish. He gently places his huge hands on Fraser's frail shoulders. "My son," he says. "I'd know you anywhere."

Fraser's eyes fill with tears. "You remember me?"

Lem shakes his head. "I've tried and tried. I remember Michelle pregnant. That's all."

"Then how did you know me?" Fraser says.

"You look just like her. Come see." Lem brings us inside. "Sit down," he says. He makes a few passes at a control panel and, suddenly, she is in the room with us behind a keyboard, a small-boned, black-haired woman with Fraser's eyes. And Lem is too, younger, stronger, and somehow whole. It's a performance on holo-disk. Michelle's face is intense with concentration and pleasure as she plays. They are both so young. The music they make is wonderful and, when their eyes meet, anyone could see how much they love each other.

Then it's over. She is gone and Lem's house is as empty as a broken heart. Fraser just stares at the place where she stood, tears streaming down his face. Lem bends close to him. "I'm sorry," he says. "I never can bear to watch that myself. I should have asked you."

Fraser gives a shaky sigh. "Can we see it again?"

How My Light Is Spent

The next time Fraser and I climb the hill, he brings his concertina. "That's great," Lem says. "Here, look at this." He spreads out a sheet of music.

Fraser looks confused. "What's that?"

"You can't read music? I'll teach you."

Fraser shakes his head. "I've never been good at learning things on paper."

"You just never had the right teacher," Lem says. They don't even notice when I slip away about an hour later. There's no point in staying. Together they make a unit, a . . . family. The unfamiliar word falls into place like the missing piece of an old-fashioned puzzle. They are a family and I am still, what did Lem say once? A lost soul.

I am a lost soul. The scum of St. Pearl. Over the next week, I call myself this and every other vile name I can think of. Because their happiness, which I wanted so badly, should not fill me with this bitter, black rage. But it does. I feel as if something is gnawing at my chest. I gave Lem and Fraser back to each other and now I've lost them both. I can't even bear to see them together.

I struggle against this feeling almost constantly—tangling

and untangling yarn on various devices in Clara's house, walking back and forth to Kildevil, lying in my bed at night where sleep rarely finds me. I only forget to be miserable in the mornings at the work camp where I've been assigned to work with the youngest ones, the toddlers. After the first day, Poppy turned up. "They said I could help you," she said. She seemed afraid I might say no, but I need her. Most of the kids are almost too easy to handle. They do what they are told out of fear. But there's one little girl, Violet. I hate to think what happened to her before she came here because if anyone touches her, she screams, and that's the only sound she makes. With extra help I might be able to do something for her.

The people of Kildevil come forward one by one, ashamed of what almost happened, and the work camp changes into something more like a school. Erica plunges into this work with all her heart. She even eats with the children, so most of the time I do too. Marrella, of course, refuses. She grumbles but learns to cook for herself, leaving dirty pots and dishes for me to deal with at the end of the day. I talk to Erica so rarely that I miss her almost as much as Fraser and Lem. So I'm happy when she sits down beside me one night at dinner. "Are you all right, Blake?" she says. "You look worn out."

"I'm fine," I lie.

Erica sighs. "I guess we're all working too hard. I'll be so glad when William comes home. Did I tell you? They're coming tomorrow."

"Carson, too?" I wonder if Marrella knows.

"Yes," Erica says. "They weren't able to restore Carson's leg.

Regeneration therapy has to be started immediately, and it was days before they got him to a hospital. He's very bitter. I don't know how Donna will cope."

What I say next is not for Marrella's sake, but for Donna and Carson. "You remember how upset Marrella was when the fighting happened? Maybe she'd help out with Carson."

Erica laughs. "I doubt that Marrella's concern would translate into anything as practical as hard work."

"It wouldn't hurt to ask."

"Well, you know her better than I do. I'll give it a try. Speaking of healing," she says, "have you seen Lem lately?"

"No," I say, not meeting her eyes. "Why?"

"I wondered if you'd noticed the change. He's so much more—focused. Maybe he was getting better all along and I just didn't see. But now, with Fraser, it's quite dramatic. You'll see for yourself. They're going to teach music here."

"Here?"

"Yes. Lem has ideas for the children. Fraser's quite excited." She reaches over and takes my hand. "Blake," she says, "you did a good thing for both of them." I only nod, hoping she will mistake my silence for modesty. And she must be too tired to see me as she usually would because she rises to leave. "That might be a good idea about Marrella. Donna will certainly need the help. I'll talk to Marrella. And try to get some rest, dear. You look exhausted." Then she's gone. It seems I can help everyone but myself. I push my tray away and sigh. They also serve who only stand and wait.

I didn't think Lem and Fraser would teach the toddlers, but

the next morning they march into the Rotunda with heavy bags that clatter to the floor. When Poppy sees Lem, she leaves the children and follows him like a shadow. While Fraser unpacks, Lem comes directly to me. "Blake, where the hell have you been? I've missed you." Erica's right. He's changed.

"Oh, busy. You know. With the children, at Clara's."

His silence forces me to peek up at him. He's looking directly into my eyes, like anyone would. "I don't care what you have to do. Make time for us. Come and see me tonight."

I look away. "Oh, sure," I say, not meaning it.

"Promise me, Blake, please." His voice is urgent. "I've found stuff. About your past. You have to know."

I feel as if someone just hit the back of my knees. I sway and Fraser, coming to join us, puts his arm out. "Whoa," he says. "Steady."

"What did you find?" My voice is a whisper.

Lem looks troubled. "It's complicated, Little Wheat." That name almost makes me smile. "It's best if I take you through the documents step by step so we can piece it together."

Suddenly I'm aware of the wailing of more than one toddler. "The children," I say. I'd forgotten them.

Lem smiles. "That's what we're here for. Look. We've set all these percussion instruments up like a Balinese gamelan. Let's get the kids over here. Poppy, can you help us?" Poppy somehow obeys without taking her eyes off Lem. We spend the rest of the morning helping the toddlers try the instruments. It's a mixed success. Some are terrified by the noise. Violet cannot be coaxed out of a corner. Lem makes notes. "For next time," he tells me.

After lunch it's time to go to Clara's. "I'll walk with you," Fraser says.

"What about the instruments?"

"I'll get my half later, on my way back up to Lem's. I'm staying there now. I've never met anyone like him," Fraser says as we head for town. "He works like crazy. I study music, we plan lessons for the kids, then he spends every night trying to find out what happened to you."

This is more than I can bear. "Won't you tell me?"

"I don't know, Blake. He says you've got to hear it first."

"I thought he'd forgotten me. Now that he has you, I mean."

"No. He said it's even more important to find out now because you brought me to him and you still have no one."

The gnawing inside me stops. Lem's wrong. "I thought I had no one too," I tell Fraser, "but that's not true."

"We kept expecting you," Fraser says. "Where have you been?"

I smile. "I guess I got lost." He shakes his head but doesn't ask.

Fraser spots the military vehicle in front of Donna's house before I do. "Look," he says. We break into a run but stop short in front of Clara's house, afraid of intruding. Carson isn't the only one going home today. Other faces peer out of the van. Donna and William step out as a chair lowers itself into the street.

In it sits the shell of Carson Walsh. He is hunched forward, shaved head down, hands lifeless in his lap. It's as if the past few months have used up his life, leaving him an old man. William and Donna hover around him as the van pulls away. Fraser takes a step forward, but I grab his arm. "No," I whisper, dragging him to Clara's house. "He doesn't want us to see him like this." I can't say how I know, but I'm sure. "Give him time."

When Fraser leaves, Clara gives me a winder and bobbins. I set up by a window facing Donna's house. I feel guilty about spying, but I can't stop myself. Soon William leaves and, shortly after, Marrella arrives. She's wearing a tunic and leggings and a blue headscarf—the clothes she wore the day Carson first saw her. For the next half hour, every skein of yarn that touches my hands tangles instantly. How can I wait to find out what's happening? But I don't have to. Marrella comes out again far too soon. Before I can look away, she sees me. To my surprise, she comes to Clara's door. "Can I come in?" she says.

"Of course. I'll get Clara."

"No, don't. I'd rather talk to you." I try to pretend this is perfectly normal. I go back to work and she sits with a heavy sigh. "This is going to be a lot harder than I thought," she says.

"Why? What did you expect?"

"I thought he'd be so pleased to know a bio-indicator was looking after him, he'd perk right up." She lowers her voice in case Clara is near. "I thought he'd be happy to see me."

"Isn't he?" As soon as the words leave my mouth, I realize how cruel they sound.

Marrella colors. "No." After an awkward pause she says, "You're doing that all wrong." She takes the winder, untangles the wool, expertly winds a bobbin, and hands it back to me.

I'm astonished. "Where did you learn that?" It seems everyone can do this work but me.

"I was apprenticed to a weaver after my grandmother died.

The dyes and yarns set off my allergies. That's how I got to be a bio-indicator. Look, there's no point in seeing Carson again today. Let me teach you how to wind these properly."

I look at the yarn, already tangled in my hands again. "I'd be happier if you could teach me how to have allergic reactions." For a nanosecond, I think she's going to slap me. But then she starts to laugh. By the time Clara comes to see what's going on, we have laughed ourselves helpless. But by the end of the day, I know how to use a bobbin winder.

The Master Thief

.

We eat at home tonight, in honor of William's return. I say nothing about Lem's discovery—partly because Carson's problems
overshadow my own and partly because I am too terrified to talk
about it. William tells us what happened in St. Pearl. "When
Carson realized they'd lost the chance to restore his leg, he just
gave up," he says. "He won't take therapy now. It's his heart that
needs healing most."

After we've heard all about Carson, he moves on to the other
reason he was in St. Pearl—the university. "Of course, I wasn't the
only one with the idea," he says. "We're fairly sure something can
be set up by next fall. It won't really be a university at first, but it
will give people hope for the future." I glance at Marrella. She
looks as unhappy as I feel.

After the meal, it's clear that Erica and William are anxious to
be alone. "I think I'll go see Lem and Fraser," I say as casually as I
can.

Erica looks surprisingly serious. "Should I come with you?"

Lem must have spoken to her. "No, stay here with William."

She looks uncertain, then says, "If you're sure," and kisses me
good-bye.

Walking up Ski Slope in the dark, I remember the first time I came here with a basket in my hand. That girl didn't even know her name. Now I will find out even more. But when I see Lem, I know this is not a happy story.

"Come in, Little Wheat," he says. "Fraser, get her some of that stew." He's stalling.

"I've eaten, thanks. You know why I'm here, Lem. Please."

We sit at the kitchen table. Fraser pulls up a chair. Lem takes a sheet of paper out of a folder. "I found this notice." He hands it to me. After the electronic header, it says, "MISSING CHILD. Blake Raintree, aged two years, one month. Taken from her mother in St. Pearl, Terra Nova Prefecture, on the night of August 25, 2354."

"Taken. What does that mean?"

"I wondered too. Once I had a date, I could start checking the archived newslist. That was for the resistance. Only approved members could access it, and the accounts were masked. But they were still pretty cautious about what they posted. This is what I found." He hands me a second piece of paper. "The toddler was snatched from a chair at an outdoor café," it reads. "The poor mother is frantic. Frankly, we're afraid she was taken for organs, but we're still looking. She has a microdot embedded in her left wrist. If anyone can help, please contact us."

"But I remember that!" And I tell Lem and Fraser about the yellow bowl in the pool of light, the arms that grabbed me.

"There's more," Lem says, handing me another paper. "This is different. From the archive of an e-zine. A publication. I've marked the part about you."

The article is dated October 2354 and is headed "DISAPPEAR-ING CHILDREN IN ST. PEARL." About halfway down, at Lem's mark, I begin to read. "Emily Monax, a former professor of English literature, arrived in St. Pearl this summer with her two-year-old daughter, only to have the child snatched away one night soon after. 'A blonde girl ripped her out of a chair at a sidewalk café,' she tearfully related. 'I only turned my head for an instant. She even took my purse. Who would hire a child to do such a thing? I only want my baby back. I'd do anything.'" The paper falls to the table and everything fades.

"Blake, are you all right? You look faint." Lem's voice seems very far away.

"She stole me."

"Who did?" Fraser asks.

"Hilary. She said she found me. Why would she steal me from my mother?"

"Do you want to stop?" Lem asks. I shake my head. "There's one more," he says. "This is the hardest. Do you want me to read it to you?" I nod. "It's from the e-list again. The header reads: 'Regarding the Child Blake Raintree.' It says, 'A few weeks ago, I was looking for information on a missing child. This is to let everyone know the mother is now on location. She decided to go public, unleashing a predictable chain of events.'"

"What does that mean? I don't understand."

"'On location' means she was picked up by the Commission. When her story was published, they noticed her."

I look at the e-zine article on the table. My eyes catch on words, and I read them out loud. "'I only want my baby back. I'd do anything.' She knew what she was doing, didn't she?"

"I think she did," Lem says.

Then I realize something. "But if she ended up in Markland, wouldn't Erica have known her?"

Lem shakes his head. "I asked. She didn't know anyone named Emily Monax."

"Erica knew all of this?" I can't believe she didn't come with me.

"No, Blake. I didn't want anyone to know before you did. Not even Erica. I only asked her if she knew the name."

"Is there any way of finding out what happened to her?"

"Yes. But I had to be sure you'd want me to look before I started."

"Where?"

"In the Archive of the Lost."

"What's that?"

"A list of everyone who died in the technocaust. I'll only look there if you want me to."

My next words are less than a whisper. "I have to know."

"I understand," Lem says. We sit silent for a long time. Finally Lem says, "Blake, why don't you stay with us tonight? I can slip down and tell Erica."

Lem's being kind. If he tells her, I won't have to repeat the story. "Thank you," I say. When he leaves, Fraser wraps me in a blanket and gives me a cup of hot milk, which I drink before I even notice what it is.

"Why did she do it, Fraser?"

"I don't know. Why don't you tell me about her?"

So I do. But it's as if I'm seeing Hilary for the first time, my own voice telling me things I always knew but never suspected. "She used to tell me how I got my name. She had a name picked out for me, but I insisted I was Blay Raytee. So that's what she called me."

"And she said she found you? You wouldn't have a name picked out for someone you just found, would you?"

"No, and she gave in because she was afraid someone would hear me."

"She knew they might be looking."

"You're right. It all makes sense. Why didn't I see it before?"

"You had no reason to."

Tears spill down my cheeks. "She took good care of me, Fraser. She taught me to read." And I tell him the rest. How she died saving me from the death squad. "She took my life away and then she saved it. How do I forgive her for loving me? How can I hate her for dying for me?"

Fraser takes my hand. "It took me nearly sixteen years to forgive Lem just for not remembering me. Give yourself time."

When I finish crying, I'm overcome with sleepiness. "I'm tired," I say.

He puts his arm around me. "Then sleep."

Drifting off, I think how nice it feels to sleep lying against someone again. Just like with Hilary. I know there's something wrong with this thought, but I'm too sleepy to figure it out.

Sometime in the night, Fraser leaves me. I wake in the morning, lying on the bench alone with a pillow and blankets. How can I face the day? Then I imagine Poppy trying to cope with

Violet and the other children alone. I can't leave her to that. I slip away without waking Lem and Fraser.

Walking down the hill, I see and hear nothing. At least I have a name for the voice on the cassette. Emily Monax, a former professor of English literature. And she loved me enough to risk her life. Just like Hilary. Damn her! Why did she take me? I'd give anything to know and now I never will.

Erica is waiting for me in the kitchen alone. She hugs me. "I'm sorry," she says. "Maybe I should have come."

I try to smile. "Lem and Fraser took good care of me."

"They both love you a lot," she says. "And so do I."

This time the smile comes easier. "I'll be glad to get to work."

"You want to work today?"

"The kids need me. It's good to be needed."

When we leave the house after breakfast, Erica says, "Look, it's snowing." Fat white flakes fill the air, exploding as they hit the ground. Winter has finally arrived.

The Winter of Our Discontent

After the excitement of the fall, winter is like a wet blanket. Everything Erica predicted comes true. There's no sign of democracy yet. Commission-run supply lines break down as people abandon jobs that no longer pay. We work harder and have less. Walking past the wharf one day, I hear a old man grumble, "The Commission wasn't so bad. We knew where our next meal was coming from."

At least William is back with what Erica calls his moral authority. I never really understood his role before. Now just a kind word from him, or a pat on the shoulder, and people stand taller and work harder. "He lightens the burden for all of us," Erica says, and she's right.

Clara's house becomes a refuge for Donna and Marrella, alternately. They need relief from each other more than from Carson's gloom. Lucky for me, because both are good teachers and both are willing to help me now that Clara's patience has been exhausted. With almost constant coaching from them, I'm finally ready to attempt my first piece of weaving. One day, while helping me set up a loom, Donna says, "I'd never thought I'd speak ill of a bio-indicator, but I do all the real work. I don't know why she comes

249

here. She isn't helping Carson, and she certainly isn't helping me."

"There isn't any change at all?"

Donna sighs. "Carson acts like we're not even there." Then she smiles. "Look, Blake, you've got that on backward again. Take it off and turn it around." Donna pats my hand. "I shouldn't say this, but without you I'd probably go day to day without laughing at all." Once this might have hurt, but we've all stopped pretending I can do this work.

As I finally sit down to the loom, I hear shouting. I pay no attention, but Donna sits up. "That's coming from my house," she says. She bolts for the door and I follow. As we rush into her house we hear a crash. A dish comes flying out of a doorway. "That's Carson's room," Donna says. We find Marrella taking dishes off Carson's lunch tray and trying to smash them against the wall. Her aim is bad. She doesn't even notice us.

"Look at me!" she yells, smashing another dish. "Just look at me. React." She bursts into tears. "I can't do this anymore, Carson. It's like trying to love a block of stone." As she picks up the one remaining dish, a mumble comes from Carson's chair. Marrella hears it too, and stops, the dish poised for flight in her hand. "What did you say?"

Donna and I lean forward, not daring to breathe. Carson's voice is weak from lack of use, but his words are clear. "You deserve better."

Marrella is still crying, but I hear the relief in her voice. "I deserve better! Miss Perfect. That would be me, would it? Let me tell you something, Carson Walsh. It's going to take you the rest of your life to figure out just how imperfect I am. Start with this."

She kneels in front of him and undoes her turban. Meters of material fall to the floor. When she's finished, she faces him, her head more bare than his. "Look at me," she says again, but tenderly this time.

Carson does. After a long minute, he runs his hand over the stubble on her head. "I think I met your barber," he says.

A few weeks later, Marrella and I are walking home through a wet snow. "Donna said she would have had her own temper tantrum ages ago if she'd known how much good it would do Carson," she tells me.

"You're getting along better now, aren't you? I barely see you at Clara's anymore."

"Everything's easier now. Carson thinks he's ready to go to the military hospital in Corner Brook. Do you think you could do my UV readings for a while? I'd like to go with him."

"Of course. I'm good at that. I'll miss you at the loom, though."

"You're getting better," she says. "You'll be fine without me."

It's true. It's been days since I've had to undo my work and start over again. It seems entirely likely I might finish my first piece of cloth. But that doesn't change this sudden empty feeling. "Maybe I'll just miss you." I sound as surprised as I feel.

"Don't count on it. I bet Erica won't, either," Marrella says. She's cheerful, though.

But when she talks to William, she hits an unexpected wall. "No," he says. "Absolutely not."

"But Blake can do my UV readings or you can set up that robot again."

William forces himself to speak calmly. "Marrella, Blake didn't pass the tests. You did. When classes start in St. Pearl next fall, you'll be there with all the others. In the meantime, we're making up a preparatory course of study. You'll start as soon as it's ready."

Tears spring to Marrella's eyes. "This is so unfair. You can't send me to St. Pearl. What about Carson?"

"He's doing well now. It's only three years. He'll wait for you."

"Three years!" Marrella pushes away from the table so quickly, she knocks over her chair as she runs from the room.

After an awkward pause, I say, "Would anyone mind if I go to her?"

Erica looks relieved. "Please."

Once again Marrella is facedown on her bed. "It should be you," she says into her pillow.

"I wish," I say. "But you're the bio-indicator."

"This is so wrong." I can't argue with that. She sits up. "Could we tell him the truth?"

"The truth? Tell him we conspired to fool him? That you became a bio-indicator because of a bunch of lies? And when we're finished, where will we be? You'll have no position and I'll have no home. Don't even think of it," I whisper furiously, trying not to show how scared I am. Everything I have is at risk.

"When you put it like that," Marrella says, "it doesn't sound like a good idea."

"It's not. Let me think. Maybe I can come up with something. But please don't tell."

"I guess I owe you that. But I'm not going to St. Pearl."

Long into the night I try to think of some way to keep Marrella out of university. I forget to worry when I'm with the kids in the morning, but the problem returns at the loom. I pass the shuttle back and forth easily. Clara comes to watch. She's spending more time with me these days. I must have been an embarrassment to her until Donna and Marrella helped me along.

"That's quite a respectable piece now, Blake," she says. "Soon you'll be ready for your headscarf ceremony. I remember mine. I was so happy to commit myself to the craft for the rest of my life. I think it was better than my wedding day."

That's what a headscarf ceremony should be, like a wedding day. Every time I think of mine, I want to cry. How can I stand up in front of everyone pretending to be happy? How can I promise to spend the rest of my life struggling with something I do so badly? I can't. "Clara," I say, "I just realized I have to do some-thing. It's urgent. Can I leave?"

Clara is surprised, but she agrees. As much as I dislike this work, I've never asked for time off before. I go to Donna's house. "Come on," I tell Marrella. "We have to talk to William."

"You've thought of a way out of this? Oh, Blake, you're so clever. I knew you would." She doesn't even ask what I plan to do.

We have to drag William away from a science session with kids at the grand hotel. He doesn't look pleased. "Couldn't this have waited?" he asks.

"No, it couldn't. You see, Marrella and I have lied to you. A lot." Marrella's mouth falls open.

William looks surprised but says, "Go on."

It takes time to tell the whole story. I don't spare myself or Marrella. I feel like I'm tearing my life to pieces. When I'm finished, William asks Marrella for her side of the story. She won't look at me now, but she tells the truth. Finally William sits back in his chair, all his questions answered. He says nothing for such a long time the silence begins to seem like a punishment in itself. "This is very serious," he finally says. His face has darkened. I can almost feel his anger.

Here it comes, I think. The end of everything. But in a small way, I feel better. At least I'm finally out from under the burden of lies.

"When I consider the mistake we almost made." He's yelling now. "Blake, do you know how rare it is to find someone who can pass these tests the way you did? Do you have any idea, any clue, how gifted you are? You would have thrown all that away. Why?"

The force of his anger is more than I can bear. I burst into tears. "I wasn't," I sob, "I'm not—the bio-indicator." I point to Marrella. "She is."

He looks as if I've gone insane. "What's that got to do with anything?"

I'm so surprised, I stop crying. "I thought you had to be a bio-indicator."

This gives him pause. "Of course not," he says after a moment. "We've looked for intuitive learning among bio-indicators because we had access to them. I looked in Kildevil, too. We couldn't very well look in Commission-run work camps, could we? It has nothing to do with being a bio-indicator."

"But you said I couldn't have my investiture unless I passed!" Marrella is indignant now.

William looks embarrassed. "That was wrong of me. I had to get your attention somehow. I didn't know what else to do."

"So you lied too. Does that mean I don't have to go to St. Pearl?" Marrella's ability to manipulate a situation takes my breath away.

"Marrella, you're not allowed to go to St. Pearl," William says, but he's smiling. "Blake's the one who belongs in a university."

"And what about those awful UV observations?" She can never resist pushing him.

"You are still the bio-indicator. Those observations will be with you for the rest of your life. Now you'd better leave us." Marrella scowls, but she doesn't waste time. For once I wish I were the one going out the door. William sits on the edge of his desk in front of me. "How could I have been so blind? Marrella was doing so badly. The moment you came, things started to fall into place. I was too relieved to wonder why. And Erica was so happy to have a sympathetic child in the house, I let her take charge of you. I should have seen what was going on. It was my pride that blinded me. I couldn't bear to think I might not be able to find the right kind of person. All the other Masters found at least one.

"Now you have to learn why the choices you made were the correct ones. The Way teaches us to look beyond appearances. It's good science, too. Just as the books helped you to choose the lichen and the shrew over the asters and the moose. The most interesting things are often not the obvious ones." He shakes his head. "I knew that, and yet I didn't see you."

"I didn't want you to," I say. "I wouldn't have become a bio-indicator. But when I found out about the education, it nearly broke my heart."

"And you still didn't tell me the truth."

"I thought it was too late."

"But why did you decide to tell me now? Did Marrella make you?"

I shake my head. My cheeks burn with shame. "I am a pathetically bad weaver. I couldn't face the headscarf ceremony."

When I look up, he's smiling. "Lucky for me."

The Aeolian Lyre

.

On a warm afternoon in April, I put my notebook on William's desk. "That's it," he says. "You've finished. We'll need to find extra work for you to do over the summer."

"I'm sure you'll think of something." Erica says William is working me too hard, but I love it. Ideas do not tangle like yarn.

I find Erica in the kitchen. She isn't needed at the school as much now. The fighting is over, not only on the island, but everywhere. The military is slowly beginning to reorganize everything, and young recruits are helping us run the grand hotel. It's just enough to ease the burden for everyone. She smiles. "Finished? Lem would like to see you. I'm coming." Something in her voice makes my heart beat faster, but I say nothing. I've been expecting Lem to find out more about my past for months.

"Fraser still won't talk about you going away?" she asks. I shake my head. "He's just afraid you'll change," Erica says. I don't reply because I know it's true. In fact, neither of us wants to talk about it. How can I tell him I won't change when I'm not sure myself?

Lem and Fraser are sunning outside the house. "I guess you know why I asked to see you," Lem says. My throat closes over, so I nod. "Actually, it didn't take long to find her, Little Wheat. The Archive of the Lost is pretty straightforward. She died just a few months after Michelle."

"They might have known each other," Fraser says softly. "I like to think they did."

All these months I've believed I harbored no hope. Now, as the last spark dies painfully, I know I was lying. "Why did you wait to tell me?" I ask.

Erica speaks. "We've been looking for something else."

"And we found it," Lem says. "Last week I made contact with a woman in St. Pearl, Rose Tilley. She knew your mother, Blake, in Markland. She knew her well."

"You found someone who knew my mother? Will she talk to me?"

"More than that. She wants to meet you. When she found out you'd be coming to St. Pearl, she asked if you'd like to live with her. She says she has a lot to tell you."

I will finally meet someone who knew my mother. "Thank you for waiting," I tell Lem and Erica. "This means a lot to me."

Later, when we walk back down the hill, Erica asks, "Are you all right?"

"I guess. I used to think I could never be a real person without her. You and William and Fraser and Lem have changed that. But I wish I could have known her. And I still wish I understood why Hilary took me."

I think I'm fine, but that night, for the first time in months, the dreams come back again. I am looking at the sky, with my head on my mother's arm. Only this time, I turn my head and there she is. My mother. She smiles and says, "I will never leave you unless I have to," in the voice I know from the recording. When I wake, I can't recall her face, but I feel as if she's been with me.

A few days later, I'm sitting outside the grand hotel with Poppy and the toddlers when I see Fraser walking down the hill. He stands taller now that he's with Lem, as if his father has given him something to reach for.

"I came to tell you there's going to be a ceremony at the crest of the hill tomorrow. Everyone is coming."

"Why didn't I hear about it before?"

"Maybe it's a surprise," he says. He sits beside me. "How are you now?"

"A little better." I tell him about the dream. "It helps to know I'll meet someone who knew her." I sigh. "I just wish I understood about Hilary."

"Me too. How did she manage with just the two of you on the streets?"

"She was a master thief." Even now, I can't keep the admiration from my voice. "We had the protection of a Tribe because she stole for them. Anything she needed, she could steal."

"And when she needed someone to love, she stole you."

I can't speak at first. It seems so obvious. "And I'm supposed to be the clever one," I finally say. "She built her whole life around me. She was only a child, but she was such a good mother." We say nothing for a long time. When I look up, Violet is standing in front of me with pieces of a broken toy. "Blay fix it," she says, and she plops down into my lap.

I stroke her hair and rock her. "I wish I could."

"I don't know," Fraser says. "She's talking now and she doesn't scream when you touch her. I'd say you have."

"Maybe. But Fraser, will there ever be a time when there are no kids like Violet? Or kids like Hilary, who need love so badly that they have to steal it? Will there ever be a time when kids get all the love they need?"

Fraser looks at me for a long time, his warm brown eyes steady. Then he looks away. "If I have anything to do with it, there will be." And that's when I know that nothing in St. Pearl will keep me from coming back to him.

The next afternoon is cloudy and chilly, but it seems everyone in Kildevil is climbing to the crest of the hill. Erica makes me wait until the children from the grand hotel have gone, too. I'm bursting to know why. "What's happening?"

"Never mind," she says. "Put on something warm and let's go see."

I rush upstairs and open my drawer. There, beside my Object, is the sweater Fraser made for me. I take it out and put it on. When Erica notices, she says nothing. But William says, "I'm not sure a serious scholar should let herself be bound to a boy." As I open my mouth to argue with him, I notice the laughter in his eyes. "I hope you're not going to be like Marrella now," he continues.

"Have I ever?" I ask, and we laugh.

It's a long, long climb to the crest of the hill. I haven't been here since the day of the first test. The place is thronged with people now, but when I look back the way we came, the hills are still flung out before us like the cloths of heaven.

When Fraser sees his sweater, he blushes. "Do you mind?" I ask him.

"Mind? I figured you'd find some fellow in St. Pearl who reads as well as you and that'd be the end of me."

"Fraser, I'm taking this sweater with me. Not only that, it's a bit tight now. You'd better make me another."

He smiles. "I'll make you a whole closetful. You'll never have to wear anything else. But come with me now; you're needed."

Lem is organizing people into groups around something wrapped in a huge piece of canvas. "Over here," Fraser says, "take hold." He places me in line along a piece of rope.

"What's going on?"

"Lem had us up the ski slope, slaving away on this for months. But he wants to tell you himself. Here he comes." Beyond Lem, I see Marrella and Carson. Carson moves slowly, but his artificial limb works well. Marrella smiles when she sees me. Fine blonde down covers her head.

I wave to them and turn to Lem. "What is this?"

"The kids at the hotel told me about Memory Day, Blake."

I swallow hard. "They did?"

"Yeah. It's time for a new Memory Day. So we can remember what really happened. I wanted your mother and Michelle and all the others who died to be up here where the world is beautiful, to get them out of the Archive of the Lost. I want them to hear the songs." He raises his voice. "Everyone ready?" A chorus replies and he points to us. "When I count to three, pull as hard as you can. The rest of you hold your lines and stand by."

We pull while others push the great canvas lump from below, and it begins to rise. Finally it settles with an earsplitting screech into the waiting base. Lem brings me forward. "Pull this," he says. I do, and the canvas flutters to the ground. Before us is a huge aeolian harp, made from the rusting towers of Ski Slope. Hundreds and hundreds of names have been etched onto the beams, overlapping until they form a web, like lichen on rock. As the beams rust and weather the names may disappear, but we'll know they were there.

The harp stands solid and proud against the sky. A strong spring breeze blows, and it vibrates with a song of renewal, with the voice of hope. I close my eyes and wish. I wish that somehow, Michelle and my mother, even Hilary, will hear the song and know it is for them.

Author's Note

The future I've envisioned in *The Secret Under My Skin* is not the way things have to be, but it is the future I'm afraid we'll create if we don't work to change things. I firmly believe the next generation can do a better job of taking care of the earth and its people than we have until now.

The Secret Under My Skin takes place in an imaginary future, but the setting is very real. Gros Morne National Park is the largest national park in Atlantic Canada, located on the west coast of Newfoundland around a huge fjord called Bonne Bay. The park has been a UNESCO World Heritage Site since 1988.

There is no grand hotel or town called Kildevil, but Killdevil Mountain exists. There osprey glide and dip beneath the salt water to catch fish. The landscape, the hills, and the shallow inlet of Bonne Bay are pretty much as I've described them. The Green Gardens hiking trail passes by ancient volcanic vents and leads to the Tablelands, a small part of the Earth's mantle which was pushed to the surface when two continents collided millions of years ago. The bare, bright orange rock of the Tablelands looks like the surface of the moon.

Gros Morne National Park is a real place, but anyone who has ever visited knows it's full of magic.